CHANGING PACE

CHANGING PACE

by

J. Marcus Evins

Dedication

In memory of my father, James "Will" Evins, who never published but filled notebooks with stories about life, the world, and the people around him. I once told him I wanted to someday write a novel. His advice – just start writing - was simple and direct.

I was reminded of those words as I worked on this book. In many ways, it is a continuation of the stories he never shared with the world. And in writing it, I feel a little closer to him.

Acknowledgements

Writing a novel is never a solitary effort. While the words on the page may be mine, this book wouldn't exist without the encouragement, support, and belief of others.

To family and friends who listened patiently, offered feedback, asked how it was going, or simply reminded me to keep going—thank you. You inspired the work in ways big or small, knowingly or not, and I'm grateful.

A special thank you to my wife, whose enthusiasm helped bring Changing Pace to life—especially when she suggested we vacation at one of the very places where the story unfolds.

Shout out to my son, Marcus, who as a firefighter and fitness trainer, convinces me every day that there are real-life super heroes that walk amongst us.

Chapter 1

The first time Travis's cell phone vibrated should have been enough to discourage him from entering the Commonwealth Lounge. Pressing the mute button silenced the phone, but not the nagging voice inside his head. Another long day at work had worn his patience thin, and the thought of going home immediately afterward offered no promise of relief. Besides, he knew he'd already lost the battle of will when he turned into the lounge's parking lot. Unable to delay the inevitable, Travis shut off the car, checked his phone for additional messages, and headed toward the entrance.

Once inside, he nodded toward a few familiar faces as he made his way to his favorite table. From there, Travis could not only see what was happening inside the lounge but also watch the traffic flowing in and out of the Greyhound Bus Station across Arthur Ashe Boulevard. A departing bus caught his attention. He watched it slowly make its way down the boulevard before disappearing and he wondered what it might feel like to be one of its passengers.

The server's arrival brought him back to the present. He watched as the attractive young woman placed a menu and napkin-wrapped utensils on the table. Something about her reminded him of Karen. Perhaps it was her mocha brown complexion or how her natural hair was brushed into a ponytail, the way Karen sometimes wore hers. When their eyes met she smiled.

"Hello, sir. Welcome to the Commonwealth Lounge," she said, smiling again. "My name is Nicky. What can I get started for you?"

"I'm sorry—what was that?" Travis asked.

"What can I get started for you?" she repeated. Travis was certain she'd caught him staring and diverted his attention to the menu, although he had no intention of ordering from it.

"I think I'll start with a shot of Hennessy and a Coors Light, in the bottle," he said.

The server nodded and walked away. Travis thought about Karen again. They were among the handful of Black employees at Lucent Technologies and were not only coworkers but also good friends. Karen was somebody he could talk to when he needed someone willing to listen. He decided to text her, but when he tapped his phone's display, the earlier texts from Elana stared back at him. Reading them again, he changed his mind about reaching out to Karen and considered the true source of his anxiety.

Six months ago, when he became the interim IT manager, human resources had practically guaranteed the position would become permanent. The HR director had assured him that he would only have to sit through an interview to make it official. But that was before Bradley Stillman was hired three months later. Now, every project-related recommendation he made was either second-guessed or questioned by Bradley. Even more unnerving, senior management had begun turning to Bradley with their IT-related questions—although Travis was supposed to be the IT department's supervisor.

Travis considered the situation at work until he was distracted again by a bus entering the station across the street. Its doors opened, and he watched passengers unload before returning his attention to the lounge. As he scanned the room, he had to admit there wasn't much to the place—just a handful of tables, a few booths, and a bar. Two television screens provided background noise—one over the bar and the other positioned for viewing from the dining area.

Since discovering the lounge, it had become a refuge where, on days like today, he could disconnect before heading home. He'd never told Elana about the place because it lacked the extravagance she seemed endlessly drawn to. Karen, though—he was certain she would appreciate its unpretentious vibe. He considered texting her again but decided to wait when he noticed the server approaching with his order.

"Here you are, sir. One cognac and a Coors Light in the bottle," she said, placing the drinks on his table.

"You're new here, aren't you?"

"New? Oh, yes," she said. "This is my second week. Is it that obvious?"

"No, not at all. You're doing fine. I just knew I hadn't seen you before," Travis said, then decided to change the subject. "Is it me, or is it busier than usual tonight?"

"I think you're right. It has picked up a little. Sometimes we get quite a bit of walk-in traffic from the bus station."

Travis nodded and followed her gaze across the street before continuing.

"Well, look, Nicky. I don't want to hold you up."

"No worries. I'll check back once you've had a chance to look at the menu."

"Thanks, but I won't need the menu. I'm just having drinks," Travis said, and handed the menu to her.

"Mind if I share your table?"

A man slid around Nicky and into the seat across from Travis without waiting for a response. He appeared to be in his mid-thirties, with dreads tied in a bun, and wore a tracksuit Travis felt was too much for the warm August evening. He grabbed the menu out of Nicky's hand and flipped it open.

"So, what's good, baby girl?" He looked up from the menu, exposing a bottom row of gold teeth before adding, "Besides you."

"Just what's on the menu, sir," Nicky said. "Why don't I give you a few minutes to look it over."

"Nah, I'm ready. How about the Philly Steak Sub, chips, and a medium Coke."

"I'll get that right out for you," she said, then looked toward Travis. "You sure I can't get you anything else?"

Travis shook his head, but before Nicky could leave, the man spoke up again.

"Hey, baby girl, ask 'em to put extra onions on that sub. By the way, when are you going to let me get your number so we can hook up?"

"My number?" Nicky began, turning to walk away. "My number is server seven. I'll make sure you get those extra onions, sir."

Once the server disappeared, the man pulled out his phone and began typing. As Travis stared at the television, he was beginning to feel the lounge had become too busy to enjoy. He decided to quickly finish his drinks and then head home.

"Damn, that woman is some kind of fine," the man said, sliding the phone into his pocket. He leaned toward Travis and extended his fist. "Not too friendly, though. Name's RJ."

"Travis, man," Travis said, and the two men bumped fists. "What woman are you talking about?"

"Come on, man," RJ said. "I'm talking about our server. You know, number seven."

"Oh, Nicky. She seems like a nice person," Travis said, and then, hoping to change the subject, asked, "You just get off one of the buses across the street?"

"Nah, man, I'm meeting a friend. His bus should have been here by now," RJ glanced toward the station, then back at Travis. "So, I guess you didn't have any luck with baby girl either?"

Travis smiled at the suggestion, and instead of responding, held up his left hand to display his wedding band.

"What's that supposed to mean?" RJ laughed. "You married dudes crack me up. I saw you two grinning at each other before I came over."

"She's alright, I guess," Travis said, "but she just took my order, that's all. Besides, I love my wife."

"Yeah, right," RJ shook his head, then went back to tapping on his phone until Travis motioned toward the television.

"Hard to believe how bad this fentanyl thing has gotten," he said. "They're talking about the raid that took place in Elizabeth City, North Carolina, where the feds busted a major drug ring a couple of years ago. They said it might still be a source of a lot of the fentanyl-laced drugs coming into the Commonwealth."

"Yeah, I heard something about that," RJ said. He glanced again toward the bus station, then pulled out his phone and tapped the screen. "I wonder where baby girl is with my Philly Steak?"

Travis continued listening as the reporter went on about the raid and the efforts to reduce the continued influx of fentanyl-laced drugs into the Commonwealth. After a few minutes, RJ leaned in his direction again.

"Look, man. I gotta bounce," he said, standing. "I think my man's bus just pulled in."

"But, what about your order?" Travis asked.

RJ tossed a few crumpled bills on the table. "It's yours if you want it,"

Before Travis could respond, RJ headed toward the exit. Through the window, Travis watched him jog across Arthur Ashe Boulevard toward the bus station.

At first, he was annoyed about the abandoned meal. Then he decided it might be a good idea to keep it—just in case Elana hadn't cooked. Lately, home-cooked meals weren't something he could depend on, and the Philly Sub was beginning to sound good. Travis had just finished the last of his drink when his phone vibrated, displaying another message from Elana. This time he replied immediately.

"Getting ready to leave the office," he texted, then added, "Sorry about not responding to your earlier texts."

"So, where's the guy who ordered the Philly Steak and chips?"

Travis looked up from his phone to see that Nicky had been replaced by a different server. Her blonde hair, dyed bright red, and oversized tortoise-shell glasses made her look as though she were trying too hard to create a style that contrasted with her otherwise plain appearance.

"He had to leave, but I'll pay for it," Travis said, handing her his credit card. "So, what happened to Nicky?"

"Nicky?" the woman repeated as though unsure who Travis was speaking of.

"The server who took the order," Travis continued.

"Oh, you mean Nekeesha. She decided to take her break," the woman said, while placing the tray on the table and picking up the empty beer bottle and shot glass. "Is there something else I can get for you?"

"Yeah, you can add another one of those to my check," Travis said, pointing to the empty beer bottle. He decided the change in servers was the result of RJ's remarks. "And can you wrap the sub to go?"

Ignoring the woman's frown as she picked up the tray, Travis checked his phone and was relieved that Elana had responded to his text. Her response was an unfamiliar abbreviation that he repeated out loud, unaware that the server had returned with his beer.

"I'm sorry, sir. Is there something else?" she asked, while placing the beer in front of him.

"No, nothing else. I was just trying to figure out a text I received."

The server glanced at Travis's phone.

"Oh, same shit, different day," she said, then giggled. "I'm sorry—I mean same stuff, different day."

Travis looked at Elana's message again, then back at the server.

"SSDD. It's the abbreviation for same stuff, different day," the server repeated before walking away.

Travis sipped the last of his beer. After a while, he wondered where his order was. The more he thought about Elana's text, the more anxious he felt himself becoming, so he decided not to wait. Once he was in the car, Travis scrolled through Elana's texts again and decided he should call her.

"Hello." Elana's voice sounded tense. Travis could hear a television playing in the background.

"Hey, I'm on my way home," he said, trying not to sound as guilty as he was beginning to feel.

"So, you're just leaving the office?"

"Yes, I—"

"I don't want to hear it, Travis," Elana interrupted. "Do you know I texted you over two hours ago, and now it's almost seven-thirty?"

"Elana, I—"

Travis could no longer hear the television in the background. Feeling more frustrated than angry, he tossed the phone onto the passenger seat. As he shifted into drive, he told himself the promotion to IT manager would fix everything—it had to. At least, that was what he hoped, as he drove home, uncertain of the reception awaiting him.

Chapter 2

At one time, home was the only refuge Travis needed—as long as Elana was by his side. They'd met when he was taking evening classes at Virginia College. The first time he saw Elana Santos was in the campus bookstore. She wore faded jeans, an oversized coat, and a wool beanie cap pulled down just above her eyes. Travis was immediately captivated by Elana's detached demeanor as she searched the bookshelves, seemingly unaware of the attention her beauty attracted.

When Elana turned in his direction, her dark brown eyes sparkled with intelligence and warmth. At first, she responded to his awkward smile with pursed lips, making Travis feel all of his thirty-two years. Then, before disappearing into the crowded bookstore, she smiled in a way that seemed both genuine and inviting. He didn't see her again on campus until a few months later at a Black Lives Matter rally. This time, encouraged by the memory of that smile, he risked starting a conversation.

They began dating despite a seven-year age difference. Elana completed her graduate degree in nursing, and shortly afterward, they married. It had all happened so quickly. At the time, Travis was an IT project manager at Lucent Technologies and believed his salary was enough to support their small family. Besides, Elana had promised that once she passed the nursing exam, she'd easily find a position at a local hospital to help with expenses.

Travis wasn't sure when it became clear that Elana would never keep her promise. While he slowly climbed the pay scale at Lucent, she spent more time—and more money—shopping for things they could barely afford. After buying the house she wanted, his salary—even with several increases over the years—barely covered their monthly expenses. Elana's excess spending pretty much took care of anything left over. Despite their strained finances, she wore the latest fashions and drove a new 2025 BMW. Travis still wore the clothes he'd owned when they met over seven years ago and drove the same 2011 Honda Accord.

This morning, Travis dressed quietly. He knew that if he woke Elana, she'd start up again about his drinking and spending more time at work than at home. He figured it would be easy enough to avoid waking her since he'd slept in the guest room after their argument the night before. Maybe that's why the sound of her voice startled him as he headed toward the front door.

"I'm glad I caught you before you left," she said.

"I didn't mean to wake you," he said, unsure of the direction the conversation might take.

"How could anybody sleep with all the racket you were making, Travis? I just hope you didn't leave me a mess to clean up."

"All I did was take a shower, Elana. There's no mess."

"You mean to tell me you waited until this morning to take a shower? The way you looked when you came home—you should have taken one last night."

"What do you mean, the way I looked? I was just tired."

"I bet you were tired, Travis. So tired that you couldn't respond to the texts I sent you."

"So, we're doing this again? Things got busy yesterday. I didn't see your texts until I was leaving the office, and I called as soon as I could to let you know I was on my way home."

"That's such a lame excuse, Travis. So, when did your office start serving cocktails?"

Travis picked up the bag containing his laptop before responding.

"Christ, Elana. I thought we were done with this last night. What else do you want me to say?"

"You know what, Travis? You don't have to say anything. I could tell you had been drinking as soon as you came through the front door."

"I really don't have time to argue with you this morning, Elana. I can't afford to be late."

"Who's arguing? I've said all I'm going to say about your drinking. Besides, the reason I wanted to catch you was because I need seventy-five dollars for a hair appointment I have this afternoon."

"Seventy-five dollars, Elana? I don't think we can afford to spend that much on a hair appointment this week. Don't we need groceries? Maybe if you wait until payday, I —"

"Wait until payday?" She interrupted. "Isn't that almost two weeks away? You know what, Travis—just forget it."

Elana started toward the stairs, then turned to face Travis. "You know what? I'm really tired of this shit. We never have money for the things I want, but you always seem to have enough money to drink or whatever it is you do."

"That's not true, baby," Travis said resisting the urge to remind her of the money she regularly spent.

"Oh, so now I'm your baby? You'd think you would want your baby looking her best."

"Of course I do, Elana. Things are just tight right now. I promise once I'm promoted to IT manager, we'll have the extra money to do more of the things you like."

"Travis, you're talking about the future. I'm talking about something I need right now—today. It's not like I get my hair done every week, since I've been wearing these braids. Why can't I just charge it?"

"Fine. Go ahead, Elana," Travis said at last. He knew it wouldn't matter if he told her the credit card was almost maxed out again. "Use the VISA. But no more than seventy-five dollars."

"Now, was that so hard?" Elana smiled the first time since coming downstairs. "By the way, I'm going to the gym this morning. So, I'll swing by the grocery store afterwards if we can spare another hundred."

"Sure. I guess that'll be okay," Travis said. He stepped toward Elana and attempted to kiss her goodbye. She turned her head, and his lips brushed her cheek. He looked at her again before pulling the front door open.

"You need to go, Travis, before you're late," Elana said over her shoulder as she headed toward the stairs. "I don't want to be the reason why you don't get that promotion—especially with things being so tight and all."

In his car, Travis looked at the Honda's cracked dash and worn seats. He glanced at the house and frowned. He wondered if there was any way to restore their relationship to a time when Elana eagerly waited for a goodbye kiss every morning. Her kisses had once been all he'd needed to face the daily challenges that came his way. Travis glanced at the house again before opening the glove compartment and removing the bottle of cognac he kept there. He unscrewed the cap and took a sip. After a second sip, Travis glanced at the house one last time before slowly backing out of the driveway.

Chapter 3

Lately, working at Lucent Technologies brought Travis little relief from the stress caused by Elana's lack of attention and financial excess. He'd joined the company in 2008 when Lucent occupied an office so small that most of its staff worked remotely from home. Since then, the company had grown, gone through several reorganizations, and eventually relocated to a larger building with more than a hundred employees in cubicles. Management had since expanded into four departments—human resources, marketing, finance, and information technology. It was during Lucent's growth that Travis progressed from web programmer to IT project manager. It was a position he'd held until six months ago, when he became interim IT manager.

At the time of his appointment, Human Resources told him he would need to sit through an interview before the position became permanent. The interview was supposed to be a mere formality to satisfy EEOC requirements. Back then, the promotion sounded like a sure thing. Now, as Travis thought about the interview scheduled for tomorrow, things felt less certain—especially since

Lucent Technologies had shifted its focus primarily to artificial intelligence-related projects. He'd taken courses at Virginia College to broaden his skill set, but his limited knowledge of artificial intelligence had become apparent to management. As a result, three months ago, management reopened the vacant IT project manager's position Travis once held and hired Carnegie Mellon computer science graduate, Bradley Stillman.

Bradley was supposed to report to him. Instead, they butted heads from the start. Bradley rarely kept him informed about the IT department's projects. That made it harder for Travis to update senior management. Satisfying that requirement before his weekly meeting with the Chief Technology Officer, Andrew Drucker, was why calling Bradley was the first thing on Travis's agenda.

"Good morning, Bradley. This is Travis," he said, trying not to sound too desperate. "Can we meet for about thirty minutes this morning so you can bring me up to speed on the projects the team is working on?"

"Okay, let me get that together for you," Bradley said. "I'll stop by your cubicle as soon as I roll everything up."

"Hey, Bradley," Travis said. "The sooner the better. I'm supposed to meet with the CTO at ten-thirty and I really need to give him a complete update on what the team is working on."

"Sure thing. I'll see you shortly," Bradley said, then hung up.

Travis went back to reviewing emails. One from the CEO's administrative assistant, contained slides for the CEO's weekly managers' meeting. As Travis began reviewing the slides, his thoughts drifted back to the difficult time he was having with Bradley. He recalled how when he was IT project manager, he had provided updates to the CTO immediately after meetings with the analysts. Now, although Bradley reported to him, he had to practically demand updates.

Instead of completing his review of the materials provided by the CEO's administrative assistant, Travis decided to look over the information he planned to present to the CTO. But he knew that without the project updates from Bradley, his report would be incomplete. It was just about nine-thirty when he saw the CTO walking toward his cubicle.

"Good morning, Andrew," Travis said once he felt the CTO was close enough to hear him. "Are we meeting in your office or in the conference room at ten-thirty?"

Andrew glanced at him as though he hadn't planned to stop. A look of confusion blanketed his face before he responded.

"Oh, our meeting won't be necessary, Travis. I ran into Bradley. He gave me a pretty thorough update. I'm pretty sure I have everything I need for this afternoon's manager's meeting with the CEO. Bradley said he'd let you know we'd spoken."

"Bradley gave you an update," Travis repeated. "He didn't mention having to see you. I don't understand."

"Yes. He left my office about fifteen minutes ago," Andrew said. "He had everything I needed on a flash drive. I was on my way to return the drive to him, but I can leave it with you if you're going to see him."

"Sure," Travis said. He took the drive from Andrew and felt his anger growing. "I'll make sure he gets it."

"Let Bradley know how much we appreciate the good work he's doing," Andrew said. "It looks like we're on track to meet the milestones we're shooting for."

Travis watched Andrew head back toward his office. He looked at the flash drive and turned it over in his hand several times before placing it on his desk. He stared at the drive a moment longer before plugging it into his computer. After reviewing the contents, he copied the files to his computer and dialed Bradley's phone number.

"Hey, Travis. I was just getting ready to call you," Bradley said, answering the phone on the first ring. "I got tied up with a customer. Is there still time for me to brief you before your ten-thirty with the CTO?"

"Don't worry about the meeting, Bradley. That's not why I called."

"So, you need something else?"

"You can come pick up your flash drive whenever you get a chance."

"What flash drive, Travis? I don't recall giving you a flash drive."

"It's the one you gave to the CTO this morning."

"Oh, that flash drive. I —. Well —. Look, I'll just come get it right now," Bradley said, then hung up.

A few minutes later, Bradley was standing outside Travis's cubicle. Travis waved him in, and Bradley took a seat.

"Look, Travis, before you say anything, I was on my way to see you when I ran into the CTO," Bradley rattled off, then stopped to catch his breath. "He asked me what the team was working on so, I gave him the drive I was going to give to you."

Travis stared at Bradley, then yanked the flash drive from his computer and tossed it on the desk.

"Do me a favor, Bradley. The next time the CTO asks you for project-related information, I would appreciate it if you'd tell him to check with me. I'm supposed to be the one who provides weekly updates to him about what the IT Department is doing."

"Well, he didn't seem to mind me giving him the information."

"That's not the point, Bradley. There's such a thing as a chain of command. How would you feel if your analysts provided the CTO with project updates without your knowledge?"

"Travis, I guess you don't consider the chain of command broken when Karen provides you with project information. More than a few times I've looked for Karen and found her over here in your cubicle. I'm pretty sure she keeps you updated on everything the team is doing."

"Bradley, Karen has nothing to do with this. And yes, we talk, but not about any specific project." Travis sat up straighter in his chair, then leaned in Bradley's direction. "Besides, what difference does it make if Karen and I discuss projects I'm already responsible for?"

"Look, Travis. I don't know what you expect me to do. If the CTO asks a question I'm not going to act like I don't know the answer if I do," Bradley said. He picked up the flash drive and walked toward the door. "I'm probably the only one who can explain the projects anyway. Do you even know which algorithms we're using—or how the data's managed?"

It took every bit of self-control for Travis not to immediately respond. His hesitancy came partly from his dislike for Bradley, and partly from knowing he'd regret anything he said. It was also because he knew what Bradley said was partially true. He didn't understand all of the technical details underlying the projects the team was currently working on. But, just as Travis was about to respond, he noticed the CTO approaching.

"Oh, there you are, Brad," the CTO said and stepped inside Travis's cubicle. "I was on my way to see you. Are you busy?"

"Not too busy if you need me for something, Andrew," Bradley said. "I was just picking up the flash drive you left with Travis."

"Well, if I can steal you away for a few minutes, I have a couple more questions about your projects. I have to admit, some of this stuff is a little over my head." The CTO smiled and turned in Travis's direction, "Will you excuse us?"

Travis nodded and watched Bradley follow the CTO toward the conference room. When the CTO entered the room ahead of him, Bradley turned and smiled at Travis, who tried to act as though he hadn't noticed.

When the conference room door closed, Travis thought about Bradley's comments. Bradley was right—Karen had been keeping him in the loop. After all, he couldn't rely on Bradley. But Karen wasn't just someone who provided him with project updates. They had met when she interviewed for the applications analyst position about five years ago.

During the interview, he'd immediately realized she was more than just another pretty face; she brought innovation and intelligence to the team of IT professionals he supervised at the time. Since then, they had worked together on various projects. She not only proved to be a supportive team player, but in time became a close friend, to the point that many around the office referred to her as his work wife. Ironically, as his bond with Karen flourished, his marriage with Elana deteriorated.

Travis looked up from his computer monitor just in time to see Karen heading in his direction.

"Hey, you," Karen said once she was inside his cubicle.

"Hey, Karen," he said. "What's up?"

"Are we still on for lunch?" she asked and stepped out of the cubicle. "If so, we need to leave now. I want to be back before one-thirty."

Travis quickly logged out of his computer and caught up with Karen as she headed toward the elevators.

* * *

Travis and Karen ate lunch together just about every workday. Even when they brought lunch from home, they ate together in Lucent Technologies' lunchroom. In the beginning, when Karen was his direct report, lunch was an opportunity to brainstorm ideas about the projects they were working on at the time. Now that Bradley was Karen's direct supervisor, their lunches together were less focused on work.

"So, what do you have going on at one-thirty?" Travis asked once he'd given the server his order.

"Not much really," Karen said. "Bradley wants to review the algorithms for the deep learning project."

"He stopped by my cubicle this morning and never mentioned that he had a meeting scheduled for this afternoon," Travis said. "I don't know how many times I've asked him to let me know when team meetings are scheduled."

"I don't think this is going to be a team meeting," Karen said. "He said he just had a few questions about the projects I was working on. It didn't sound like Natalie or Ben were going to be there. But then again, you never know about Bradley. He can be pretty vague sometimes."

"Well, if he was planning a meeting for this afternoon I wouldn't be able to attend anyway. I have the CEO's managers' meeting at one-thirty."

"Speaking of managers," Karen said. "I'm sure you're excited about the interview tomorrow."

"I don't know if excited is what I'm feeling lately, Karen. I'm definitely not feeling as confident as I did a few months ago."

"Why not, Travis? I thought human resources said the interview was just a formality when you were placed in the interim position."

"That's what they said then, but with everyone at Lucent excited about AI, I'm not sure how management feels about keeping me in the position permanently. Whenever I talk to senior management, my promotion is never mentioned, and lately, the CTO has been talking more to Bradley about project-related stuff than to me."

"I'm sure you'll be fine. Maybe what you're feeling is just nerves. After all, a promotion to IT manager is a pretty big deal."

"You could be right, I guess. Still, you have to admit, Bradley has been getting a lot of attention lately. Did you know he met with the CTO this morning without my knowledge and updated him on the team's projects?"

"No, but maybe you shouldn't worry so much." Karen sighed, then glanced at her phone before continuing. "I really doubt senior management would choose Bradley over you, Travis. You have seniority and have held down the interim IT manager's position for the past six months. I'm sure by now everybody knows Bradley is just a kiss-ass."

Travis hoped Karen was right. The promotion would not only come with added responsibility but also a considerable pay raise. As he thought about the promotion, instead of imagining Elana by his side, he wondered how life would be with a woman like Karen. They were a successful team at work, and he imagined the bond they shared would carry over into other aspects of life. He watched Karen as she typed a message on her phone. He smiled when she looked up, but noticed a change in her demeanor.

"Everything okay, Karen?"

"Yes. Everything's just fine," she said. "Are you ready to head back to the office?"

"Yeah. I guess we should. I do have the managers' meeting at one-thirty, and you have your meeting with Bradley. You sure you're okay?"

"I'm okay, really." Karen slowly rotated her head from side to side before continuing. "Craig called the office. Someone told him I had gone to lunch—with you."

"Well, that shouldn't be a big deal. Everybody has to eat."

"I know, but he just texted me to enjoy my lunch date. And he said to say hi to my boyfriend."

Travis watched Karen's eyes moisten. He was aware of her boyfriend, Craig, and from what he could tell, the relationship was on its last leg. According to Karen, although they still shared an apartment, they were basically just roommates now. She'd already given Craig an ultimatum to either move out of the apartment by the end of the month or she would move in with her sister, Kiara, and he would have to sign a new lease. Travis wished there was something he could do to uplift Karen's spirits, but she remained quiet during the drive back to the office.

* * *

"So, how was lunch?" Bradley asked as soon as they walked off the elevator. Travis could tell by the smirk on Bradley's face that he couldn't care less.

"It was pretty good," Travis said. "You should come along sometime, Bradley."

"I appreciate the offer, but I wouldn't want to intrude," Bradley said. "By the way, Karen, you received a call shortly after you left for lunch. Somebody named Greg... Craig... something like that. He said it was important that you return his call."

"Thanks, Bradley," Karen said, exchanging glances with Travis.

"Okay then," Bradley said. "It's almost one-thirty, Karen. Are you ready?"

"Sure," Karen said, looking toward Travis again. "You got anything else?"

"No. Not at the moment," Travis said, then turned toward Bradley. "Let's plan to discuss the projects you and the team are working on by the end of the week."

"Yeah, sure thing, Travis," Bradley said with the usual sarcasm, then returned his attention to Karen. "You, ready?"

A few minutes after Karen and Bradley disappeared, Travis's cell phone lit up.

"Team meeting," Karen texted.

"Figures," Travis replied.

"Talk to him about it," she texted.

"Rather talk to you," he replied.

"When?" she asked.

"After work?" Travis texted, and immediately regretted the suggestive tone of his text and waited nervously for a response. After a few minutes, he turned off his phone and headed to the conference room.

* * *

The one-thirty managers' meeting began as usual, with each manager summarizing their department's priorities and goals. Each tried to convince Lucent Technologies' CEO, Patrick Oberman, that their department's concerns outweighed the others. As usual, the marketing manager, Chad Cunningham, stressed the need for more advertising, which always conflicted with the finance manager, Scott Keslo's, emphasis on reducing costs. Travis listened to the two argue back and forth until the CEO finally intervened.

"Gentlemen, I think we can table the advertising question until I've had an opportunity to review next quarter's advertising costs in more detail," he said. "I'll expect you two to crunch the numbers and send me a written proposal by this Friday. Let's move on to Human Resources. Janice—do you mind?"

The human resources manager, Janice Powell, cleared her throat before directing everyone's attention to the projector screen displaying Lucent Technologies' organizational chart. Senior management was at the top of the chart, followed by the four departments—Human Resources, Finance, Marketing, and Information Technology. Janice began by referring to the financial manager's point about reducing costs.

"I think everyone would agree that Lucent Technologies has seen a lot of growth over the past few years. As a result, we've begun to experience some overstaffing."

"Excuse me, Janice," Travis interrupted. "I'm not sure I understand what you mean by overstaffing."

"To put it simply, Travis, with Lucent's recent restructuring, there is now some overlap in job responsibilities. The reductions will allow us to do more with less. I think—"

"Janice, I don't want to waste everyone's time going over something that's already been covered," the CEO interrupted. "A copy of your slides and the related background information were sent to everyone this morning. Let's move on to the slide showing the proposed reductions."

"Yes, I'll put it up right now," Janice said. She advanced to the requested slide before continuing. "The bolded position titles are under consideration."

No one commented. Travis flipped through the meeting packet and curse himself for not reviewing the slides earlier. If he had, he would have noticed personnel reductions were being considered not only in the Financial and Marketing departments but also in Information Technology. The proposed cut to IT would eliminate Bradley's position as IT project manager, with its duties absorbed by the IT manager position he currently held. After allowing the managers to review the slide, the CEO motioned to Janice.

"Thanks, Janice. I'll respond directly to managers who've submitted justifications for retaining any of the proposed cuts. So, ladies and gentlemen, if there's no additional business to discuss, we're going to adjourn. Andrew, we'll take a look at your team's project status once everyone leaves."

"Is there a timeline for when the reductions will take place?" Travis asked, unable to hide his concern. "I mean, who decided which responsibilities the IT manager would take on?"

The CEO looked toward the CTO, then back at Travis.

"Travis, these reductions have been under consideration for some time and Andrew agrees there is quite a bit of overlap between the IT manager and IT project manager positions. Both positions report to him. Who else besides our Chief Technical Officer is in a better position to decide?"

Travis looked at Andrew, then back at the CEO, unsure of the best way to express his concerns.

"Travis, you're probably not going to see any other reductions," Janice offered. "The only other personnel change I'm tracking in the IT department involves the QA analyst role. As you know, Ben Williamson has given his two-week notice."

"Sure, I know Ben's leaving, but I think—" Travis began, but the CEO cut him off.

"I think we've discussed personnel changes enough for now. A decision regarding the proposed reductions hasn't been made yet. But let me be clear. I'm the one who will make the final decision on reductions. This meeting is adjourned."

* * *

Back in his cubicle, Travis couldn't stop thinking about the proposed cuts. He was frustrated—not only because the CTO hadn't asked for his input, but also because he didn't know how the changes might impact his potential promotion to IT manager. As he flipped through the meeting slides again, he noticed the lights in several nearby cubicles going off. He checked his phone and was disappointed that Karen hadn't responded to his last text.

As a few more cubicles darkened, Travis powered down his computer and switched off his lights. Before heading out, he texted Karen again, asking if she wanted to meet for drinks at the Commonwealth Lounge. He'd always been able to count on her encouragement and support. Maybe now she could help him overcome the increasing uncertainty he felt about tomorrow's interview.

Chapter 4

Karen dropped the bag containing her laptop onto the chair near the door; relieved to find Craig wasn't home. As usual, the apartment reeked of marijuana and the coffee table in front of the television was littered with beer bottles. Karen picked up the empty bottles and a half-eaten box of chicken and broccoli that had leaked soy sauce onto the chair cushion.

She tossed everything into the kitchen trash can and looked around the room. It was hard to ignore the sink filled with dirty dishes and the feeling that life had been a lot simpler before she let Craig move in. Unfortunately, the few minutes of relief Karen thought she might enjoy vanished when she entered her bedroom.

"Craig, what are you doing in here? I thought we agreed—my room was off limits. Craig, wake up!"

"Damn, Karen, what's the problem?" Craig said, struggling to a seated position on the edge of the bed. "I was watching TV and I guess I must have dozed off."

"What's the problem, Craig?" she said. "Where do you want me to begin?"

"You know something, Karen?" he said. "You can be a real bitch sometimes. Karen's eyes moistened as she looked at the man who, not too long ago, had shared her bed. His once neatly groomed hair hadn't been cut in months and was now plastered on one side of his head. He squinted at her through bloodshot eyes, apparently unaware of the trail of slobber that had dried on his cheek.

"Please get out of my room, Craig. I want to take a shower and change my clothes."

"Go ahead. Shit, it wasn't too long ago we showered together. Maybe you forgot you're supposed to be my woman."

"Please, Craig. I've had a long day, and I don't have the energy for this right now."

"So, I guess you must have used up all your energy when you went to lunch with your boyfriend."

"Boyfriend? Craig, I have no idea what or who you're talking about," Karen said. "Look, can't I just get out of these clothes so I can take a shower, please?"

"Don't think I don't know you have a thing for that dude at work. What's his name?" Craig paused and looked down at his lap for a moment, then back at Karen. "Travis. That's his name, right?"

"Craig, I've told you a thousand times. Travis is just a coworker—nothing more."

"Is that what you call someone you text all the time and go to lunch with every day?" Craig asked.

Karen didn't respond. She couldn't deny her feelings for Travis and wasn't about to apologize for their friendship. Besides, despite having strong feelings for him, he was married—although Karen suspected not happily—but so far, she had respected the boundaries his marriage created.

"Well?" Karen said, returning her attention to Craig.

"Well, what?" he asked.

"Look, just go in the other room so I can take a shower. Maybe I should start locking my bedroom door when I'm not home."

Craig struggled to his feet and stared at Karen for a moment before heading for the door. At the doorway, he stopped and turned back toward her.

"Go ahead and take your damn shower, Karen. Fuck you and Travis."

Once Craig finally stumbled out of the room, Karen slammed the door and locked it. She walked over to the bed and was about to sit down, but the image of Craig lying there repulsed her so much that she sat in one of the nearby chairs instead. After checking her phone for additional messages, Karen undressed and jumped in the shower. As soon as she turned off the water and wrapped herself in a towel, she heard a knock on the bedroom door.

"What now, Craig? I just got out of the shower and I'm trying to get dressed."

"Hey, look, Karen. I just want to say I'm sorry about what I said earlier, okay?"

Karen remained still and continued listening. This was the part she hated the most—the insincere apologies and promises.

"Karen, you hear me, babe? Can you just open the door so we can talk? You hear me, babe?"

Karen cringed every time Craig called her *babe*. She listened to him as she continued drying off and began dressing. Lately, it was the same thing just about every day. She'd come home from work and he'd be either asleep or nodding in front of the television. They'd argue, and then he'd apologize and make promises he'd never keep. It hadn't always been like this. When she first met Craig he seemed like someone who could finally take her mind off of Travis. But now, as she listened to Craig outside of her bedroom door, the only thing on her mind was Travis.

"Hey, babe. Come on. I know you can hear me."

"Craig, I'll be out when I finish putting my clothes on."

Karen slipped on a pair of jeans and one of her favorite blouses. She moisturized her face and applied some light makeup. Satisfied with the way she looked, Karen brushed her hair, then reached for her favorite perfume, which she tucked into her purse with her cell phone. When she finally opened the bedroom door, she was greeted by the skunky odor of marijuana.

"Took you long enough," Craig said, offering her the joint he was smoking. "You want some of this?"

"No, I don't, and you shouldn't either," Karen said. She walked over to the refrigerator and peeked inside. "I thought you were supposed to start a new job today?"

"Yeah, I went down there, but I left early." Craig took a long drag from the joint and knocked the ash into an empty beer bottle. "You sure you don't want some of this?"

"How can you leave early the first day on a job?" Karen asked.

"Look, babe, that job wasn't the right fit, okay," he said, sucking on the joint again and blowing a stream of smoke in her direction. "Besides, I know I can do better."

Karen shook her head, then picked up her keys and headed toward the door.

"Craig, I'm going out to get something to eat. I'll be back shortly."

"So, Karen, do you really think you can just come home from work, change clothes, and leave? And why are you all dressed up?" Craig stood slowly, as if he might approach her. Karen placed her hands on her hips.

"Craig, don't even think you have anything to do with what I wear or where I go. Don't forget you're supposed to be moving out by the end of the month."

"And there you go with that shit again," he said. "I thought we agreed that once I found another job, we'd renew the lease."

"No, Craig. What we agreed was that living together wasn't working, and either you would move out by the end of August, or I would," Karen said. "The end of August is only two weeks away and it doesn't look like you're trying to do anything but hang around the apartment and get high."

Craig sat down and relit the joint. His intense stare made Karen nervous. She regretted not having responded to Travis's earlier text before coming home. Her phone vibrated, interrupting the silence.

"You answering that?" Craig asked, a cloud of smoke escaping from his mouth as he spoke.

"It's probably just work," Karen said without looking at her phone. "I'll check it later."

When the phone vibrated a second time, Karen removed it from her purse and looked at the display. She noticed Travis had sent two additional texts. In the first, he asked if she was going to be able to meet with him, and the second contained the address of a lounge located across from the Greyhound Bus Station on Arthur Ashe Boulevard.

"Yeah, I bet it's just work," Craig said. "How about letting me see for myself?"

"Craig, I don't have time for this right now. I'll be back in a little while," Karen said. She muted her phone and slid it back into her purse.

"You know, just because we're going through a rough time right now, Karen, doesn't mean you have to disrespect me."

"Craig, nobody's disrespecting you. There's nothing in the refrigerator, and I'm hungry. I just want to get something to eat. I really don't understand the problem."

"Okay, then I'll go with you. Where are we headed?"

"Didn't you just finish eating Chinese?"

"Nah, that was lunch. Let me wash my face and change shirts. Won't take me but a minute."

Karen watched Craig leave the room. Once she heard water running in the bathroom, she pulled out her phone and began typing.

"Can't make it. Too much drama," she texted. Then, remembering Travis's interview, she decided to send him another text: "Good luck tomorrow. You'll do fine."

"So, you ready or what?" Craig asked. He came back into the room, pulling a dingy white t-shirt over his head. "Where are we going?"

Karen slid her phone back into her purse and looked at Craig. She shook her head, unable to believe she had let herself end up in this situation.

"You know what, Craig, I've changed my mind. You can still go if you want to."

"What? I thought you said you were hungry."

"I was, but I've lost my appetite. Don't let me stop you though."

"Come on, Karen. Don't be like that."

"Be like what, Craig? As usual, you're trying to make something out of nothing. I just can't keep doing this."

"Baby, it's not too late for us if we want this to work. You once said you loved me."

Karen walked over to the refrigerator and grabbed a bottle of water.

"I once thought I did," she said, then walked back to her bedroom and closed the door.

* * *

As Travis sat in the Commonwealth Lounge, he was no longer thinking about the personnel reductions at Lucent or the interview scheduled for tomorrow. Instead, he watched the traffic going in and out of the bus station across the street and wondered if Karen had taken his earlier text seriously. Since she hadn't responded, Travis had sent her another one, asking again if she was willing to meet him for a drink. Then, as an afterthought, he'd sent a text with the location of the lounge.

While he sipped a second beer, waiting for Karen to respond, Travis thought about his relationship with Elana and the possible promotion to IT manager. Both seemed like part of the same dream—one that was beginning to feel less and less real.

"How are you doing this evening, sir?"

Travis looked up to find Nicky, the server from the night before, standing at his table. She stared at him as though attempting to read the expression on his face.

"Oh, I'm doing okay. I've already ordered, though," Travis said, holding up his beer bottle. "So, is it Nicky or Nekeesha?"

"It's Nicky, sir. I..."

"And please, call me Travis," he interrupted.

"I just came over to apologize for the other evening," she said with a smile, then added, "Travis."

"Apologize? Apologize for what?"

"I probably seemed a little short with your friend the last time you were here," she said.

"My friend? Nah. I didn't know that guy. He just wanted a seat near the window."

"Well, I still want to apologize for the way I acted. It's just that every time he comes in..."

"Oh, so he's a regular?" Travis asked. "I can't say I've ever seen him in here before."

"He was here a couple of times last week with another guy." Nicky shrugged, glancing toward the kitchen. "Every time I see him, he tries to come on to me. It gives me the creeps."

"I can't imagine why he would do that," Travis said with mock surprise, until he realized from Nicky's expression that she was taking him seriously. "Look, I'm just kidding, Nicky. You are an attractive young woman. I'm sure you have plenty of guys trying to talk to you all the time."

"Not so much, Travis, and when they're not your type, it can be pretty annoying," she said, glancing again toward the kitchen. "Especially when you're working. Speaking of which, it looks like my order's up."

Just as Nicky was turning to leave, Travis pulled a twenty-dollar bill from his pocket and handed it to her.

"What's this for?" she asked. "I'm not your server tonight."

"It's for last night," Travis said.

"But I..." Nicky stammered. Before she could finish, Travis continued.

"You went on break before I could tip you. I was hoping to see you again so I could give it to you."

Nicky thanked him and tucked the bill into her pants pocket. She waved in Travis's direction before rushing toward the kitchen. Travis watched Nicky for a moment longer before pulling out his phone. He noticed a text from Karen that said she wouldn't be able to meet him. Disappointed, he finished his beer and ordered another shot of Hennessy, which he downed quickly. When he stood to leave, Travis stumble backward into something—or someone. He turned and saw a man stooping to retrieve a duffel bag from the floor.

"My bad, I didn't see you, man," Travis said. "Let me help you with that."

"Nah, I'm good," the man said. A backpack hung from one shoulder. When he stood, he slung the strap of the duffel bag over the other shoulder. He was about Travis's height, with the same medium-brown complexion. Someone who didn't know any better might have assumed they were brothers, even though Travis wore a short natural and the man's hair was sponge-brushed. Travis extended his hand.

J. Marcus Evins

"Name's Travis. I guess I need to look where I'm going."

"Not a problem. I wasn't watching where I was going either," the man replied while shaking Travis's hand. "Name's Orlando."

"Look, Orlando, let me make up for almost knocking you down. If you're drinking, I'm buying."

"Wish I could, man. But I have a bus to catch," Orlando said. "Appreciate the offer, though."

Travis shook Orlando's hand, then watched him exit the lounge and disappear into the bus station across the street. After checking his phone again, Travis walked to his car and headed home, unable to shake the dread he felt about tomorrow's interview.

Chapter 5

The first thing Travis saw when he pulled into the driveway was Elana leaning over the front porch railing, talking to their next-door neighbor, Maurice. Her tight shorts accentuated her long, tanned legs, and the snug V-neck T-shirt she was wearing left little to the imagination. Travis noticed Maurice's eyes lingering on her—until the sound of the car caught his attention. The drinks he'd had at the lounge were not enough to dull the jealousy he felt when Maurice slowly raised his hand and waved. Elana glanced in his direction, then disappeared into the house.

Travis took his time getting out of the car, hoping to give the impression he wasn't bothered by their appearance on the porch. Despite living next door for almost six years, Maurice was not someone he considered a friend. It wasn't that Maurice wasn't friendly or sociable enough. At six-two with chiseled features and a gift for gab, Maurice was anything but unsociable. But what Travis couldn't stand—apart from Elana suggesting that he resembled the singer Maxwell—was that every conversation with Maurice inevitably circled back to his favorite topic—Maurice.

To avoid, or at least delay interacting with Maurice, Travis headed toward the mailbox at the end of the driveway. He was pretty sure Elana hadn't checked the mail; she never did, even though she was home all day. At the mailbox, he sorted through the usual bills and junk mail. By the time he walked back up the driveway, to his relief, Maurice had also disappeared.

When he entered the house, Elana was sitting in front of the television. Her cell phone vibrated almost immediately, and she began talking to the caller before Travis could say hello. Even though Elana was on the phone, he could feel her eyes on him as he walked by. After Travis placed his cell phone and laptop on the dining room table, he sorted through the mail again before tossing the junk mail in the trash and heading toward the kitchen with the remaining bills.

In the kitchen, Travis stared into the nearly empty refrigerator. It was obvious Elana hadn't gone to the grocery store like she said she would after her morning workout. After searching through the cabinets, Travis found a jar of peanut butter and made a sandwich using the last two slices of bread. As he poured the last of the milk into a glass, Elana entered the kitchen.

"I'm surprised you haven't already eaten," she said. "I thought you might have grabbed something on your way home since you're getting here so late."

"Come on, Elana. It's not that late," Travis said. He glanced at the time displayed on the microwave. "It just took me a little longer to finish things up at work, that's all. At least I'm home earlier than yesterday."

"Not by much. It's almost seven-thirty, and yesterday you got home around eight," Elana said, handing Travis his cell phone. "I heard it vibrate. It looks like you missed a text."

Travis glanced at the phone's display, then at Elana. "So, what's going on with Maurice?"

"Maurice?" Elana repeated the name as though she was uncertain about who Travis was talking about. "Oh, you know how he is. He was just chatting. Did you talk to him?"

"No, I didn't get a chance. I checked the mail before coming in. He was gone by the time I made it to the house. Besides, I think it's you he's more interested in talking to anyway," Travis said, eyeing Elana's outfit. "Especially when you're dressed like that."

"Don't be ridiculous, Travis," she said, rolling her eyes. "Maurice is just being neighborly. And this is what plenty of women wear to work out. Didn't I tell you I was going to the gym today?"

"I know, but I thought you were going this morning," Travis said.

"I planned to, but I was running late and decided to work out after my hair appointment," Elana said. "All I needed was a touch-up. Anyway, Maurice was talking about his job. Did you know he's getting promoted again? This will be his second promotion since we've known him. Speaking of which, have you heard anything about your promotion?"

"Not really," Travis said. "I still have an interview to sit through. It's scheduled for —"

"I still can't believe you have to interview for a job you've been doing for over a year," Elana interrupted. "That doesn't make any sense."

"Actually, it's only been six months," Travis said. "Besides, HR said the interview is just a formality."

"So, when is the interview supposed to be?" Elana asked but continued talking before Travis could answer. "Did they at least tell you how much more money you'll make? We can definitely use it."

"I can agree with that," Travis said, patting the stack of bills in front of him and immediately regretting it when Elana rolled her eyes toward the ceiling and pursed her lips.

"Anyway, maybe once you're making more money, I can stop wearing these braids and start getting my hair done every week again—like I used to. I know you want me looking my best," Elana said, spinning around and striking a pose as if she were a runway model.

As he watched Elana, Travis forgot about the stack of bills, the dry peanut butter sandwich he was eating for dinner, and her obvious lack of concern about the most important interview of his career tomorrow.

"Oh, so you like what you see?" Elana teased.

"Of course I do," Travis said and wrapped his arms around her waist.

"Stop, Travis. I'm tired," Elana laughed, slipping out of his grasp. "I'm really sore from my workout. I think I'll take a shower and turn in early. You might want to do the same."

Travis watched Elana head upstairs. He wondered if the suggestion that he go to bed early was an invitation to join her. For a moment, he considered the possibility—until the bathroom door closed. Once he heard Elana turn on the shower, he picked up his phone and checked his text messages. He scrolled past Karen's earlier message, and clicked on one he hadn't read, wishing him luck on tomorrow's interview.

After deleting both texts, Travis grabbed two bottles of Coors Light from the refrigerator and returned to the table. Sipping from one of the bottles, he tried to sort through the bills again. His thoughts drifted back to Karen, and he wondered what she meant by "too much drama." He was pretty sure it had something to do with her boyfriend, Craig. He considered the interview scheduled for tomorrow, but by the time he finished his second beer, his thoughts had returned to Elana.

* * *

When Travis entered the bedroom, it took a few seconds for his eyes to adjust to the faint glow of the nightlight. He undressed quietly, slid under the sheet, and reached for Elana's warmth. She stirred slightly, moaning softly as she turned toward him. Encouraged, he pulled her closer as she snuggled against him. When their lips met, her eyes snapped open.

"What are you doing, Travis?" she asked as she rolled away. "I told you I was tired."

"But I—" Travis hesitated, his voice trailing off.

"But you what? You're drunk, aren't you? I can smell alcohol on your breath."

"No, don't be ridiculous, Elana. I only had a couple of beers. I just thought we could—"

"You thought we could what, Travis? I told you I was sore from my workout. What you need to do is go to sleep."

"Okay, already, Elana. I'm sorry. Just go back to sleep."

Travis lay still, chastising himself for misreading the situation. In the dim light, he watched Elana as she rolled over to face away from him. Soon, her soft snores broke the silence, and he closed his eyes. Travis wasn't sure how long he'd been asleep when Elana's voice startled him.

"Wake up, Travis," she said, shoving him several times.

"What? What's going on?" he asked, now fully awake. "Are you all right?"

"No, Travis, I'm not all right. I can't sleep because you're snoring."

"Snoring? I just fell asleep," he said, confused.

"Travis, maybe one of us should sleep in the other bedroom," she said.

"How about if I just turn in the opposite direction?" Travis said.

"You know that's not going to work, Travis," Elana said. She jumped out of bed and grabbed her cell phone from the nightstand. "Don't worry about it. I'll go."

Despite her irritation, Travis couldn't ignore how sexy Elana looked as she rushed toward the bedroom door wearing only her bra and panties.

"Wait, Elana," he said, sitting up. "You don't have to leave. I'll go."

Without a word, Elana returned to her side of the bed and slid under the sheets. Travis got up and looked in her direction, but she'd already turned away. He grabbed his clothes from the floor and stumbled down the dark hallway to the guest room. Once inside the room, Travis dropped his clothes in a pile. He sat on the edge of the bed, trying to make sense of what had just happened.

Unable to sleep, Travis crept downstairs and quietly opened the dining room cabinet. In the dim light, he felt around until he found what he was looking for and twisted off the cap. He tilted the bottle to his lips and felt the bittersweet liquid burn down to his nearly empty stomach. After taking another sip, Travis began to feel the liquor's calming effect and decided to take the bottle with him to the guest room. Still unable to sleep, he lay in bed thinking about his life—and whether a promotion would make any difference. Then, just before daybreak, he drifted off to sleep. The empty liquor bottle slipped from his hand and rolled under the bed.

Chapter 6

The interview wasn't the first thing Travis thought about as he squinted at the sunlight cascading through the bedroom window. He was unable to register a single thought through the fog created by his lack of sleep and the alcohol he'd consumed the night before. His head throbbed, and when he remembered why he was in the guest room, the throbbing increased. It was only after noticing the clock on the nightstand and realizing he was going to be late for work that he remembered the interview.

Searching for something to wear only made Travis more anxious. He decided there was no need to check the bedroom closet where Elana was sleeping. He wasn't ready to face her anyway—especially after what had happened last night. Besides, it was unlikely she had done any laundry. Looking around the room, Travis noticed the pants and shirt he'd worn the day before in a pile on the floor. He laid them on the bed and smoothed out the wrinkles before heading for the shower.

J. Marcus Evins

* * *

"Hey, neighbor," Travis heard a familiar voice behind him as he hurried toward his car. "You're leaving for work a little later than usual this morning, aren't you?"

It was just his luck that, of all days, Maurice happened to be outside when he was running late. He continued toward his car, hoping to avoid conversation with the man, but he could hear footsteps behind him. He turned to face Maurice.

"Damn, Travis, you look like shit. You feeling okay?"

"I'm good, Maurice," Travis said through clenched teeth. "I'm just running a little late. I'll have to talk to you later, okay?"

"Yeah, okay." Maurice laughed. "You know, Travis, I could have loaned you my iron if you needed one."

Travis glared at him without responding and continued to his car. Once he was in the Honda, he looked up after struggling with his seat belt to see Maurice still watching with a smile on his face. When the seat belt finally snapped together, Travis adjusted his rearview mirror and realized he hadn't shaved. He caught a glimpse of Maurice shaking his head before turning around and walking back across the lawn toward his house. Maurice hadn't gone far when Travis stepped out of the car to see why it wouldn't start.

"Any idea what's wrong?" Maurice reappeared at Travis's side just as he lifted the hood. "Tell you what, Travis. How about you get behind the wheel while I jiggle a few wires?"

"No. That's okay, Maurice. I'm pretty sure I can figure this out."

"Come on, Travis. You know what they say. Two heads are better than one. You know this is almost like an old Honda I had a while ago. I bet it's just a loose wire or something. Look, I can grab my toolbox and—"

"No, you don't need to get your toolbox," Travis said, cutting him off. "I'm already late for work. Let's go ahead and try jiggling the wires."

Once he was back in the car, Travis felt his desperation growing. It was already after nine o'clock and Maurice's incessant chatter under the hood only heightened his anxiety. As a last resort, Travis reached for his phone, tapped on the number to the office, and just before he pushed "send," Maurice peeked in the window.

"Go ahead. Give it a try. See if she'll turn over now."

Travis dropped his phone in the passenger seat and twisted the key in the ignition. He listened as the engine whined painfully before finally starting. Maurice slammed the hood closed and walked back around to where Travis sat in the car.

"Man, you really need a new ride. At the very least, you probably need new wires. And I'm smelling a lot of gas. I don't know." Maurice shook his head. "Then again, maybe you just flooded her. Did I ever tell you, before I got my Lexus, I had an old Honda like this one and—"

"And I really have to go now, Maurice," Travis said, cutting him off. He waved, shifted the Honda into reverse, leaving Maurice standing in the driveway.

* * *

It was almost nine-thirty when Travis drove into Lucent Technologies' parking lot. Normally, he would have been pissed that someone had parked in his assigned spot, but this morning he had more to worry about. Besides, he hoped parking as far as possible from the entrance to the building would make his late arrival less noticeable.

Before Travis got out of the car, he glanced in the rearview mirror at the stubble on his face, then reached for the glove compartment. When the door dropped open, the toiletry bag he kept there wasn't the first thing that caught his attention. Instead, he pulled out the bottle of cognac, and his throbbing head almost convinced him that there might be truth in the idea of drinking the hair of the dog. Instead of giving in to temptation, Travis tossed the bottle back in the glove compartment, grabbed the toiletry bag, and headed for the building.

Once he was at his desk, Travis checked the interview schedule and confirmed the first person was scheduled for ten o'clock. He was second on the list and scheduled for eleven. Elated to have enough time to at least shave, he grabbed his toiletry bag. Unfortunately, Claire, the CEO's administrative assistant, stopped him before he made it to the bathroom. She told him he had been moved up on the schedule because the person who was supposed to interview at ten had reconsidered. Now, scheduled for a ten o'clock interview, Travis had only enough time to grab his sports jacket before Claire ushered him into the conference room.

A few minutes later, Travis was seated in a chair across from a table where the members of the interview panel sat. As their eyes met, he felt his uneasiness growing and the familiar conference room seemed to shrink. His boss, Andrew Drucker, sat directly across from him. To Andrew's left was Chad Cunningham from Marketing, and next to Chad was Scott Keslo from Finance. Natalie Nguyen, an analyst Travis had directly supervised before Bradley came on board, sat on Andrew's right. Although he knew everyone on the interview panel, each person introduced themselves. After introductions, Andrew explained the interview process, and the questions began.

The first few questions were about the IT manager's responsibilities, which Travis felt comfortable answering, and he began to relax. Chad cleared his throat loudly before continuing with the next question.

"So, Mr. Pace, can you describe the various types of support an IT manager provides to an organization?"

Chad looked up from the list of questions as did the other panel members and waited. Andrew Drucker interrupted before Travis could answer.

"To be clear, Travis, what we want to know is what are some of the ways you've supported the individual stakeholders or departments here at Lucent Technologies. As interim IT manager two of your peers are on the interview panel. How would you describe the support you've provided to their departments?"

Travis looked at Chad and then Scott. As far as he was concerned, outside of an occasional email and his attendance at staff meetings, he seldom interacted with either of them.

"Most of our interaction occurs during meetings, but I've always made myself available to the different departments," Travis began. "Trying to get up to speed as the interim IT manager has kept me pretty busy. But, like I said, I've always made myself available."

Travis looked at the panel's emotionless faces, unable to interpret how they had received his answer before continuing.

"I'm sure, as I gain more experience, I will be able to provide more in the way of support."

"Okay, thank you," Chad said, and turned toward Natalie, who directed her attention to Travis.

"Mr. Pace. Can you —"

"No, wait a minute, Ms. Nguyen," Andrew interrupted again. "Travis, you mean to tell me you don't know the most obvious ways you provide support to your internal customers as the IT manager?"

Unsure of how to respond, Travis remained silent and listened as Andrew continued.

"What about the computers? What about software? What about all of the technology each of our employees uses? Wouldn't you agree those are resources the IT manager is responsible for?"

"Yes, but I guess I—"

"There's no guessing here, Travis. The IT manager should know the full scope of his responsibilities. Please go ahead, Ms. Nguyen. Sorry for the interruption."

Natalie looked around the room before continuing.

"Mr. Pace, can you define the term sexual harassment and describe the two types that can occur in the workplace?"

"I'm not sure I understand the question," Travis said. He was still trying to recover from the exchange with Andrew and hoped his response would allow him more time to consider how best to answer the question.

"You mean you don't know the definition of sexual harassment, Mr. Pace?" Natalie asked.

"No. I mean yes," Travis said. "I mean, I know the definition of sexual harassment, but I guess I'm not familiar with the two types."

"Okay, so you don't know the two types, Mr. Pace," Natalie said and glanced at Andrew Drucker.

"Let me give you an example of one type," Andrew said unexpectedly. Everyone in the room looked in the CTO's direction. "Let's say you supervise a team consisting of both men and women. You give special attention to one of the women on your team. Several of the other team members feel the woman is benefiting from the additional attention given to her. You follow me, Travis?"

"Yes. I think so," Travis said. "But I'm not sure I'd agree that an incident of sexual harassment has occurred until there's evidence the woman has actually received some sort of benefit."

"Well, Travis, although you might not agree, this scenario could lead to one of the types of sexual harassment often referred to as quid pro quo—or "this for that," Andrew said. "Do you think we could have that sort of problem at Lucent?"

"No. At least not that I'm aware of," Travis answered. He couldn't help but feel that Andrew's question was suggestive of his relationship with Karen.

"Oh, and Travis," Andrew said, "the other type of sexual harassment is called hostile work environment. In my opinion, one type can lead to the other. We don't need either type occurring at Lucent Technologies."

Andrew rocked back in his chair as though he was certain his point had been made.

"Thank you, Andrew," Travis said, then added, "I'm pretty sure neither type exists at Lucent Technologies."

"You can't be too sure, Travis." Andrew looked toward Natalie. "Okay, let's wrap this up. Ms. Nguyen, do you or the other panel members have any other questions for Mr. Pace?"

Natalie slowly moved her head from side to side. The other panel members remained silent.

"Travis, do you have any questions for the panel?" Andrew asked.

"No, I just look forward to hearing from you," Travis said.

Andrew thanked Travis, then announced the panel would be taking a break. As Travis walked toward the door, he heard a chair scrape loudly across the floor and turned to face Andrew.

"So, how are you doing this morning, Travis?" Andrew placed his hand on Travis's shoulder. "I mean, is everything going okay?"

The question made Travis more nervous than he'd been sitting in front of the interview panel. It was as though the CTO was asking a question to which he already knew the answer.

"Sure, everything's going great, Andrew. I just hope I did okay."

Instead of responding, Andrew smiled, but his attention seemed to be on something else. Travis turned to see what had captured Andrew's attention and saw Bradley seated in the waiting area, dressed in a blue suit, pressed white shirt, and tie. A leather-bound portfolio rested in his lap. Suddenly feeling uncomfortable, Travis shook Andrew's hand and headed toward his cubicle.

* * *

"Hey you," Travis looked up a few minutes later to see Karen at the entrance of his cubicle. "Have you already finished your interview?"

He nodded and looked in the direction of the conference room without responding.

"Is everything okay? How did it go?"

"Okay, I guess."

"Just okay? So, what kind of questions did they ask you?"

"I can't go into too much detail right now, Karen," he said, scanning the area outside his cubicle. "Maybe later."

"How about over lunch?" Karen suggested. "You look like you could use a break. We could go to the cafeteria down the street."

"To tell the truth, Karen, I don't think I'm going to lunch today. The interview kind of threw me off schedule and I have to catch up on a few things." He shifted his chair forward and looked toward the conference room again.

"Travis, are you sure everything's okay? Who are you looking for?"

"Nobody, Karen. Look, I'll catch up with you later this afternoon. Maybe after you come back from lunch."

"Okay, Travis—but are you sure everything's okay?" Karen leaned forward and lowered her voice. "I mean, is everything okay between us? I really wanted to meet you after work yesterday, and I'm sorry I wasn't able to."

"Oh no. We're good. I know what you're dealing with. I hope it didn't seem like I was putting any pressure on you."

"You? Put pressure on me? Of course not." Karen smiled slightly. "You actually help take some of the pressure off. Anyway, I'll see you after lunch. Okay?"

Travis watched as Karen walked toward the elevators. Once she disappeared, his thoughts returned to the interview and the image of Bradley sitting outside the conference room. Until today, he hadn't considered Bradley a serious contender for the IT manager position. Now, it was clear how naïve he had been.

Instead of dwelling on the possible outcome of the interview any further, Travis grabbed his shaving kit. Once inside the restroom, he stared at his reflection in the mirror. His eyes were red and the stubble made his face look dirty. As he shaved, Travis wondered if the interview panel had seen anything as bad as what he saw staring back at him.

Shortly after he returned to his cubicle, the conference room door opened. Bradley walked out, followed by the CTO. They shook hands, chatting like old friends. Travis watched their chummy exchange, unable to recall a time when he'd disliked two people more. As Bradley walked away, the CTO motioned to a woman dressed in a business suit seated in the waiting area and escorted her into the conference room.

An hour later, the conference room door opened, and the CTO escorted the woman to the elevators. Once the CTO returned to the conference room, the doors remained closed for nearly another hour. When they opened again, Chad, Scott, and Natalie walked out. The two men headed in the direction of their cubicles, while Natalie walked in Travis's direction on her way to the IT Department.

"Hello, Natalie," he said as she passed the entrance to his cubicle. He could tell she wasn't trying to make eye contact.

"Oh, hi, Mr. Pace. Do you need something?"

"No, just saying hello. I'm sure you've had a long day."

"Yes, it has been a long day, Mr. Pace."

"I hear the team's making a lot of progress toward meeting the AI project milestones. I'm sure you've had a lot to do with that."

"Not just me, Mr. Pace. It's been a team effort. Bradley deserves a lot of credit for moving things along."

Travis noticed Natalie kept averting her eyes as she spoke. It was as though she didn't want him to see what her eyes might reveal. Her behavior seemed especially odd since he had not only been her direct supervisor but had also chaired the interview committee when she was hired. Travis had always felt she was pretty friendly, even though their conversations were always work-related. Now, it felt as though he was talking to a stranger— and the feeling made him more paranoid about the possible outcome of his interview.

"Well, look, Natalie, I don't want to hold you up," he continued. "I guess I'll see you at our next meeting. Keep up the good work."

"Sure, Mr. Pace. Oh, and I'm glad you're feeling better," Natalie said, as she turned and continued toward her cubicle.

"Feeling better," Travis repeated, barely above a whisper. "I've never felt better."

After the conversation with Natalie, Travis's thoughts drifted back to the interview. When he wasn't thinking about the questions he'd been asked, he recalled the image of Bradley in his blue suit, the leather portfolio resting on his lap.

It was almost 5 p.m. when Travis noticed the gradual exodus of nine-to-fivers from the building, that he received a text from Karen.

"Hey you. Everything okay?"

"Not really," he texted.

"What can I do?" she texted.

"Wish I could see you," he texted.

"When?" she texted.

"@ the lounge in one hour," he texted.

"OK. I'll text if I can't make it," she replied.

Travis turned off his phone's screen. He watched the cubicles around him empty and become dark. Most days since becoming the interim IT manager, he'd found plenty of reasons to work beyond five. Today, as he thought about meeting Karen at the lounge, he couldn't think of any.

* * *

Travis had almost finished his second beer when Karen walked into the Commonwealth Lounge. She was dressed more casually than he'd ever seen her in faded jeans and a black T-shirt. Her kinky curls, normally brushed into a ponytail, were now parted on one side. A small handbag dangled from her shoulder.

Anyone could tell she wasn't one of the lounge's regulars. Most of them wore the look of weariness from just getting off a bus across the street and were often weighed down by luggage, kids— or both. Travis couldn't ignore the attention Karen received as she made her way to his table. She smiled and slid into the seat across from him.

"Wow, you really look nice, Karen."

"Oh, stop, Travis. You see me at work every day."

"Just calling it like I see it. Can I get you something to eat? Or maybe something to drink?"

"I'm not hungry, but I'll have whatever you're drinking."

After placing an order for two more beers, Travis watched Karen look around the lounge and wondered if she felt uncomfortable meeting him after work. She met his gaze with a smile.

"So, what do you think?" Travis asked, not sure what else to say.

"About what?"

"The lounge."

"I don't know. I guess it's kind of cozy."

"I hope you being here isn't going to cause any problems. Neither of us needs that."

"It's okay. I told Craig I was stopping by my sister's house after work. That'll cover me for at least a couple of hours. Oh, and just so you know, he's still moving out by the end of the month."

Travis nodded, uncertain what to make of Karen's revelation or the sudden elation he felt.

"Well, look, I'm really glad you came, Karen," he said. "I think I owe you an apology for the way I was acting earlier. I guess the interview left me a little rattled."

"I could tell something was wrong," Karen said, leaning closer to Travis and touching his hand. "I was really worried about you. So, what happened?"

"I'm pretty sure I screwed up today, Karen. Last night I got into it with Elana again and couldn't sleep. I woke up late and rushed out of the house without shaving. I was even wearing the same clothes I had on the day before. I just hope my sports jacket hid the wrinkled shirt I was wearing."

"Wow, Travis. I'm sorry to hear that you think the interview didn't go well. I have to admit you didn't seem like yourself this morning."

"That bad, huh?"

"Not really. You just looked tired. I guess I didn't even notice you hadn't shaved or that you were wearing the same clothes. Maybe the interview committee missed it too. Things might not be as bad as you think."

"Nah, I can feel it. I screwed up. The entire time, it felt like I was in an episode of *The Twilight Zone*. Everyone on the interview panel seemed like strangers—even Natalie. Did you know she was on the interview committee today?"

"Natalie Nguyen? No, I hadn't thought about it, but now that you mention it, I guess that's where she must have been most of today."

"Yeah, Natalie was one of the interviewers, but even she didn't seem like herself. I talked to her after the interviews were finished, and she was giving me the weirdest vibe. I'm serious. I mean, I get her formality during the interview, but afterward she kept calling me Mr. Pace. You'd never know we've been on a first name basis since she was hired. It was really weird."

"It probably doesn't mean anything. Natalie can be a little offbeat sometimes. But seriously, what happens if you don't get the position? Right now, there are no other vacancies in our department, and if there were, you'd be overqualified."

"Honestly, Karen. I don't know what I'd do. Maybe find another job. Who knows? Maybe it's time for me to explore my opportunities beyond Lucent Technologies."

"Maybe we both should. I've been thinking about leaving Lucent for a while now," Karen said. "Maybe you and I could go into business together. You know—do some consulting or contract work. I just feel like I could use a fresh start."

"Yeah, a fresh start is just what I need," Travis said. He gestured toward the Greyhound Bus Station. "Hey, maybe we should just cross the street right now, jump on a bus, and disappear."

Travis laughed at his attempted humor, but noticed Karen's expression didn't change.

"I wish it were that easy," she said, barely above a whisper.

Travis watched as she looked in the direction of the bus station, trying to read her expression. There was so much more he wanted to say, but was distracted by someone familiar entering the lounge.

"Hey, I know that guy." Travis nodded toward Orlando as he entered the lounge. Travis raised his beer bottle in the man's direction. Orlando acknowledged Travis with a smile while stopping to answer his cell phone.

"So, who's that?" Karen asked.

"Just somebody I bumped into when I was here last night. I mean, I actually bumped into him and knocked him down—or at least the bags he was carrying. I offered him a drink afterwards, but he was on his way across the street to catch a bus. Speaking of which, are you ready for another one of those?"

Karen nodded and Travis ordered another round of beers. He also asked the server to give Orlando whatever he wanted to drink. Shortly after they finished their drinks, Travis and Karen got up to leave. Orlando was still on the phone as they passed his table. Travis waved and Orlando raised his glass in their direction.

"That was really nice of you," Karen said once they were outside.

"Hey, you might not know this, but sometimes I can be a pretty nice guy," Travis said.

They stood beside Karen's car while she searched her purse for the key. Travis could tell she wasn't in a hurry to leave.

"By the way, I've always thought of you as a nice guy," Karen said, finally locating her key fob. "And I think no matter how your interview turns out, you'll be just fine."

"I sure hope you're right, Karen. The way things have been going lately, I could really use something good to happen. Anyway, thanks for coming. This was just what I needed after the day I've had."

"No, thank you for inviting me. Believe me, I needed this as much as you did."

"I guess I'll see you at the office tomorrow," Travis said. He leaned over to open the car door and Karen pressed her lips against his.

"For luck," she said. Travis searched her eyes as she moved closer. He enjoyed the warmth and weight of her body pressing into his. Her arms tightened around his waist as she kissed him again before letting go.

"Things are going to turn out just fine," she said. "You'll see. Sometimes nice guys don't finish last."

Travis waited for Karen to adjust herself in the seat before closing the car door. She smiled at him again before starting the engine and slowly driving away. Travis watched her taillights disappear, then walked over to his car.

* * *

It was almost nine o'clock by the time Travis pulled the Honda into the driveway. He turned off the headlights and rolled to a stop beside Elana's car. He remained in the car for a moment to prepare himself for a confrontation, but when he entered the house, he was surprised to find that she wasn't home. Instead, there was a note on the kitchen table that said she was out with friends.

Travis decided to call her—just to let her know he was home and had seen the note. Elana's phone rang until it went to voicemail. Her voicemail greeting caught him off guard, causing Travis to leave an awkward message before hanging up. As soon as he placed the phone on the television stand, it vibrated. He picked it up and read Karen's text.

"Thanks. I really enjoyed tonight."

"We'll have to do it again," Travis replied.

"Promise," Karen texted.

"Promise," he replied.

Travis placed his phone on the television stand, and his thoughts returned to Elana. He grabbed two beers out of the refrigerator, turned on the television, and stared blankly at the screen. By the time he finished the second beer, he'd decided it wouldn't be fair to question Elana's whereabouts after having drinks with Karen at the lounge. Instead of dwelling on it further, Travis focused on preparing for work, hoping to make a better impression tomorrow than the one he felt he'd made during the interview. He carefully pressed his favorite shirt, polished his best pair of shoes, and thought about how much better life would be if the IT manager's position became permanent.

At eleven o'clock, Travis grabbed another beer from the refrigerator and checked his phone to see if Elana had responded to his voicemail. Seeing no response, he texted her:

"How's it going?"

Travis waited a few minutes before dialing her number but before he could push "send," he heard his phone vibrate.

"You see my note?" Elana texted.

Before he could respond, another message popped up.

"Home soon."

"OK," Travis replied, though he wanted to say more.

Travis held his phone for a moment, anticipating another message, then set it on the television stand. For the next two hours, he alternated between staring at the TV screen and glancing at his phone. It was one-thirty when Travis realized he had dozed off—and Elana still wasn't home. He checked his phone again, then went to the window and peered out into the darkness.

A few minutes later, he turned off the television and went upstairs to stretch out on the bed. Travis was sure he'd be awake when Elana came home, but he fell asleep shortly after lying down. If only he had managed to stay awake a bit longer, he might have seen Elana stumble through the front door and silently take his phone from the television stand.

Chapter 7

The anger that awakened Travis the next morning was immediately replaced by nervousness as he crept down the hall toward the guest room where he hoped to find Elana sleeping. He paused at the door and watched the slow rise and fall of her chest as she snored lightly. Her hair was disheveled, and she'd obviously fallen asleep without removing her makeup. The clothes she'd worn were piled beside the bed in a wrinkled mound.

Deciding not to wake her, Travis returned to the bedroom and got into the shower. As he dressed, Travis struggled with the idea of leaving without talking to Elana. He had decided to leave for work without doing so when she appeared on the stairs, dressed only in her panties and bra.

"Morning, Travis," she said. Her voice was hoarse and barely above a whisper.

"Morning. I thought you were still sleeping," Travis said. "I was hoping not to wake you. I know you came in pretty late."

"No, I was awake," she said and held up his phone. "I just wanted to make sure you got this."

He walked toward her, and she tossed the phone onto the sofa. He picked up the phone and continued toward Elana. She turned and started back upstairs. "You left it on the television stand last night," Elana said over her shoulder as she continued up the stairs. "Don't you need it for work?"

"Yeah, I do, Elana," Travis said, sliding the phone into his pants pocket.

"I bet you do," she said, stopping halfway up the stairs and turning in his direction. "So, who is she, Travis?"

"Who is who, Elana?" Travis asked. He could feel the weight of the phone in his pocket.

"Oh, so now I'm supposed to be stupid? I'm talking about the bitch you're making promises to, Travis."

"I don't know what you're talking about, Elana, but I can't talk about this right now. I have to go to work."

"And what the fuck is she thanking you for, Travis? You know what—forget it. I knew it all along."

"Elana, can we talk about this when I come home?" Travis asked as Elana continued up the stairs. He called out to her again, but the bedroom door slammed shut.

Travis pulled the phone back out of his pocket. He couldn't believe he'd left it on the television stand. As he flipped through the messages, Travis noticed the time and rushed out the front door. Fortunately, the Honda started immediately, and best of all, Maurice wasn't lurking around to delay his departure. For the moment, everything felt perfect—except for his relationship with Elana.

* * *

The first thing Travis noticed when he arrived at work was the absence of managers. They were usually busiest in the mornings before disappearing into their cubicles until lunch. Aside from a few staff members chatting in one or two cubicles, the office seemed quieter than usual for a Thursday at Lucent Technologies. When he went to the breakroom for coffee, several employees who had been deep in conversation greeted him briefly before disappearing.

When he returned to his cubicle, Travis noticed a "Meeting in Progress" sign on the conference room door. The sign made him wonder if he was missing a meeting, so he decided to check his calendar. Before he could log into his computer, his phone vibrated and a text message from Karen appeared on the screen.

"Have you checked your email?"

"Not yet. Just got in," he replied.

"Need to talk to you ASAP," Karen texted back, immediately followed by, "Let's do lunch at noon."

"OK. See you at noon," Travis replied.

He turned off the phone's display and returned his attention to the calendar. After confirming he had no meetings, he opened his email. As he sorted through his inbox, Bradley walked hurriedly past his cubicle toward the conference room. He entered and the door slammed shut. Travis wondered if Bradley was holding another analyst meeting without telling him but immediately dismissed the thought. Karen would have mentioned it in her text.

As Travis continued reviewing emails, he noticed two from the CEO. He opened the first one and his heart sank. The message thanked him for participating in the interview process and informed him that he had not been selected for the IT Manager position. It went on to describe his new role as an AI consultant, effective September 1, and noted he would be relocated to one of the smaller cubicles in the IT department. The second email was addressed to all staff, announcing Bradley's appointment as IT Manager, also effective September 1. After reading both emails a second time, Travis sat back and took a moment to gather his thoughts. Then he opened a new message and sent a meeting request to the CEO, copying Human Resources.

* * *

It was almost noon, and Travis hadn't received a response from either the CEO or Human Resources when Karen peeked into his cubicle.

"Travis, can I come in?" she asked and without waiting for a response, she took a seat in the chair next to his desk. "I saw the CEO's email. I am so sorry."

"You're sorry? No, Karen, I'm the one who's feeling pretty sorry right now." He stared at his computer monitor, not ready to make eye contact with Karen. His voice trembled. "Six months ago, Human Resources said the interview would be a formality. I really don't need this shit right now. Maybe I should make it easy on everyone and just quit."

"You know you can't do that, Travis. You need to take a moment to think this out."

"Think what out?" He finally looked in Karen's direction, but not at her. "Everything I touch lately seems to turn to shit. Everything."

"Come on, Travis. You know that's not true."

"No, it is true. I'm serious. It's everything. Everything at work. Everything at home. Everything."

"Travis, it's twelve fifteen. Why don't we get out of here for a little while?" Karen asked. "Maybe get some lunch."

"I really don't have much of an appetite, Karen. Besides, I sent the CEO and Human Resources a meeting request. I don't think I should leave the office until I hear from them."

"You did? Well, aren't they in a meeting right now? Come on, Travis. It'll give you a chance to think about what you really want to say when you meet with them."

With some persistence, Karen was able to persuade Travis to join her for lunch at the cafeteria where they usually ate. After they were seated, Karen listened while Travis continued voicing his frustration.

"I just don't get it, Karen. I've been the interim IT Manager for six months—six months—and still they chose Bradley."

"Travis, don't beat yourself up. I think you shouldn't jump to any conclusions until you've met with the CEO. It's very possible you have a legitimate grievance if Human Resources made you a promise they didn't keep."

"And to think, Karen, up until now I thought Bradley would be the one moving to the AI consultant position when Ben left. Now I have to move to one of the cubicles in the IT Department by September 1st?"

"AI consultant position? Is that what you were told? I don't remember seeing that in the CEO's email."

"It was in an email sent just to me," Travis said. "Can you see me as an AI consultant after supervising the entire team?"

Karen shook her head and stared across the room without comment. She averted her eyes when Travis looked in her direction, and continued pushing the food around on her plate. When their eyes finally met, Travis could see her tears. She ate the remainder of her meal in silence and Travis never touched the coffee he'd ordered.

Once Karen paid the bill and they were leaving, Travis heard a familiar voice coming from the other side of the cafeteria. When he took a few steps in the direction of the voice, he saw Bradley seated in a booth with the CTO, Andrew Drucker, and the Marketing Manager, Chad Cunningham. It was apparent Bradley saw them too and began speaking louder. Travis took another step in Bradley's direction and immediately felt Karen's hand tighten around his arm. He glanced back at the booth as they left the restaurant but not before noticing a thin smile creep across Bradley's face.

* * *

As soon as Travis was back in the office, he checked his email. So far, neither the CEO nor Human Resources had responded to his meeting request. It was almost two-thirty when he saw the department managers heading toward the conference room for another meeting. Because he hadn't seen the HR manager or CEO enter the conference room yet, he felt certain they were preparing to meet with him. Fifteen minutes later, when he saw both heading toward the conference room, a feeling of doubt began to replace the small bit of hope he had been clinging to.

Shortly after the conference room door closed, an email from the CEO appeared in his inbox. The email began with an apology for the delayed response, but went on to explain that he would not be available to meet with him until next week. It ended with a request for patience and cooperation while management resolved issues related to the company's reorganization. Travis was debating whether or not to respond when he heard his cell phone vibrate and saw a text from Karen.

"You busy?"

"No," he texted back.

"Meet me at your car in ten minutes," she replied.

"What's going on?" he texted.

"Meet me in ten minutes," she texted again.

Ten minutes later, Travis sat in his car as Karen approached. She opened the passenger door and dropped into the seat. By the look on her face, he could tell she was deeply upset.

"So, what's going on, Karen?"

"Travis, I'm really worried."

"About what?"

"Your promotion."

"You shouldn't be. The CEO finally responded to my meeting request and has agreed to see me next week to discuss the reorganization. Maybe he'll rescind his decision about the IT manager position once I tell him about the assurances HR gave me six months ago. Who knows? I might be able to rebound from this after all."

"Did the CEO mention anything else?" Karen asked.

"Like what? He's probably not going to go into too much detail in an email. I'm sure once I let him know I have a possible grievance against HR he'll —"

"Travis," Karen interrupted. "I have a feeling the CEO is not going to care about what you might have discussed with HR."

"What makes you say that?"

"You're not going to like this, Travis." Karen glanced toward the office building before continuing. "Bradley's office door was open when he came back from lunch and I overheard him talking on the phone. He was telling someone you had been drinking the morning of the interview. He also said it didn't matter because he was promised the IT manager position when he was hired three months ago."

"You've got to be kidding me, Karen. That's not what HR told me when I accepted the interim position. And what sense would it make for me to drink before an interview? I had a few beers at the Commonwealth Lounge after work and a couple more once I got home, but—"

"Travis, that's not all," Karen interrupted again.

Travis tried to concentrate on what Karen was saying but her voice seemed to come from somewhere far away as he recalled how hungover he was the morning of the interview.

"I was so pissed," Travis finally heard Karen say, "so pissed that when Natalie came back from lunch, I asked her about your interview. She told me that after you left the room, everyone made comments about your appearance, and the CTO said he'd received complaints that our relationship was possibly inappropriate because you're married and we spend so much time together. She also said the CTO was certain he smelled alcohol on your breath when he talked to you after your interview."

Travis opened his mouth to speak, but no words came out. He suddenly felt the weight and trajectory of his life as it plummeted toward some immeasurable depth. He looked at Karen. Tears streamed down her face. He wanted to reach out to her but instead he wondered if he'd lost her too.

"So, what are we going to do, Travis?"

"What are we going to do?" he repeated.

"Yes, what are we going to do? You're not in this by yourself."

"Based on what you've told me, Karen, I don't know what to do. I really think I need to talk to the CEO before next week, if possible — today. I need to tell him my side of the story and about the promises made by Human Resources as soon as possible. He definitely needs to know I hadn't been drinking on the morning of the interview."

"I'm sorry, Travis. I'm just so sorry."

"Look, Karen. We'd better get back inside. You should dry your eyes before you go in."

Travis reached over and opened the glove compartment. He pulled out a box of tissues and saw the bottle of cognac. He quickly closed the glove compartment, handed Karen the box of tissues, and wondered if she'd seen it too.

"So, what's that, Travis?" Karen asked while dabbing her eyes with a tissue.

"What's what?" he asked.

"This." Karen opened the glove compartment. "I didn't know you kept liquor in your car."

"That's been in there for a while, Karen. You can look at the bottle and tell I've only taken a couple of sips out of it."

"So, why is it in your glove compartment, Travis?"

"You know I like to have a drink now and then, Karen. But never during the workday."

"Never, Travis?"

"I said never, didn't I? Don't tell me you're starting to believe what they're saying is true."

"I didn't say that, Travis. I guess I'm just really confused right now. Let's just go back inside."

"You go first, Karen. Considering everything that's happened, I don't think it would be good for us to go in at the same time."

Travis watched Karen disappear into the building before opening the glove compartment and pulling out the bottle. He thought about what Karen had shared and the suggestion he'd been intoxicated during the interview. He thought about Elana and the idea of facing her when he returned home with the news that he wasn't getting the promotion.

Slowly, he twisted the cap off the bottle of cognac. A sip would help numb the painful realization that the IT Manager position might never be his. A few sips later, he tossed the nearly empty bottle back into the glove compartment. As Travis headed back toward the office building, he decided he couldn't afford to wait until next week to meet with the CEO to straighten things out. He needed to meet with him today.

* * *

If someone had asked Travis if he remembered what time it was when he walked up to the conference room door after returning from his car, he would have said no. All he would remember was that when he knocked, no one answered, so he opened the door anyway. Inside, he noticed Bradley seated at the table. The CEO, CTO, and department managers were also seated around the table. Claire, the CEO's administrative assistant, was at one end of the long conference table, presumably taking notes on a laptop.

"Can I help you, Travis?" the CEO asked, his face twisted into a frown. "As you can see, we are in a meeting."

"Yes, I know, sir. I'm sorry," Travis said nervously. "I sent you an email and —"

"And I told you I was unable to meet with you until next week," the CEO interrupted. "Is there something you didn't understand?"

"I just think..." Travis paused, struggling to avoid looking at the faces seated around the table, "I just wanted to say I think we should meet sooner than next week. It's important."

"Travis, I understand your concern," the CEO said, "but if it's any consolation, I'll see what I can do to fit you in sooner, but I won't be able to check my schedule until I finish here. For now, please excuse us so we can continue our meeting."

Travis's eyes lingered on the CEO for a moment before glancing again at the faces around the table. Everyone looked as though they were holding their breath. Even Claire, who had continued typing when he first entered the room, stopped and looked at him with the same expression as the others. Without another word, Travis slowly pulled the door shut as he left the room. He would have gone back to his cubicle for the rest of the day, satisfied that he had at least gotten the attention of the CEO. But instead, as the door clicked closed, Travis heard the sound of laughter and instinctively pushed the door open again.

"Did I say something funny?" Travis asked as he walked back into the conference room.

The CEO immediately turned in his direction.

"What is it now, Travis?"

"I couldn't help but hear laughter when I left the room," Travis said. "I think after working for this company for nearly sixteen years, if nothing else, I deserve some respect."

"And as of right now, you have it, Travis," the CEO said. "Now, I must insist that you leave."

Travis reached for the doorknob as if to leave but Bradley leaned over and whispered something in the financial manager's ear. Bradley shook his head and nudged the financial manager again. Both looked at Travis with exaggerated smiles. Bradley snickered.

"By the way," Travis said, looking in Bradley's direction, "you need to stop by my cubicle after this meeting."

"Stop by your cubicle?" Bradley repeated. "For what?"

"Just come see me afterward," Travis said, turning toward the door as if to leave.

"Not likely," he heard Bradley say under his breath with his usual sarcasm.

"Bradley, you will come see me after this meeting," Travis said, raising his voice, no longer able to conceal his annoyance.

"Travis, control yourself," the CEO said. "Either you leave this room right now, or I will be forced to call security."

"I guess I'm no longer Bradley's supervisor," Travis said, turning toward the CEO. "So, now I get it. I see why you weren't in such a hurry to meet with me."

"Travis, I want you out of this conference room. As a matter of fact, take the rest of the day off. It's apparent you're not feeling well. Go home and come back tomorrow when you're ready to be the professional I know you're capable of being."

"Go home? You want me to go home?" Travis repeated. "First, you give my job to someone who's only been with the company for three months after I've given over fifteen years. Now, you're telling me I need to go home and everything's going to be okay, Mr.

Oberman. No, I'm not going anywhere until I've had a chance to talk to you."

The CEO jumped to his feet and motioned toward his administrative assistant. "No, Travis, you need to leave right now. Claire, call security. Let them know that Travis Pace is to be escorted from this building immediately."

As Travis turned to leave the conference room, he realized the door had remained open the entire time. The usually busy office was now pin-drop quiet, and he was certain anyone within earshot had heard the commotion in the conference room. Now, it felt as though every eye in the office was on him as he walked the short distance to his cubicle in slow motion. Two of Lucent Technologies' security officers were waiting for him by the time he reached his desk. The taller of the two looked like a retired wrestler, and the other one could have easily passed for Barney Fife. They were immediately joined by the CEO.

"Mr. Pace is to be escorted out of the building and not allowed back on the premises," the CEO said. He then turned to Travis. "Please make sure you take all of your personal belongings when you leave."

"Mr. Oberman," Travis began, as the exhilaration he'd felt only moments ago slowly gave way to the sobering reality of what was happening. "Can we at least talk about this?"

"Travis, I don't know what else there is to talk about. You're lucky I didn't fire you yesterday after you showed up for an interview intoxicated. What were you thinking?"

"But, Mr. Oberman, that's why I needed to talk to you as soon as possible. I hadn't been drinking. This is all a big misunderstanding."

"And Travis, I was willing to discuss your concerns when we met, but after your outburst this afternoon, I've run out of patience. I hope you can get your life together, but there is no longer a place for you at Lucent Technologies."

J. Marcus Evins

"So, you're letting me go?" Travis asked, searching the CEO's face. "You're letting me go after more than fifteen years, all because of a misunderstanding?"

"Travis, an official letter of termination will be sent to your address of record as soon as possible," the CEO said, motioning to the security officers. "Please assist Mr. Pace with packing any personal belongings, then escort him off the premises."

The CEO stared at Travis for a moment, shook his head, and then walked back toward the conference room. The security officers immediately stepped into Travis's cubicle, but he refused their assistance. Instead, he tossed the few personal items he kept in his cubicle into one of the boxes they provided, grabbed his sports jacket, and headed toward the elevator.

* * *

It wasn't until he was outside that Travis realized the security officers were still behind him. He turned and glared at the two men, but they continued following him until he reached his car. Once inside, Travis turned the key in the ignition. Although the Honda started immediately, it quickly died. Looking up from the dashboard, he saw Barney Fife elbow the wrestler. They both laughed and continued watching. Travis got out and raised the hood, tugging on each battery cable before sliding back behind the steering wheel again and twisting the key. The car still wouldn't start. A tapping sound startled Travis. Realizing it was Barney Fife, he lowered the window.

"If it won't start, you'll need to call for a tow."

"Okay, I'll do that, but you two don't have to wait out here," Travis said. "I don't plan to be here any longer than I have to."

"You should probably go ahead and make the call." The security officer stared at Travis for a moment, then motioned toward his partner, whose head was under the Honda's hood. "What do you think, Chuck?"

"I don't know. It'd probably start if there wasn't so much corrosion on the battery terminals," the wrestler said, slamming the hood closed. "On the other hand, he could've just flooded it. I'm smelling a lot of gas."

"Look, Pace, even if your car won't start, you still need to leave the premises," Barney Fife said. "You can either call a tow company or we can call one for you."

"I don't need you to call a tow company for me," Travis said. "If I need a tow, I'll call for one myself."

Frustrated, Travis twisted the key in the ignition again. This time, the Honda shuddered, then slowly rumbled to a noisy idle. He immediately shifted the car into reverse, forcing Barney Fife to jump out of the way. When he shifted the car into drive, the wrestler stumbled backward. When both security officers were clear of the car, Travis drove around them once before heading toward the parking lot exit. He honked the horn and stuck a hand out the window as if to wave goodbye, but instead extended his middle finger. He laughed at the confused looks on the men's faces, but his amusement quickly faded as the reality of what had just occurred hit him. The sound of his phone vibrating brought him back to the moment. He glanced at the message on the screen before tossing the phone on the passenger seat and pressing the gas pedal to the floor.

Chapter 8

Travis couldn't remember the last time he'd been home so early or so sober. The only signs of life in the neighborhood were a few kids, still out of school for the summer, who were willing to brave the late-afternoon August heat. He was glad that, at least, Maurice wasn't outside. Today would have been the worst day to endure the man's questions about why he was home so early. He still hadn't decided what he was going to tell Elana, let alone a nosy neighbor. He couldn't imagine how she was going to respond to his being fired, especially after confronting him that morning about the text messages he'd received from Karen.

As Travis considered his options, he retrieved his cell phone from the passenger seat. He swiped the display and saw a new text from Karen.

"Where are you?" But before he could respond, another text appeared. "Call me when you're able to talk."

He dialed Karen's number. The phone rang once, and she answered.

"Travis, what the hell happened? I heard security had escorted you out of the building."

"I don't know, Karen. I guess things got out of control."

"Was it because of what we talked about in your car?"

"No. Not really. I guess I'm just tired of taking crap from everybody."

"Does Elana know?"

"No. I just got home and haven't gone in the house yet. I was sitting in the car trying to figure out what to tell her when you texted. She was already pissed about some other stuff when I left for work this morning."

"Are you going to be okay?"

"I don't know. The more I think about it, I probably shouldn't have come home so soon, considering everything that's happened."

"Maybe you should give yourself more time to think things out before you go in the house. Is it too late to leave?"

"I think so. I'm pretty sure Elana has already seen my car in the driveway. She might even be looking at me right now."

"Is there anything I can do?"

"Honestly, Karen, at this point I don't think there's much anybody can do."

"I wish I could see you, Travis."

"I don't know if that's a good idea."

"I know. You're right. I just thought..." Karen began but didn't finish.

"Look, I think I should just face this head-on," Travis said. "I'll text or call you later, okay?"

Travis ended the call. He stared at the house and wondered again what he would say to Elana. Karen was right—he should have given himself time to sort things out before coming home. He could have stopped by the lounge and figured out the best way—or even the best time—to break the news to Elana, but now it was too late. The feeling of dread intensified as he got out of the car and walked to the house. He paused for a few seconds before unlocking the front door and stepping inside.

As usual, the television was tuned to one of the home shopping shows, but Elana's chair was empty. Travis stared at the television screen, contemplating whether if he could delay telling Elana what had happened. Maybe he could just say he had left work early because he was upset about the argument they'd had that morning and wanted to get home as early as possible to work things out. Then, maybe in a few days, he'd have it all figured out and might not have to tell Elana he'd been fired at all. A buzzing sound diverted Travis's attention, and he reached into his pocket, only to find his phone's screen black. The buzzing continued, and he noticed Elana's phone on the dining room table.

When he picked up the phone, he heard bumping sounds coming from upstairs. As Travis slowly climbed the stairs, the sounds became louder and the source more apparent. At the bedroom door, he saw Elana's legs draped over Maurice's shoulders. Her eyes were closed, and the musky odor of sex filled the room. Each of Maurice's thrusts resulted in more moans as the headboard bumped against the wall. Travis entered the bedroom to the sound of Elana's orgasm. When her eyes opened, she pushed Maurice away and motioned toward the door.

"Travis, be cool, man," Maurice said as he rolled away from Elana and landed on the floor. He looked up at Travis and grabbed a pair of shorts lying next to the bed. He tried to put them on, while gesturing frantically toward Elana. "It's not my fault, man. She invited me over."

"You motherfucker. I'm gonna kill your ass," Travis said as he ran toward Maurice. The younger, more athletic man easily sidestepped Travis to avoid being hit. Travis rushed toward Maurice again, this time stumbling and falling to his knees.

Maurice grabbed the rest of his clothes and ran out of the room. Travis, still on his knees, swung around and glared at Elana.

"Don't say shit to me, Travis," she screamed. "Don't you say a goddamn thing."

Instead of responding to Elana, Travis ran out of the room and down the stairs just as Maurice escaped through the front door. Instead of pursuing Maurice, he ran back upstairs—just in time to see Elana crawling across the bed to the other side of the room to keep him from reaching her.

"What the fuck, Elana?" Travis shouted, unable to catch his breath.

"No. Fuck you, Travis. I'm glad you caught us. And just so you know, it's not the first time."

"Not the first time?" Travis stepped toward Elana. He was still unable to control his breathing or the pounding in his chest. "You're telling me this is not the first time you've been with that motherfucker, Elana?"

"Travis, just stay the fuck away from me," Elana said as she slipped into her panties and bra.

"You know what? Fuck you, Elana. You're a sorry bitch," Travis finally managed. "I should have known. All the shit I've done for you. I ought to —"

"You ought to what? I'll call the police and have them lock your sorry ass up."

"Fuck you and the goddamn police, Elana."

"No, fuck you, Travis. You think you can have your fun and I can't. You think I'm stupid."

"Fun? What fun are you talking about, Elana?"

"Oh, you don't think I know about the late hours—about why you don't respond to my texts—about the bitch you're always texting."

"It's not what you think, Elana. Karen—she's just a coworker who—"

"Who you're fucking. I don't want to hear it, Travis. As a matter of fact, why don't you go to her ass right now and leave me the fuck alone."

Elana ran past Travis into the bathroom and slammed the door. He heard the lock click, but tried the door anyway. For a moment he remained outside the bathroom door. He felt himself become angrier as the image of Maurice and Elana's lovemaking replayed in his head. He yanked on the doorknob.

"Please go away, Travis," Elana yelled from inside the locked bathroom. "I hate your black ass."

"Elana, open this goddamn door," Travis said. He yanked on the doorknob again.

Frustrated, Travis kicked the bathroom door. Then, feeling a sudden burst of adrenaline, he ran down the stairs and out of the house. He crossed the lawn and pounded on Maurice's front door, pausing for a moment to listen for a response. Hearing nothing, Travis pounded on the door again. Still, there was no answer. Walking to the edge of the porch, he looked around and noticed one of Maurice's cars was gone. Instead of remaining on the porch, he stepped onto the lawn, picked up a stone paver, and flung it through Maurice's front window.

When he returned to his house, he found the front door locked. Trying his key, he realized the door had also been deadbolted. After trying the door again, Travis walked out on the lawn and looked up at the bedroom window.

"Hey, Elana, open the door," he yelled.

There was no response, but Travis was sure the blinds moved slightly.

"Elana, come on. I know you can hear me."

He walked around to the back of the house and tried the door, only to find it deadbolted too. Next, he peered through the kitchen windows but saw no sign of Elana. In the distance, Travis heard a door slam and assumed Elana had finally unlocked the front door.

Relieved, he ran to the front of the house, only to find some of his belongings scattered across the lawn. Now, angrier than before, Travis pounded on the front door. He could hear the sound of Elana sobbing on the other side.

"Elana, open the door. You can't just throw my stuff out here on the lawn."

"Go away, Travis. I hate you. I hate this marriage."

"Elana, let me in before I knock down this goddamn door," he shouted, slamming his fists on the door several times. "You're accusing me of shit I haven't even done."

"Go ahead, knock the door down. I've already called the police. They'll be here any minute."

"Why would you do that, Elana? Why would you call the police? Come on, Elana. Just open the door."

As if the possibility of Elana calling the police wasn't enough, Travis noticed that some of the neighbors had come outside of their homes. Not wanting to make more of a spectacle of himself, he began gathering the items strewn across the lawn and tossed them into the trunk of his car.

Afterward, Travis sat in the car staring at the house. He thought about how happy he and Elana had been when they first moved in and how it no longer felt like home. He twisted the key in the ignition and let the car idle. A light drizzle began as Travis shifted the car into reverse. He needed someone to talk to and a place to sort things out. Without considering it further, he backed out of the driveway and headed for the lounge. At least there, he could get the drink he'd wanted earlier—and definitely needed now.

* * *

As he headed toward the Commonwealth Lounge, Travis realized he hadn't given any thought to where he would spend the night until he saw the sign for a Rodeway Motel. Since the motel was not far from the lounge, he decided to check if there were rooms available. When he saw the faded awning and worn carpet leading up to the motel's entrance, he knew it wouldn't be anything fancy. His suspicions were confirmed inside the lobby, where he was greeted by a musty odor and outdated furniture. He heard the low murmur of country music playing somewhere behind the front desk. An elderly White man, preoccupied behind a glass partition, didn't acknowledge Travis's presence until he was just a few feet from the desk.

"Can I help you, sir?" the man asked, peering over his bifocals but otherwise remaining expressionless.

"I'd like a room," Travis said.

"What size room are you needing?" the man asked.

"I'm not sure. What do you have available?"

The man tapped on a computer keyboard a couple of times, stared at the monitor, and then responded.

"How long are you staying?"

"Maybe a day. Maybe two. I haven't decided yet."

"Well, let's see. We've got two standard rooms available," the man said, tapping the keyboard again. "One with a king-size bed and one with two queens. Either room is one hundred-three dollars plus tax. Both are non-smoking."

"I'll take the one with the king-size bed," Travis said, pulling out his wallet and handing the man his credit card. He watched as the man entered some information, then swiped the card. There was a beep. The man swiped it again, frowning slightly. Finally, he looked up at Travis.

"Want to try another card? This one's been rejected."

"Rejected?" Travis leaned forward. "Can you try it again? Something must be wrong with your reader."

"Nope, nothing wrong with the reader. I've already swiped it twice. Says here it was reported stolen."

Travis immediately realized Elana must have reported the card stolen. He pulled out his wallet and began counting the cash it contained.

"We do take cash," the man said, tapping the edge of Travis's credit card on the counter. "But you have to leave a deposit. You'll get it back once you check out."

"So how much is the room with the deposit?" Travis asked.

"Let's see," the man said, tapping the keyboard again. "Three hundred fourteen dollars, three cents."

Travis counted a little over a hundred dollars in his wallet and patted his empty pants pockets.

"I don't have enough cash on me, and I didn't bring my other card," Travis lied. "Let me get that card from you, and I'll come back with the cash."

"No, sir, I can't," the man said, tossing the card in a drawer. "Once I receive a code forty-three, I have to hold it. You'll need to contact your card issuer."

Travis looked at the man and scowled. He considered trying to use his debit card to pay for the room, but decided not to risk additional embarrassment. Instead, Travis thanked the man and planned to visit the bank that issued the card in the morning. On any other day, he might have caused a scene by demanding the card back, but today was not that day.

Chapter 9

Once he reached the Commonwealth Lounge, Travis ordered his usual shot of Hennessy and a bottle of Coors Light. He quickly downed the shot of cognac, then sipped the beer while considering the reality of his situation. It didn't take long for him to conclude that sleeping in the Honda for one night might be his only option. As he observed the hustle and bustle around him, Travis realized that while nothing seemed to have changed about the lounge, everything in his life had. He kept watching people come and go from the lounge until his loneliness became unbearable.

"Are you able to meet me at the lounge?" Travis texted Karen. A few minutes later, his phone vibrated.

"Maybe. How long will you be there?" Karen replied.

"A while. Nowhere else to go," he texted back.

"Sorry," Karen replied.

"Not your fault," he typed.

"I'll let you know when I'm on my way," Karen answered.

Changing Pace

Travis stared at the phone until the display went dark, then waved to one of the servers. He ordered another shot of cognac and drank it immediately. He sipped the remainder of his beer and, as the calming effects of the alcohol began to take hold, tried to make sense of what had happened.

One thing he knew for certain was that his marriage to Elana was over. It had been heading toward self-destruction for a long time, but her affair with Maurice had crossed a line from which there was no return. He also thought about his job at Lucent Technologies and knew, even if he hadn't been fired, any position other than IT manager was not the future he had envisioned. As far as he was concerned, both his marriage and his job had been traveling on the same road of inevitability. Yet, despite everything that had occurred, Travis felt a strange and unfamiliar sense of freedom.

As he contemplated his future, Travis stared across the street at the Greyhound Bus Station and wondered, as he had many times before, what it might feel like to get on a bus and leave it all behind. He became so absorbed by the idea of escaping the catastrophe his life had become that he decided to walk over to the bus station. When he stepped outside the lounge, Travis noticed the increasing clouds darkening the sky. The drizzle that had begun earlier had now become a steady shower, prompting him to quicken his pace across Arthur Ashe Boulevard.

Inside the bus station, Travis walked over to the screen displaying the schedule. The many destinations made him realize how small his world had become since moving from Baltimore fifteen years ago. He hadn't been looking at the schedule long when he felt a tap on the shoulder.

"So, what are you doing over here?"

"Oh, hey," Travis said as he turned to face a man wearing a Nike tracksuit and matching baseball cap. The man looked familiar, but he was unable to recall his name. "I'm just checking out the schedule."

"I'm glad I ran into you again. I wanted to thank you for the drink," the man said, extending his hand. "I don't know if you remember, but my name is Orlando."

"Okay. Yeah, Orlando," Travis said, shaking his hand. "It was no problem at all. I figured I owed you for almost knocking you down the other day."

Just then, Orlando's phone vibrated.

"Excuse me for a minute," Orlando said. Travis watched as he walked a few steps away. He decided the tracksuit and cap were the reason he hadn't recognized Orlando. They made him look younger than he remembered. Once Orlando finished his phone conversation, he walked over to the ticket window. Travis could tell by his body language that he was not in agreement with whatever was being discussed.

"Everything okay?" Travis asked when Orlando walked back to where he was standing.

"Not really," Orlando said. "They're saying my bus broke down at the last stop, so there's going to be a delay."

"How long of a delay are they talking about?" Travis asked.

"They don't know for sure. The person at the window said they'll either repair the bus or send out a replacement. They should have an update in a couple of hours," Orlando said, glancing at the schedule. "So, what time does your bus leave?"

"It's not," Travis said, then quickly added, "What I mean is, I was over at the Commonwealth Lounge and just needed some fresh air. So, I walked over."

"Well, it's good seeing you, man," Orlando said, looking around the station and shrugging. "I guess I might as well get comfortable. Looks like I'm going to be here for a while."

Travis watched Orlando struggle to put a backpack and duffel bag on his shoulders before heading in the direction of a row of plastic chairs against the wall. He walked over and sat next to him.

"Hey look, I'm going to head back across the street. It's not going to be comfortable sitting on these too long." Travis tapped on the hard plastic chairs for emphasis. "Why don't you let me treat you to a beer while you're waiting?"

"That might not be a bad idea," Orlando said. He looked at his phone and then glanced at the departure and arrival times displayed on the screen. "As long as you let me buy. You treated last time."

"Let me help you with your bags," Travis said.

"Nah, I'm good. I've been lugging these things around for so long, they're like a part of me."

Orlando swung the duffel and backpack onto one shoulder before they headed toward the exit. The rain had picked up, and they jogged across the street to escape getting soaked. Orlando motioned to the server as soon as they were seated and placed their order. Once the drinks were brought to the table, Travis immediately downed another shot of Hennessy and took a sip from the bottle of beer. He watched as Orlando scanned the lounge.

"Look, man, I'm going to the restroom," Orlando said. He swallowed his shot of cognac and took a few more sips of beer before standing. "Go ahead and order another round if you like."

Travis watched Orlando collect his duffel bag and backpack, then head toward the restrooms on the other side of the lounge. Once he lost sight of Orlando, he pulled out his cell and tapped Karen's name.

"Still at the lounge," he texted, then waited a few seconds before sending another. "Can't wait to see you."

Travis stared at the cell phone as if to will an immediate response from Karen, but none came.

J. Marcus Evins

"Is everything okay?" Orlando asked when he returned from the restroom.

"I wish I could say everything was," Travis said. He laid his phone on the table and returned his attention to Orlando, who remained standing for a moment, staring across the street at the bus station before sitting down.

"Man, I wonder what's going on with that bus," Orlando said finishing the remainder of his beer. "My boss is raising hell about me not making it back tonight."

"Oh, you don't have to tell me about bosses," Travis said. "This is probably the worst day of my life because of my former boss."

"The worst day of your life? Come on, Travis. You look pretty chill for someone experiencing the worst day of their life."

"So, what would you call the day you lose not only your job but also your wife?" Travis asked.

"Hey, you're kidding, right?" Orlando asked.

"Wish I was, man. This has been one shitty day for sure," Travis said. He finished the rest of his beer and motioned for the server to bring another round to the table. "And right now, I can't say tomorrow is going to be any better. I feel like I've lost everything."

"So, if you don't mind me asking, what happened?"

"To tell the truth, Orlando, I'm still trying to figure it out. One minute I thought I was inching my way up the ladder at work, and the next minute I realized there was never really a ladder. At least not one for me."

"No ladder. That's pretty deep, man," Orlando said. He tilted his beer bottle toward Travis before taking another sip. "But I think I get what you're saying."

"All I know, man, is that everything about my life has become extremely complicated. And work isn't the worst of it," Travis said. "So, Orlando, let me ask you something, and I'm not trying to get into your business either. You married?"

"Nah, man. I'd definitely consider it if the right person comes along. So far, I haven't met the kind of person I would be willing to make that kind of commitment to."

"Well, you'd be doing better than most if you ever find the right person," Travis said. He paused and motioned toward the server to bring two more shots of Hennessy to the table. "I thought I had the right one, but she turned out to be the wrong one."

"I hear what you're saying, but that's hard to believe."

"Hard to believe? What makes you say that?"

"The other night when you and your lady were in here, it seemed like you two were really into each other."

"The other night," Travis repeated, even though he knew exactly who Orlando was talking about. "Oh, no, man, you're talking about Karen. She's someone I work with. I mean, someone I used to work with, since now I'm out of a job. We're just friends."

"Just friends? Nah, Travis, that's not what I saw. I wasn't trying to spy on you two or anything, but I followed you out to the parking lot the other night. I wanted to thank you for the drink, but when I saw you two standing at the car I decided it might not have been a good time to interrupt."

"Oh, you must have seen me walk Karen to her car?"

"Sure did, and you two were looking real cozy. I decided to keep it moving and went back in the lounge," Orlando said. "So, you think maybe she could be the right person?"

"Who knows, man," Travis tilted the bottle of beer upward and drained it. "I tell you one thing, we probably wouldn't be having this conversation if she were my lady instead of the bitch I married."

"Whoa, man. I think we need another round," Orlando said, and caught the server's attention. He ordered another round of drinks and asked for the check.

The server returned with their drinks, and for a moment, both men drank in silence. Orlando checked his phone again and began typing while Travis's thoughts drifted back to Karen. He was beginning to dread the idea of waking up hungover tomorrow morning in the Honda, and Karen's arrival meant the possibility of a loan for a room. But when he pulled out his phone, Travis was again disappointed. He was just about to send Karen another text when Orlando jumped up from his seat.

"Look, man. I think I'm going to head back across the street so I can check on the status of my bus," Orlando said. He placed enough money on the check to cover their drinks, then picked up his duffel bag and backpack.

"Maybe I'll walk over with you," Travis said and stood. "I could use some fresh air."

"Up to you, man," Orlando shrugged, then laughed. "You sure you're not waiting for a bus?"

"Hey, who knows. The way things are going lately, maybe I'll grab a ticket myself while I'm over there," Travis said. He watched Orlando stagger slightly under the weight of the bags he was carrying. "You sure you don't want me to help you with those?"

"No, no, I've got 'em." Orlando repositioned the bags and headed toward the exit.

Outside, it was raining much harder, and Travis wondered if going back to the bus station was a good idea. As soon as they entered the station, Orlando walked over to the ticket window. Travis could hear the conversation between Orlando and the person at the window.

"No, sir. The bus to Elizabeth City has been delayed. There's a flood watch in effect, so it could take longer than expected."

"So, there's no other bus going to that location?" Orlando asked.

"Not tonight, sir. The next bus going to Elizabeth City isn't leaving until tomorrow morning. If you like, I can book you for the next bus or give you a refund."

"I don't think either option will work for me," Orlando said. "You think I can get an Uber or Lyft from here to Elizabeth City?"

"I don't know, sir. I can give you their numbers if you like," the cashier said. She disappeared from the window for a moment, then returned with a slip of paper containing the numbers for the ride services and handed it to Orlando. Orlando moved away from the window, and the cashier glanced at Travis and smiled.

"Can I help you, sir?"

"Oh, no. I'm with him," Travis said and pointed in Orlando's direction.

Travis moved away from the ticket window and took a seat in the waiting area. Orlando remained standing. He took out his phone and began dialing the numbers the woman had given him. Travis listened to Orlando's conversation for a moment before checking his own phone to see if he'd received anything from Karen. He was disappointed to find no response to his texts and noticed his phone's battery was down to five percent. Ignoring the low battery, he texted Karen again, hoping for a reply. When he pushed "send," he was momentarily elated when he heard the phone vibrate, only to realize it was the sound of the battery dying, along with his hopes of hearing from Karen.

Chapter 10

"Karen, what's wrong?" Kiara asked when she answered the phone. "Are you crying?"

Karen took a deep breath before responding to her sister. Not wanting to go home, she had been driving around for some time after leaving work, hoping to make sense of what had happened that day. Now she was parked outside of her sister's house.

"Karen, are you still there?"

"Travis got fired today, Kiara, and I think it's partly my fault."

"You're kidding, right? Where are you anyway? Are you home?"

"No, I'm outside."

"Outside? Outside where, Karen?"

From her car, Karen watched Kiara open her front door and step out onto the porch. She placed her hands on her hips and stared in the direction of Karen's car before waving for her to come in. Karen slowly opened the car door and walked toward the house. Kiara hugged her younger sister before guiding her through the door.

"So, what's going on, Karen? What's got you so upset?"

"It's like I said. They fired Travis today. When we last talked, he was trying to schedule a meeting with the CEO to discuss an interview he had yesterday. I found out later he had been escorted out of the building by security."

"And how again is that your fault, Karen?"

"Just before Travis got fired, I told him about a conversation I overheard between Bradley and someone he was talking to on the phone. He said Travis was intoxicated during the interview along with some other stuff about how he had been promised the IT manager position when he was hired three months ago."

"Wait a minute, Karen. Who is Bradley?" Kiara asked.

"You know, Bradley Stillman. He's the guy I told you they hired a few months ago whom I can't stand."

"Okay, so I still don't understand why you think it's your fault that Travis got fired, Karen."

"It's not just that, Kiara. There's also some talk going around the office that my relationship with Travis is inappropriate."

"Karen, I hate to be the one to say I told you so, but this was a road you didn't even have to go down. If it were me, I would give Travis some space to allow him to figure this out on his own. Travis is not just a grown-ass man—he's a grown-ass married man."

Karen looked at her sister, but before she could respond, her phone vibrated. She glanced at Travis's text message, letting her know he was at the Commonwealth Lounge and wanted to see her. After exchanging several more text messages with Travis, she laid her phone on the coffee table and shook her head. She was so distracted while texting Travis that she hadn't noticed Kiara leave the room.

"Was that him?" Kiara asked when she returned. She set two empty wine glasses and a bottle of Moscato on the coffee table.

"He's at the lounge where I met him the other evening and wants to see me, Kiara. I told him I'd try to make it."

Kiara uncorked the bottle of wine and filled both glasses. She slid one of them in front of Karen. "Here, you probably could use this. It's something I picked up yesterday. Let me know what you think."

"I think I'm going to pass, Kiara. I can tell from Travis's texts that he needs someone to talk to. I don't think I should drink anything before driving over to the lounge."

"Here's an idea, Karen. Don't go anywhere. Instead, just tell him to go home and talk to his wife. I can't believe this man has you whipped like this. I thought you said you hadn't even given him any yet."

"Kiara, it's not like that."

"So, tell me, Karen." Kiara took a sip of wine before continuing. "What's it like?"

"It's complicated." Karen's phone vibrated. "I should go. That's probably him again."

Karen looked at her phone and pursed her lips. She looked at Kiara, shook her head, and rolled her eyes toward the ceiling before placing the phone back on the table. Then, she took a long sip from the glass of wine in front of her.

"Well," Kiara said as she finished her glass of wine and poured herself another, "are you leaving or what?"

"That was Craig, Kiara," Karen said, drinking the remaining wine in her glass. "I'm so tired of his sorry ass, I don't know what to do. I really don't need his shit right now."

"Just tell him you're planning to stay here tonight."

"That's what I told him Wednesday when I met Travis at the lounge. I don't think he—"

"Karen, stop right there," Kiara interrupted. "Who cares what he thinks? Sometimes you can be too accommodating when it comes to men. Aren't you two supposed to be going your separate ways at the end of the month anyway?"

"Sure, but I just don't want to deal with any unnecessary drama from him before then, Kiara," Karen said, standing to leave. "Look, once I'm at the Commonwealth Lounge, I'll text Craig that I stopped by your place. I'm not going to be at the lounge too long anyway. I just want to see how Travis is doing."

Karen could see the concern on Kiara's face but was sure her sister didn't understand the bond she shared with Travis. He'd always been there for her, and she was going to be there for him now. She watched the look of concern on Kiara's face change to one of annoyance when the doorbell rang.

"I wonder who could be at my door. Nobody should be dropping by here without calling me first," Kiara said. She tiptoed toward the door, but before she could reach it, someone knocked several more times and rang the doorbell again. She looked through the peephole, then walked back toward Karen and whispered.

"It's Craig, Karen. What do you want to do?"

"Craig? What in the hell is he doing here?" Karen whispered. She tiptoed to the peephole and could see Craig standing on the porch. His image became distorted as she watched him step toward the door again to push the doorbell and then walk back to the edge of the porch. Kiara tapped Karen on the shoulder.

"So, what do you want to do? Why don't I just tell him you aren't here?"

"Come on, Kiara. Craig's not that stupid. I'm pretty sure he's already seen my car by now."

"Well, his stupid ass had better stop knocking on my damn door and ringing my doorbell like he's crazy," Kiara said and began walking toward the door. "Look, I'm going to ask him what his damn problem is."

"Wait, Kiara, let me talk to him," Karen pulled lightly on her sister's arm and went to the door. She looked through the peephole again before opening the door.

"Craig, what are you doing here?"

"I texted you a couple of times and you didn't answer. I figured you were at Kiara's. So, I just thought I'd drop by."

"Drop by for what, Craig? Can't I visit my sister without you stalking me?"

"Stalking you? Come on, Karen. It's not even like that. You normally get off from work around five, and now it's seven o'clock. Can't a man worry about his woman?"

"Look, Craig, this needs to stop," Karen paused and looked out toward the street. "How'd you get here anyway? I thought your car was in the shop."

"It is. I caught a ride with Dontrell. He stopped by the crib earlier, so I asked him to drop me off when I saw how late it was getting."

"Where's Dontrell now? How were you planning to get back to the apartment?"

"Well, when I saw your car, I figured I could catch a ride with you. So I told him he could leave."

Karen looked at Craig and shook her head. She could tell he had probably been drinking and smoking weed before coming over. She thought about Travis at the Commonwealth Lounge and wished she'd left before Craig showed up. She could have been spending time with Travis instead of babysitting Craig's insecurities.

"Give me a minute, Craig," Karen said, stepping back into the house. She closed the door before he could respond and walked back into the living room where Kiara was sitting.

"Hey, Kiara. I'm going to leave now."

"Is everything okay, Karen? Craig sounds like he's had a few."

"No, everything's not okay, Kiara. Lately, Craig's like this all the time. I'm going to have to give him a ride back to the apartment. One of his trifling-ass friends dropped him off, so he doesn't have a ride."

"Damn, girl. I know you said you were tired of Craig, and I can definitely see why," Kiara said. She walked over and hugged Karen, then pushed her far enough away to look into her eyes. "Make sure you text me as soon as you get home, okay? He worries me."

"Sure, I'll text you once I get home. But it's not Craig I'm worried about. I just hope Travis—"

"Look, Karen," Kiara interrupted, "you've got way too much going on right now. First, you need to do something about Craig. I'm pretty sure Travis is going to be okay. Just call him tomorrow."

"I sure hope you're right, Kiara," Karen said, and hugged her sister again before walking out the front door.

Chapter 11

Travis pushed the power button on his cell phone again before accepting that the battery was dead. He doubted he had a charging cable in his car and decided to let Orlando know he needed to head to the nearest store to buy one. Orlando was still on the phone, and from the defeated tone in his voice, Travis could tell things weren't working out as he had hoped. A few minutes later, Orlando walked over to where Travis was sitting.

"You wouldn't believe how hard it is to get a ride out of this place. None of the ride services are willing to do a one-way trip that far."

"I'm not trying to get into your business, Orlando, but just how far are you trying to go?"

"Elizabeth City, North Carolina. It's about a hundred and thirty miles from here. I guess I can't blame anybody who doesn't want to drive that far without a return fare, but my boss doesn't want to hear that. Maybe it's not too late to rent a car."

Despite having problems of his own, Travis could empathize with Orlando. It reminded him that he wasn't the only person with issues beyond their control. As he thought about Karen, he began to accept that she wasn't coming to the lounge, and sleeping in the Honda was now his only option. That's when a possible solution to both his and Orlando's problems occurred to him.

"What if I give you a ride to Elizabeth City, Orlando? It's not like I have anywhere else to go."

"You, give me a ride?" Orlando repeated. "In what?"

"My car. How'd you think I got to the lounge—walk?"

The serious look on Orlando's face erupted into laughter. He sat down beside Travis, glanced at his phone, and finally responded.

"So, where's your car?"

"Parked over at the lounge."

"I don't know, man. We've both had a few drinks," Orlando said. "You sure you're sober enough to drive in this rain?"

"Look, man, the rain sobered me up," Travis said. "Besides, everything that's happened today has me feeling pretty wired."

"Where's your car again?"

"Like I said, it's over in the parking lot behind the lounge. All I'd need is some gas."

"Well, if you're serious, I can make it worth your while."

"As long as you give me gas money, we're good."

"One other thing, Travis. I think I should do the driving."

"Nah, man. Like I said, I'm feeling okay to drive. Besides, you've probably had as much to drink as I have."

"Nah, Travis. You started drinking way before I did tonight. I tell you what. I'll make it more than worth your time. I'll pay for your gas and throw in a couple hundred for helping me out. That should be enough for you to grab a hotel in Elizabeth City. You could spend the night there and drive back in the morning."

Travis thought about Orlando's offer. He could definitely use the money. He could also use a good night's sleep after everything that had happened. Besides, maybe Orlando was right. He had been drinking before they ran into each other, and Orlando could be in better shape to drive. He finally decided to let Orlando drive to the gas station down the street before deciding whether or not to let him drive the rest of the way to Elizabeth City.

"Okay, Orlando. It's a deal. I'm ready when you are."

"Man, I'm more than ready," Orlando said. "Let's get out of here."

As they headed toward the parking lot, Travis wished it was not raining so hard. He and Orlando were soaked by the time they reached the Honda. Orlando tossed his duffel bag, backpack, and tracksuit jacket into the back seat and slid behind the wheel. When he turned the key in the ignition, the car whined, shuddered, and then died. Orlando scowled as he glanced at Travis.

"Give it another try. She can be a little hard to start sometimes. Just don't give it any more gas until it turns over."

Instead of responding, Orlando twisted the key in the ignition. This time, the Honda started. Orlando revved the engine before letting it idle.

"Had me worried for a minute," Orlando said. "So, where's the closest gas station?"

"You sure you're all right?" Travis asked while struggling to fasten his seat belt. Once the belt finally snapped, he hoped Orlando was in better shape to drive than he was.

"Yeah, man, I'm good," Orlando said, using the palm of his hand to wipe away the condensation forming on the windshield. "Want to put the location into Google Maps?"

"Don't need it," Travis said. "I'm going to show you a way that avoids some of the traffic and runs directly into Sixty-Four West. After that, it's a straight shot."

"Straight shot to Elizabeth City, right?" Orlando asked.

"Yeah. I see signs for Elizabeth City every time I've gone to Virginia Beach," Travis said. "We just need to get some gas before we go too far."

Travis gave Orlando directions to the nearest gas station. By the time the car eased onto the boulevard, the rain was falling much harder, and an occasional rumble of thunder could be heard. When they arrived at the gas station, Travis ran into the store while Orlando pumped gas. Inside, Travis filled two cups with black coffee and grabbed several bottles of 5-Hour Energy Drinks. At the register, he noticed a display case containing phone chargers and added one to his purchases.

"Hey, where's your restroom?" Travis heard Orlando ask and turned around just in time to see him entering the store.

"In the back. Just past the dairy case," the cashier said, waving Orlando in the direction of the restrooms. Travis paid for the drinks and waited for Orlando at the entrance. He hadn't noticed that Orlando was carrying his bags when he entered the store, but couldn't help noticing them once he came out of the restroom.

"Man, you could have left those in the car," Travis said, nodding toward the bags hanging from Orlando's neck and shoulders. "Whatever's inside is going to get soaked in this rain."

"It's cool, man. I'd rather chance getting them wet than stolen. Besides, all my stuff is wrapped in plastic. These days you can't be too careful."

"I guess you're right. But look, I think I'm okay to drive now that I've had some fresh air and a couple sips of coffee."

"Nah, we're good, man. We had a deal, remember? Besides, you're still looking a little wobbly."

Travis considered insisting on driving, but he followed Orlando back to the car, slid into the passenger seat, and handed him one of the cups of coffee. Before he could say anything, Orlando pulled out his wallet and handed him three one-hundred-dollar bills.

"Hey, man. You gave me one too many," Travis said as he attempted to hand one of the bills back to Orlando.

"Nah, man. You keep that. You're doing me a big favor. Especially on a night like this. Shit, I couldn't even get any of the people I know in Richmond to give me a ride. Yeah, you keep that. That should be more than enough to pay for a room in Elizabeth City."

Travis folded the bills and slid them into his pants pocket. He then gave Orlando directions to the shortcut. As they drove, Travis wondered why Orlando was catching buses if he could afford to pay the kind of cash he'd given him for a ride. Eventually, he became less concerned about the money. What bothered him more was the huge smear the wipers were making across the windshield. Orlando didn't seem bothered, but Travis reprimanded himself for not replacing the wipers months ago when he first noticed they were worn.

A couple of miles from the gas station, Travis could barely make out the dimly lit sign of the motel he had visited earlier. Seeing the motel again reminded him of his unresolved situation with Elana—and the credit card. As they continued past the motel, Travis directed Orlando to make a right at the next intersection. Orlando turned onto the dimly lit road leading to the shortcut Travis promised would take them to I-64 West.

"Are you sure this is the way?" Orlando asked after they had driven a couple of miles down the dark road. "I'm sure glad we gassed up already. Doesn't look like anything is on this road but us."

"We'll be on Sixty-Four before long," Travis said while trying to conceal his own nervousness. "I've come this way hundreds of times."

"I think I'll feel a whole lot better when we see some signs for the highway," Orlando said. "I can barely see through this windshield."

"Spray a little wiper fluid on it," Travis said. "Maybe that'll help clear it up some."

The wiper fluid mixed with the rain, clearing some of the smearing on the outside, but the inside of the windshield remained hazy with condensation. Travis watched Orlando lean closer to the windshield while at the same time using one hand to wipe away the haze.

"Do you have anything I can use to wipe the windshield?" Orlando glanced in Travis's direction. Travis pressed the glove compartment lock and the door dropped open. He fished around the compartment until he felt the box of tissues.

"Hey, what's that?" Orlando looked over at Travis and then down at the open glove compartment. "Oh, so you're holding out on me, man."

"What's what?" Travis asked, closing the glove compartment.

"I see that bottle you're hiding," Orlando said, grinning. "I could use a sip right about now."

"You serious, man? I don't know if that's a good idea. Can you even see out of the windshield? Besides, the bottle is almost empty.

"Look, Travis, I got this. A sip is all I need. I can see just fine."

Orlando reached for the glove compartment, and when he did, Travis could feel the Honda begin to hydroplane. Orlando didn't seem to notice how fast he was going, or that the car had lost traction as it glided over the puddled water on the road. Just as Travis was about to tell Orlando to slow down, a deer galloped onto the road. In an attempt to avoid the deer, Orlando jerked the steering wheel but couldn't maintain control of the car. Travis felt himself lose consciousness as the car slid down the embankment and slammed into a tree.

* * *

J. Marcus Evins

Travis opened his eyes. A tree looked as though it was growing through the middle of the Honda's engine compartment. The rain had stopped, but a dense fog blanketed the area around the car. In the darkness, he could hear Orlando moaning. With some effort, Travis freed himself from his seat belt and pushed open the passenger door. He remained seated for a moment, letting the shock subside, then struggled to his feet before limping around to the driver's side. Inside the car, he could barely make out Orlando through the fogged-up window, struggling with his seat belt. Blood trickled down one side of Orlando's face from a gash above his left eye. Travis yanked on the door handle, and after several unsuccessful attempts, he ran back to the passenger side of the car.

"Can you get free?" Travis shouted, sliding into the front seat beside Orlando. "Let me see if I can move the steering wheel out of the way."

He pulled the steering wheel release lever, and it moved slightly.

"Okay, man," Travis said, doing his best to stay calm. "Let's get you out of here."

"I can't move my left foot," Orlando groaned. "I think it's stuck under the brake pedal."

Travis reached under the steering wheel, hoping to free Orlando's foot. As he felt around inside the dark car, he could tell Orlando's foot was wedged under the brake pedal in a way that suggested it could be broken.

"Grab my stuff from the back seat," Orlando said, groaning again. "I think I can pull my foot out."

Travis quickly grabbed Orlando's belongings from the back seat, placed them under a nearby tree, and hurried back to the car.

"Okay, I took care of your stuff," Travis said. "Any luck getting your foot unstuck?"

"No. Do you have a crowbar or something in your trunk?" Orlando asked through gritted teeth. Travis could tell from Orlando's labored speech that he was in extreme pain.

"I don't have the keys, man," Travis said. "Can you pull the trunk latch?"

Orlando grimaced but didn't respond. Travis opened the glove compartment, pulled out a flashlight, and shined it around the car's interior. Seeing nothing useful, he stepped back outside to search the immediate area. As he shined the light toward the front of the car, he noticed smoke coming from beneath the crushed hood, and smelled the unmistakable odor of gas.

"Hey, Orlando, you still with me?" Travis asked, making his way back to the passenger door.

He peered inside and saw Orlando slumped over the steering wheel, motionless. Travis crawled into the car and tugged on Orlando, but he couldn't move him. Frustrated, he glanced out the windshield and saw flickers of yellow-orange flames curling from under the Honda's hood.

Travis tugged on Orlando again. Unable to move or awaken him, he decided to give freeing Orlando from the driver's side another try. When Travis got to the other side of the car, he heard a small explosion. Flames now covered the entire hood of the car. A second explosion knocked Travis to the ground, where he lay watching the car become engulfed in flames.

When Travis could no longer see Orlando through the smoke and flames, he climbed up the embankment's muddy slope. On the road, there were no signs of traffic in either direction. He searched his pockets for his cell phone but remembered it had died earlier. It occurred to him that Orlando had a phone, so he stumbled back down the embankment toward the car. At the bottom, Travis froze when he saw the Honda completely obscured by a wall of smoke and flames.

Remembering Orlando's phone, he ran to where he had placed Orlando's belongings under the tree. The duffel bag had a lock on it, but Travis was able to search through the pockets of Orlando's tracksuit jacket and the backpack. After searching for several minutes without finding a phone, he gathered Orlando's belongings and made his way back up the embankment. He walked along the dimly lit road, hoping to flag someone down. After about an hour, he spotted the faint outline of a gas station through the fog. He jogged toward it, but slowed to a walk when he saw that it was closed.

Frantically, Travis pushed on all the doors until he discovered that the restrooms were unlocked. Inside the men's restroom, Travis checked Orlando's jacket again. Instead of a phone, he found Orlando's wallet and bus ticket. He stuffed both into his pants pocket and tried to open the duffel bag again, pulling on its brass lock several times before giving up. He then remembered the motel they had passed on the way to the shortcut. It would be a place where he could use a phone to report the accident. Before leaving, Travis checked his reflection in the mirror and splashed cold water on his face. He then slipped into Orlando's jacket, leaving his soaked shirt behind, and headed down the road toward the Roadway Motel.

As he walked in the direction of the motel, Travis could hear the distant sound of emergency vehicles. A wave of panic washed over him when he realized they were probably heading to the crash site. Reaching the motel, he climbed the stairs leading to the lobby. Several people pushed past him, likely curious about the sound of distant sirens. When he entered the lobby, Travis slid Orlando's duffel bag and backpack under a chair and sat down. He was pretty sure Orlando was dead and that the police would eventually trace the car back to him. Exhausted, he buried his face in his hands, stifled a sob, and wondered when the nightmare would end.

Chapter 12

Despite the warm mid-August temperatures, Detective Phillip Kelly shivered slightly as he waited outside the Office of the Chief Medical Examiner. He didn't know if it was because of the cooler temperature maintained in that wing of the building or the mixture of uncertainty and anticipation he was feeling. What Kelly did know, as he wondered why he had been called back in six hours after his shift had ended, was that after nearly twenty-five years, his career with the Richmond Police Department was pretty much over.

Lately, he'd been watching less experienced detectives handle the high-profile cases he used to be involved in. Now, since his transfer from the department's Major Crimes Division to Special Events, he was more often relegated to cases involving domestic disputes and traffic incidents. He'd initially fought the transfer, but finally accepted the reality that, at the age of fifty-two, he lacked the stamina, physical ability, and desire he once had for more demanding assignments.

So, when he received a call from the examiner about an accident that had occurred outside of his shift, he was surprised.

Based on the incident report, filed by the officers who had gone to the accident site earlier that evening, it seemed to be an open-and-shut case. According to the report, a Black male had been killed in an automobile accident where alcohol and hazardous weather conditions were contributing factors.

Apparently, the man had lost control of the car he was driving, run off the road, and struck a tree. The only aspect of the case that deserved additional attention—and likely the reason why the examiner was still in his office after midnight—was that the car had somehow caught on fire, and the driver was subsequently burned beyond recognition. Kelly just didn't understand why an accident, where he wasn't the responding officer, required him to come in before his usual shift rotation.

After a few more minutes that felt like hours, the office door finally opened, and the chief medical examiner, Clifton Johnson, stepped into the hallway. His glasses hung low on his nose as he peered over them, seemingly ignoring Kelly's presence. He looked down the hallway in one direction and then the other, before his eyes finally rested on Kelly.

"Come on in, Phil, and have a seat," he said, continuing toward his desk without looking back to see if Kelly was behind him. "Push that door closed, would you?"

Kelly closed the office door and took a seat in front of the examiner's desk. Most of the desk was covered with file folders, neatly arranged in rows so only the tabs were visible. He watched as the man he'd known for the last fifteen years carefully removed one of the folders and flipped through its contents. Kelly listened to the barely audible sound of Cliff humming as he reviewed the contents of the folder. Kelly had just about run out of patience, but before he could ask why he was there, the humming stopped, and Cliff looked in his direction.

"I'm sure you're wondering why I asked you to come in, Phil. I realize this is well outside of your normal duty hours."

"I'd say that was an understatement, Cliff. You know I'm pretty much on regular hours since my transfer from Major Crimes."

"So, what's it been now, Phil, about a year since your transfer? I bet Terri's glad to have you at home more," Cliff said and peered over his glasses. "I can tell you haven't been missing any meals lately."

"Yeah, I guess you could say she's getting used to having me around. But I'm sure you didn't call me in after midnight to discuss my love life or my diet."

Cliff didn't respond, but instead handed Kelly the folder he had been looking over and tapped a few times on his computer keyboard before speaking.

"That's the report the responding officers filed for an accident that occurred earlier this evening over on the Northside," Cliff said.

"Yeah, so? I saw the summary on the board when I came in. Looks pretty typical to me," Kelly said. He opened the folder and began reviewing the report while continuing to listen to Cliff. "I see Lazaro and Beiring caught this one. Have they notified the deceased's family yet?"

"Yes, the family was contacted right after the vehicle owner's DMV records were pulled," Cliff said. He tapped on the computer's keyboard a couple more times, printed a page, and slid it across the desk toward Kelly. "Now, add this to the equation. That's a copy of the initial forensics report."

Kelly reviewed the information on the sheet of paper, then looked up at Cliff.

"Weren't you part of that Rock Bottom Taskforce a couple of years ago?" Cliff asked.

Kelly nodded and thumbed through the folder's contents while Cliff continued talking. As far as he was concerned, the taskforce was his last real police work before getting transferred.

The target of the DEA-led operation had been a gang based in Elizabeth City, North Carolina, that trafficked drugs, primarily fentanyl, throughout North Carolina and the Commonwealth of Virginia. The gang used rental cars and interstate buses to move their product. The task force arrested twelve of the gang's members and successfully shut down most of the routes used by the rental cars.

Unfortunately, when the operation ended and surveillance was reduced, Kelly suspected that remnants of the gang had reconstituted and continued their activities via bus. Buses were inexpensive and left a minimal paper trail, making it difficult to connect couriers to the main operation. He became so convinced that buses were now their preferred distribution method that, for some time after the task force ended, he would stop by the Greyhound Bus Station on Arthur Ashe Boulevard, hoping to observe enough suspicious activity to justify sending a red flag up the chain of command. His unofficial surveillance efforts hadn't been successful, and after his transfer, he had given up on the idea of pursuing it further.

As Kelly reflected on his taskforce experience, he couldn't figure out a possible connection with the accident. Cliff seemed to read his mind.

"When the deceased came in, I attempted to confirm the identity of the person in the car and ran a sample through CODIS, and the name that came back wasn't the registered owner of the car," Cliff said, finally taking a breath. "The name of the person that came back was one of the members of the gang the taskforce had gone after. That's why I wanted to call you in on this before I release my findings. So, what do you think?"

Kelly looked in Cliff's direction but not at him and felt vindicated. He also felt himself shiver again, and this time, it had nothing to do with the temperature of the room.

"Well?"

"Well, what?"

"You want in on this or not?"

"I don't know, Cliff. You do know I'm pretty much a desk jockey these days, don't you? Isn't what you're suggesting a little bit outside of my current job description?"

"You're kidding me, right? This doesn't sound like the Phillip Kelly I know. The man I know wouldn't let something like this slip through his fingers. I remember you saying not too long ago that the taskforce only put a dent in the amount of fentanyl coming into the Commonwealth. Well, this is an opportunity for you to do something about it."

"Okay, so what if I decide to look into this? I mean, how far under the radar can I fly, and for how long?"

"Right now, this is an active investigation. The DNA sample is considered inconclusive without corroborating evidence. It'll take at least a few days for me to get what I need to make a positive ID, and per Virginia Code, as long as the investigation is still active, we can't release the body," Cliff said. "I figure that will give you about a week, and you wouldn't be flying under the radar exactly."

"How do you figure? You're looking at a possible dead drug dealer and maybe a missing person if I'm reading this right. And who knows? Maybe the car was stolen by the deceased. Or, maybe it was sold by the registered owner."

"You're right. There are a lot of maybes. But let me ask you, Phil, is that what your instincts are telling you?" Cliff asked. "Besides, right now we're just talking about a traffic accident which is, by the way, clearly within your area of responsibility if you wanted to get involved."

The room became quiet. Kelly shuffled through the report again as he considered what Cliff was suggesting. The sound of Cliff's phone buzzing penetrated the silence.

"Okay, is she alone?" Cliff asked the caller. He glanced in Kelly's direction. "Sure. I'll be there in a few minutes. Thanks."

J. Marcus Evins

Cliff ended the phone call and returned his attention to Kelly.

"The deceased's wife is here to identify the body. She's with a neighbor who drove her down to the station. You want to walk over with me?"

"Hold on, Cliff. I'm not getting this," Kelly said. "How is this supposed to work if you already suspect the person in the car isn't her husband?"

"Right now, we're following standard procedure. The deceased's family has been notified, and they have the right to identify the remains of the presumed victim. You're the only person, besides me, who knows about the preliminary DNA results," Cliff said. Kelly watched as Cliff carefully slid another one of the folders from the stack on his desk and stood. He walked around and took a seat on the edge of the desk. "You know, meeting the wife could be a good starting point for your investigation."

After a few minutes, Cliff walked across the room and opened the office door. He looked back in Kelly's direction.

"Well, no one can say I didn't try. I guess the case will have to go back to Lazaro and Beiring. Hopefully, they don't screw this one up," Cliff said, then slowly rotated his head from side to side. "Look, Phil, do me a favor and pull the door closed when you leave. Sorry about having you come back in at such a late hour. I'll make sure you get the OT."

Kelly didn't comment. He was thinking about the promises he'd made to Terri. Promises that he'd take things down a notch since leaving Major Crimes, and that they could retire to someplace warm in a year or so. The transfer to Special Events had made keeping promises easy, and his years on the force made retirement inevitable. Yet, he couldn't deny the excitement he felt when he thought about the case. There were too many unanswered questions, and the idea of leaving a case with so much potential complexity in the hands of two rookie detectives bothered him. He'd only need to reassure Terri this would be the last one.

"Hey, Cliff," he said as he rushed toward the door. "Wait up. It might be a good idea to have the investigating detective with you while you're talking to the wife."

Cliff waited for Kelly to catch up. They shook hands, and the two men continued down the hallway together.

Chapter 13

"Are you okay, sir?" Travis thought the question was part of the dream he was having—until he heard it again. "Sir, are you okay?"

"Yeah, I'm okay," Travis said, opening his eyes. The blurred face of the speaker slowly came into focus. "I guess I must've dozed off for a minute."

The young man's accusing tone and his blond hair pulled back into a man bun made Travis feel more annoyed than threatened. He remained in front of Travis as though unsure what to do next before speaking again.

"Are you a guest, sir?" he asked. Travis could tell from the man's expression that he probably looked as bad as he felt. "If you aren't a guest at this motel, I'm going to have to ask you to leave. We don't allow loitering in our lobby."

Travis looked around the lobby. He wondered how long he'd been sitting there.

"If you are a guest, sir," the young man persisted, "would you happen to have your key card with you?"

"Look, I'm sorry. I'm planning to check in," Travis said. "I just sat down for a minute."

"Sir, you've been sitting here for over an hour," he said. "I'm sure you can understand our concern."

"Sure, no problem. I'll check in right now," Travis said and walked toward the front desk.

"Are those your bags, sir?" the young man asked, pointing at the duffel bag and backpack that had been pushed under the chair where Travis had been sitting.

"Thanks, I wouldn't want to forget those," Travis said. He went back to grab the bags from under the chair and continued toward the desk. The young man was now behind the glass partition that separated the front desk from the lobby.

"And how long will you be staying with us?" the man asked once Travis made it to the registration desk.

"How much for one night?" Travis asked. He pulled out his wallet, and the three one-hundred-dollar bills Orlando had given him.

"You sure you don't want to put this on a credit card?" the man asked. "If you pay with cash I'll have to charge you a two-hundred-dollar deposit for incidentals."

Travis did not respond immediately. The wallet he pulled from his pocket wasn't his—it was Orlando's. Two one hundred dollar bills were in the wallet. There was also a driver's license and a credit card, but the name on the cards was not Orlando.

"So, will you be paying with a credit card or cash, sir?" the desk clerk asked again.

"It'll be cash," Travis said, and laid four one-hundred-dollar bills on the counter.

After receiving the key card, Travis rode the elevator up to his room. Once inside, he pulled Orlando's wallet from his pocket and examined its contents again. For a moment, he studied the picture on the driver's license. It was clearly Orlando—just with a different name: Roy Patterson. He tossed the wallet onto the bed and thought about the tangled mess his life had become. In one day, he'd lost his job, his wife, and had been in a horrendous accident that may have killed someone—someone who had a reason to hide his identity. It felt like a terrible joke was being played on him or he was experiencing a nightmare from which he couldn't awaken. Travis turned on the television, hoping to calm his increasing anxiety. A few minutes later, the low drone of the television, combined with his fatigue, allowed him to drift off to sleep.

* * *

It seemed like only a few minutes later that Travis was awakened by the sound of someone knocking on the door. Although the knocking continued, he refused to open his eyes, hoping whoever was at the door would go away. When the knocking finally stopped, he allowed himself to doze off again—until the sound of someone opening the door jarred him completely awake.

"One minute, I have to put some clothes on," he called out, although he'd fallen asleep fully dressed. Travis glanced around the room, slid the duffel bag out of sight, and checked in the mirror on the way to the door. He peered through the peephole before unlatching and pulling the door open.

"Can I help you?" Travis looked down at the petite, brown-skinned woman standing in the doorway. He could see housekeeping carts in front of some of the other rooms.

"I'm sorry, sir. I thought you had checked out," the woman said. Her soft Latina accent immediately reduced the anxiety Travis had felt when he'd first heard her knocking at the door.

"What time is checkout?"

"Twelve o'clock," she said.

Travis frowned. "What time is it now?"

The woman glanced at her watch and then back at Travis. "Eleven forty-five, sir. If you would like to stay longer, you can call the front desk. It shouldn't be a problem."

"Thanks, I'll do that," he said, slowly closing the door.

"I can still vacuum your room if you like," the woman offered quickly, "or leave some clean towels."

"No, no. I'm fine. I'll give the front desk a call right now."

Travis pushed the door closed and walked back toward the television. He scrolled through the channels until he found a local news station. Sitting on the bed, he tried to ignore the duffel bag and backpack lying on the floor, but his curiosity got the best of him. He pulled the duffel bag toward him and tugged on the small padlock. After several unsuccessful attempts, he gave up and called the front desk.

"No worries, Mr. Pace," the desk clerk said. "You would just have to pay for the additional night. Should I put it on your credit card?"

"I paid cash when I checked in," Travis replied. "I'll need to come down to the desk to pay. Can you give me about thirty minutes?"

"Of course, sir. I see you have a deposit on your account, so I'll hold the room until you come down."

Travis thanked the man and hung up. As he walked past the mirror, he paused and looked at the stranger staring back at him. His eyes were red and sunken. His hair was matted and he could use a shave. After showering and drying off, Travis sat on the edge of the bed. He looked at the clothes he'd removed and hated the idea of putting them back on. The pants looked okay after he brushed them off, but he needed to find a replacement for Orlando's track jacket. In the meantime, he decided to put the jacket back on. As he picked it up, a wallet fell out of one of the pockets and landed on the bed. Assuming it was Orlando's, he pushed it under a pillow and headed for the elevator.

When the elevator doors opened, Travis was greeted by the aroma of bacon and freshly brewed coffee, reminding him he hadn't eaten in over twenty-four hours. He peeked in the restaurant and was immediately acknowledged by one of the staff.

"Can I help you, sir?"

"Am I too late for breakfast?"

"Yes, sir. We just finished clearing everything away. We reopen at twelve-thirty for lunch in about five minutes if you'd like to come in and wait."

"No, that's okay. Maybe I'll come back when you reopen," Travis said, waving at the man before walking away. He could feel the paranoia returning and was pretty sure he wouldn't return to the restaurant. The feeling made him consider again whether or not contacting the police about the accident was a good idea. He was certain they would eventually trace the accident back to him anyway. He just needed a little more time to figure out the best way to explain why the person driving his car was someone whose true identity he did not even know.

As Travis continued toward the front desk, he noticed the motel's souvenir shop. At least that's what the sign said above the entrance to the small, cramped room he entered. The store featured mostly toiletry items and Virginia-themed caps, hats, and mugs. Travis was able to pick up a toothbrush, razors, shaving cream, and snacks. He also looked through a rack of T-shirts until he found one that didn't have "Virginia is for Lovers" or anything too obviously related to Virginia tourism.

On the way to the register, Travis saw a display containing alcohol miniatures. He picked up two of the bottles and, for a moment, held them in the palm of his hand as though trying to determine their weight. He stared at the bottles, unable to control the sudden nausea or the trembling of his hand. Feeling light-headed, Travis carefully placed the bottles back on the shelf. It wasn't until the cashier bagged his purchases and he was on his way to the front desk that the light-headedness subsided.

When he reached the desk, he noticed the young man who had checked him in the night before had now been replaced by the older man who was on duty during his previous attempt to check into the motel. Travis hoped the man wouldn't recognize him, but he could tell by the look on the man's face that wasn't the case.

"I see you decided to stay with us after all," the man said as Travis approached. "So how can I help you?"

"I called about staying an additional night," Travis said. He gave the man his room number and watched him go to the computer. He tapped on the keyboard a few times, then looked back at Travis.

"You must have checked in after my shift," the man said. "I'm here most weeknights until eight."

"Yes, it was much later than that," Travis said.

The man returned his attention to the screen. Travis wondered if he'd bring up the issue with his credit card from the night before.

"It's going to be one hundred fourteen dollars and three cents," the clerk finally said. "Of course, we'll have to hold on to your deposit until you check out."

Travis searched his pockets and realized he'd overspent at the souvenir shop and didn't have enough money left to cover the cost of the room. Searching his pockets again, Travis pulled out what he thought was his wallet only to realize he had mistakenly brought the wrong one with him.

"We also take Visa," the man said, apparently having seen the credit card in Orlando's wallet.

Travis hesitated, but slowly pulled out the card. He didn't want to cause a scene and draw attention to the front desk after what had occurred the previous night. He wondered if the man would ask for additional identification and what he would do if he did. But when he handed over the card, the clerk quickly swiped it and handed it back without a word.

"Looks like you're all set," he said. "Enjoy the rest of your stay."

"Sure, thanks," Travis said slowly. For a moment, he couldn't move and watched the clerk walk to the other end of the counter to talk to another guest. When the guest walked away, the clerk glanced back at Travis.

"Anything else I can help you with, sir?"

"No, thanks." Travis smiled and walked a few steps away from the desk. He couldn't believe using Orlando's Visa had been that easy. But then he heard his name. He froze and turned to face the desk clerk.

"Just a minute, Mr. Pace," the clerk said. "There is one other thing. I should have caught it before."

"Is everything okay?" Travis asked, silently cursing himself for using Orlando's credit card.

"Give me just a minute," the clerk said and walked over to the computer.

Now, Travis was certain using Orlando's credit card had been a mistake. He was sure the desk clerk had discovered the error and was trying to figure out how to handle the situation. Travis watched the man type something into the computer and considered his options. At the very least, he could claim it was simply an error. At worst, he'd have to find the nearest exit out of the motel. He considered a few more scenarios until interrupted by the desk clerk.

"Just as I thought," the clerk said. "We owe you a refund of your deposit since you used the credit card. I can either pay you the amount in cash or credit it back to your card. Which do you prefer?"

Travis smiled. The clerk, waiting for a response, gave him an odd look.

"Cash will be fine," Travis said finally.

The desk clerk nodded and went over to the register. He counted out the two-hundred-dollar deposit and handed it to Travis. He thanked the man and quickly headed for the elevators. Though momentarily relieved, Travis grew increasingly paranoid about being stopped again before he could make it back to his room. It wasn't until he reached his floor, and the elevator doors opened to an empty hallway, that he finally felt a small measure of calm.

Chapter 14

As Karen drove to work the next morning, she was still bothered by Craig's unannounced visit to Kiara's house. It made her realize, more than ever, that he still hadn't accepted that their relationship was truly over. She didn't know what else needed to be said or done to convince Craig that they would be going their separate ways at the end of the month. Karen had considered moving out of the apartment before the lease expired, but she had decided to use the two remaining weeks to gradually transfer some of her belongings into storage before eventually moving in with Kiara. Besides, Craig seemed determined to wait until the very last day to move out of the apartment, which meant she'd have to wait until he was gone before turning in the keys.

When she finally arrived at work, Karen remained in her car. She squinted at the Lucent Technologies logo, trying to imagine what the company had been like when it first started. When she was hired four years ago, Travis told her that when he started working for Lucent, it wasn't like it is today—with elevators and security police scanning badges. Back then, everyone worked in one big room, and the CEO was just one of the guys working from a cubicle like everyone else.

Karen recalled her interview for the software analyst position and how Travis had quickly become the main reason she wanted the job. He was handsome, intelligent, and at that time, the only Black manager in one of the city's largest tech companies. She immediately knew they would work well together, and she hadn't been wrong. Now, just knowing Travis was no longer at Lucent made the building seem cold and unwelcoming. Karen pulled her phone from her purse and tried calling Travis a second time that morning. Once again, it went directly to voicemail.

Inside the office, Karen noticed Bradley and the rest of the analysts huddled together, talking in hushed tones. Natalie Nguyen was the first to acknowledge her. When their eyes met, Karen could tell Natalie had been crying. Even Bradley's usually smug expression was replaced by something more somber.

"Oh, Karen, I'm so sorry to hear about Travis," Natalie said, quickly walking toward her and hugging her tightly. "I know you and Travis were close."

The hug caught Karen off guard because she never thought of Natalie as an emotional person.

"I'm sure he's going to be okay," Karen said, returning the hug while glancing at Bradley and Ben Williamson. "He'll rebound from this. You'll see."

When Karen tried to make eye contact with Ben, he averted his gaze and looked toward Bradley, who slowly turned to face her.

"Karen, I don't think you understand," Bradley said. "Perhaps you should have a seat."

"No, I'm fine. What's going on?" she asked. "You guys act as though somebody died. Travis is going to—"

"Karen," Bradley interrupted gently, "Travis is dead. He was involved in an accident last night. I'm truly sorry."

J. Marcus Evins

Karen stared at Bradley as though he was speaking a foreign language that she couldn't comprehend. But what he'd said would have been incomprehensible in any language.

"What did you say?" she asked, unable to think of anything else to say. Then the ground seemed to shift beneath her and a black veil descended over her eyes.

* * *

When Karen opened her eyes, the first thing she felt was the cool compress on her forehead. Natalie, kneeling beside her, smiled sadly and helped her sit up.

"How do you feel, Karen?" Natalie asked, removing the folded, water-soaked paper towels that had been used to make a compress.

"I'm just a little woozy," she said, looking around the room. She noticed Bradley and the CEO apparently discussing what had happened, then returned her attention back to Natalie. "I can't believe I fainted. I think I'm okay now. I just need to get up."

Slowly, with Natalie's assistance, she got up and looked around the room again before stumbling toward the nearest chair. For the next few minutes, she closed her eyes and rested her head on her arms in an attempt to shut out what was going on around her.

"How are you feeling, Ms. Harris?" Karen lifted her head to see Bradley and the CEO standing next to her. "You had us worried for a minute."

The CEO smiled warmly and placed a hand on her shoulder.

"I'm fine, sir. I just—" Karen began, but was unable to finish before her eyes flooded with tears and her speech became incoherent.

"There, there, Ms. Harris. It's going to be okay. You just take a moment. I'm going to come back and check on you. Just take it easy for now."

She watched the CEO walk back to where Bradley was standing. They talked for a few more minutes before the CEO left the room. Bradley walked over to where Karen was seated.

"How are you feeling, Karen?" he asked. "I know you must be devastated. Is there anything I can do for you?"

Karen looked at Bradley and shook her head. As far as she was concerned, he had already done more than enough.

"Natalie, Ben, can you both come over here for a minute?" Bradley waited until they were close enough to hear him.

"First of all, I'm sure each of you is just as shocked as I am regarding the loss of our colleague, Travis Pace. Despite the circumstances, it's clear he contributed a great deal to Lucent Technologies, particularly in its formative years. The CEO said he would be contacting Travis's family to offer condolences on behalf of Lucent Technologies as soon as it's appropriate. Additionally, leadership has authorized flexible leave, effective immediately, for anyone who feels they need it."

"So, what are we going to do?" Karen asked.

"I'm sorry, Karen. Did you say something?" Bradley asked.

"I said what are we going to do?" she repeated before continuing. "For as long as I and the other members of the team have been here, Travis was our supervisor. I think it would be appropriate if some expression of sympathy also came from the people who worked closely with him."

"Well, I don't know," Bradley said. "I thought whatever the leadership did would sufficiently convey our collective feelings."

"Our collective feelings," Karen repeated. "What collective feelings are you talking about, Bradley? I'm talking about something from his team, not some general expression of sympathy from a bunch of people who couldn't care less."

"Excuse me, Karen. I realize you are—"

"That I'm what? You have no idea what I am right now, Bradley."

"You're right, Karen. I don't. Perhaps you and I should talk about this afterward, but first, I'd like to finish telling everyone what's going on," Bradley paused for a moment before continuing. "The CEO told me we should expect a visit from the Richmond Police Department this afternoon. A Detective Kelly should be here around one and he wants to speak with Travis's coworkers."

"I don't get it," Ben spoke up. "What information could the police possibly want from us? It's not as though a crime has been committed."

"I know, Ben," Bradley said. "I thought the same thing. All I know is they asked to talk to us about Travis. That's pretty much all the details I have right now. The interviews will be conducted in the conference room. So, I recommend anyone going to lunch should be back before one. That's all I have right now. Karen, did you want to speak to me?"

Ben shook his head and whispered something to Natalie. Karen remained silent. She'd only heard bits and pieces of what Bradley had said. She was still trying to make sense of what had happened. The sound of her name brought her back to the moment.

"Karen," Bradley repeated her name. "Why don't we go to my office and chat."

Once they were in the office, Bradley offered Karen a seat, which she refused. Instead, she remained standing, arms crossed in front of her chest, staring at Bradley.

"So, is there something we need to talk about, Karen?" Bradley took a seat on the edge of his desk and looked up at Karen. "I do understand how hard this must be for you, but I don't think Travis's death should be an occasion for us to lose respect for each other. I think everyone was fond of him."

"Were you fond of Travis, Bradley? Really?"

"Of course. I mean, he had his problems, but I thought he was an all right guy."

"Yeah, you're right. Like most of us, he had some problems. But you know what his biggest problem was, Bradley?" Karen leaned forward in his direction. She raised her voice slightly. "Do you, Bradley?"

Bradley straightened his posture but remained seated on the edge of the desk. His eyes shifted away from Karen to something beyond the closed door of his office. Unable to resist, Karen followed his gaze and saw Natalie and Ben talking nearby. Their presence seemed to relax Bradley.

"I'm not sure where you're going with this, Karen, but —"

"But nothing, Bradley. Let me finish—you had it in for Travis since you've been here. Everyone knows how you kissed up to the leadership to get his job."

"You need to be careful, Karen," Bradley said. He slid off the edge of the desk, moved around to the opposite side and took a seat.

"Careful, Bradley? Travis was careful. He took shit from you, the CTO, and the rest and never said a goddamn thing because he was trying to be careful. And now we know how that turned out."

"You know what, Karen, this conversation is over. I'm not going to stand here and accept these accusations from you. And if I were you, I'd—"

"What are you going to do, Bradley? Fuck me over like you did Travis? Don't worry, I'm leaving. In fact, I think I'm going to take the administrative leave the CEO offered," Karen said and walked toward the door.

"But what about the detective? He'll be here at one and wants to interview the members of the team. Can't you wait until after he leaves?"

Karen paused and faced Bradley. She opened her mouth as though to speak, but instead began crying. As the tears streamed down her cheeks, all Karen knew was she needed to get out of the office. Behind her, she heard Bradley call out her name, but she kept walking. When Natalie stepped toward her, she waved her away. Karen continued to her cubicle, grabbed the bag containing her laptop, and headed for the elevator. She jabbed the elevator button several times before deciding to take the stairs.

Chapter 15

Once he was back in the room, Travis turned on the television and unpacked the bag from the souvenir shop. He placed the snacks and beverages on the desk, then laid the T-shirt out on the bed. After opening a bag of chips, he twisted the cap off a drink. Just as the bottle touched his lips, he heard a vibrating sound. It took a moment for him to figure out it was coming from the backpack. When he finally located the phone, it vibrated a second time. Seconds later, a short buzz indicated a voicemail had been left. Travis slid his finger across the display, only to find the phone locked.

As he continued looking through the backpack, he found a toiletry bag and what looked like a change of clothing. After removing everything, he tossed the backpack aside and pulled the duffel bag onto the bed. He yanked several times on the padlock securing the bag, but gave up and rechecked the pockets of Orlando's jacket for a key. Finding nothing, he took a second look at the items from the backpack. This time, he shook each piece of clothing and opened every case in the toiletry bag.

Still unable to find a key, Travis stared at the duffel bag and tugged on the padlock again. When the afternoon news came on, he turned up the volume. He sat on the bed next to the duffel bag, staring at the television for a few minutes before remembering the items he'd bought from the souvenir shop. With some effort, he removed a blade from one of the razors. The blade sliced easily through the canvas duffel bag, revealing its contents. In the middle of the bag was a pistol, which Travis carefully placed on the bed. Stuffed on one side of the bag were four brick-sized packages wrapped in aluminum foil and sealed inside thick plastic. On the other side were neatly stacked bundles of money, each sealed in clear plastic.

Travis used the razor to cut open one of the stacks. He tore the band off and counted the one-hundred-dollar bills it contained. He pulled out another stack, sliced it open, and found more one-hundred-dollar bills. Unable to control his excitement, Travis dumped the rest of the bag's contents onto the bed and stacked the money into a neat pile. As he counted the fifty individually sealed packages of cash, he imagined how different things would have been with Elana if he'd had this kind of money. But thoughts of Elana were inseparable from those of Maurice. Now reminded of the last time he'd seen them together, he became so angry that he thought he might be hallucinating when he heard his name.

A reporter from one of the local news stations was interviewing a detective from the Richmond Police Department about a car accident that had occurred the night before. The detective said the body discovered at the scene was assumed to be the owner of the wrecked vehicle, and based on their investigation so far, foul play was not suspected. He went on to say that a mixture of alcohol and hazardous road conditions were likely contributing factors in the crash. In the top right corner of the television screen was a picture of him, taken a few years ago, on Copacabana Beach during a vacation when he and Elana had traveled to Brazil. His hair was slightly longer, and he needed a shave. The scene transitioned from the detective to a reporter, who added that because the body found in the wreck was burned beyond recognition, police were awaiting a positive ID from forensics. There was no mention of anyone else in the car.

Travis stared at the television. Although he felt remorse over Orlando's death, he was certain that contacting the police had become more complicated. He reasoned that doing so would result in a media circus and raise countless questions. There was no way to know what the police would do once they found out the person in the car was Orlando, not him. He'd have to explain why someone he barely knew had been driving his car, why he left the scene of the accident, and why he waited so long to contact them. The more Travis replayed the possible scenarios in his head, the more convinced he became that calling the police was no longer an option.

Orlando's phone vibrated again, but Travis reached for it too late to see the caller's number. Just as before, the phone vibrated again a few seconds later, indicating another voicemail message had been left. Travis tossed the phone on the bed and picked up one of the foil-wrapped packages. He felt its weight, turning it over several times. He picked up another package and compared it with the other three. Still not satisfied, he used the razor to slice open one of the foil-wrapped packages and wasn't surprised by the white powder that trickled out. Now, as he looked at the contents of the duffel on the bed, he was more than certain why someone was blowing up Orlando's phone.

It was then that Travis decided he needed to leave the motel. It was too close to the accident site, and he didn't want to risk any of the staff recognizing him from the news. Travis considered his options as he looked at the money and drugs stacked neatly on the bed. He decided to leave just after dark, and at the very least, dispose of the gun and drugs as soon as possible.

Travis couldn't help but wonder how far half a million dollars would take him—and if it was worth the risk to find out. As he considered his situation, he caught a glimpse of his reflection in the mirror and recalled the picture shown on the news. Running his hand over his uncombed hair, and feeling the coarse stubble on his face, he knew the first thing he needed to do. Without giving it a second thought, he grabbed a razor and shaving cream on the way to the shower.

After showering and shaving, Travis stuffed the pistol, money, and drugs into the backpack. The duffel was stuffed in the trashcan along with Orlando's other belongings and anything else he didn't have room to carry. Travis decided to keep Orlando's track jacket, even though it was something he wouldn't normally wear during the summer. He figured the jacket's pockets were large enough to hold the two packs of cash he'd opened and could be zipped closed. Before leaving the room, he checked his appearance in the mirror one last time and convinced himself that shaving his head and face made him look a lot less like the person featured in the news.

Outside of the motel, the streetlights had come on, and he welcomed the security of the increasing darkness. However, the comfort Travis felt as he walked along the shoulder of the road turned out to be short-lived. About a mile from the motel, he began to feel paranoid about the contents of the backpack and the consequences if he were stopped. As he scanned the area, Travis noticed the opening to a culvert running under the road ahead. After ensuring he wasn't being observed by passing cars, he slid down the steep embankment to see if the culvert might be a suitable hiding place.

Unfortunately, when he reached the culvert, he was disappointed to find water streaming out of its opening. Feeling discouraged, Travis climbed back up the embankment and continued down the road. A few minutes later, he came across another culvert. The opening to this one was partially hidden by a pile of small rocks and weeds. He would have missed it if not for the dim glow of a streetlight shining from across the street.

Scanning the area again, Travis slid down the embankment's steep slope. Unlike the previous culvert, this one appeared to be dry inside. Satisfied, he checked the contents of the backpack one last time before shoving it as far into the culvert as possible. Before leaving, he ensured the area looked undisturbed, patted his pockets to make sure the two packs of money were still there, and climbed back up the embankment. Once he was on the road, Travis checked his surroundings. On the other side of the road was the utility pole that cast a dim light over the area near the culvert. It supported the overhead power lines that ran along the treeline and stood out in a clearing.

Once he was sure that he could find the culvert again, Travis decided to follow the path most familiar to him. After all, he'd always fantasized about leaving Richmond one day, and now that fantasy was just a few miles away from becoming a reality. The only thing missing was Karen. But for now, Travis's biggest concern was figuring out just how far he'd need to go to distance himself from someone who might be looking for what was in Orlando's backpack.

Chapter 16

As he stood in line at the ticket window, Travis felt as if every eye in the bus station was on him. It was a relief when the agent on duty said she recognized him from the night before and insisted on exchanging or refunding the cost of his ticket. Not yet comfortable with the idea of using the money from the duffel bag, he gave her Orlando's ticket in exchange for a seat on the next bus leaving the station. The agent never asked for identification, and Travis boarded a bus less than twenty minutes later headed to Wilmington, North Carolina. Once the bus pulled out of the station onto Arthur Ashe Boulevard and he caught a glimpse of the Commonwealth Lounge across the street, his decision to leave Richmond felt less impulsive.

By the time they merged onto I-64 West, Travis began to relax. The bus was more comfortable than he had imagined. The high-backed leather seats offered a degree of privacy, and he was grateful to find a row with an empty adjacent seat. As the scenery blurred outside his window, Travis thought about how much his life had changed over the last few days. One thing was certain: he didn't want fate dictating his next steps. He hoped Wilmington would be far enough from Richmond to allow him the time and space to think, yet close enough to return for the rest of the money when he was ready.

Two hours into the trip, he dozed off, but was awakened when the bus pulled into the Norfolk, Virginia station. The stop lasted only ten minutes, barely enough time for passengers to disembark and board the bus. As Travis watched more people board the bus, he hoped no one would take the seat next to him. Unfortunately, it wasn't long before a man dropped into the seat. He nodded and smiled before inserting earbuds and focusing on his phone. Though the man seemed harmless, Travis patted his pocket to confirm the money was still there. Gradually, he relaxed enough to fall back asleep.

He might have slept until they reached Wilmington if not for a bump in the road. He opened his eyes to find the man beside him staring.

"Is everything okay?" Travis asked, watching the man remove his earbuds.

"Oh, I'm sorry," the man said. "I didn't mean to stare."

"No worries," Travis replied. "Was I snoring or something?"

"Yes, but it's not a problem." The man held up his earbuds. "I'm on public transportation a lot, so I always keep these handy."

Travis nodded and turned toward the window, hoping to discourage additional conversation.

"You catch the Greyhound often?" the man asked, undeterred.

"No, not often. This is probably the first time I've been on a bus in years," Travis said, his annoyance growing at the man's persistence.

"Yeah, I travel on the Greyhound all the time," the man said, extending his hand. "Name's Nathan."

"Name's Tra—" Travis paused, then continued, "Trammell. My name's Trammell."

"Nice to meet you, Trammell," Nathan said. "On my way to New Bern. How about you?"

Travis hesitated and was relieved when the man continued talking without waiting for an answer.

"You know, most people have never heard of New Bern. It's a small place but quiet. Not a bad place to put down roots, though," he said, then added, "I don't live there myself. No, I actually live in Richmond. My wife drove down to visit her parents—they retired there. I'm going to meet her to spend time with the in-laws, then we'll drive back to Richmond tomorrow. So, you and your wife do much traveling together?"

"My wife?" Travis repeated. "No, not really."

"Oh, don't mind me. My wife says I'm always jumping to conclusions. I guess I thought when I saw your ring..." Nathan paused before continuing. "Hell, I don't know what I was thinking. Anyway, it's like when I was looking at you earlier. You looked so familiar. I thought I'd seen you somewhere before—maybe in Richmond. You spend any time there?"

"No, never have," Travis lied. The mention of the wedding band reminded him of Elana and Maurice. The thought made him desperate to remove the band as soon as possible.

"So, where did you say you were from, Trammell?" Nathan asked.

"D.C.," Travis said, blurting out the first thing that came to mind.

"D.C.," Nathan repeated. "Could have sworn I'd seen you someplace. I never forget a face."

Nathan became silent for a moment, tapping on his phone before turning back to Travis.

"This is going to sound crazy," Nathan said, his tone somber.

Travis suddenly felt trapped as he stared at Nathan in anticipation of what he might say next.

"You don't have to worry, though," Nathan said. "That is, as long as you don't ever go to Richmond."

"Go to Richmond?" Travis repeated, his voice trembling slightly. "Why wouldn't I want to go to Richmond?"

"Well—and this is the crazy part," Nathan said. "You ever heard of a doppelgänger?"

"A what?" Travis asked, unsure if Nathan was serious or just toying with him.

"A doppelganger. You know, like a double," Nathan explained. "Maybe I've seen your doppelgänger in Richmond. Did you know meeting your doppelganger is bad luck?"

"No, I hadn't heard that before," Travis said, unable to control the feeling of paranoia as the bus rolled to a stop. "Hey, look, excuse me, Nathan. I think this is where I get off."

Travis slid past Nathan into the aisle. As he walked toward the front of the bus, he glanced through the windows and wondered where he was. Just before stepping down the stairs, he leaned toward the driver.

"Excuse me, what stop is this?" he asked, certain it wasn't Wilmington.

"This is the Washington, North Carolina bus stop," the driver said. "But, if I remember correctly, your ticket said you were going to Wilmington. You've got two more stops before we get there."

"I just want to stretch my legs," Travis said.

"Help yourself but I'm only going to be here for fifteen minutes," the driver said, peering through the bus window. "You know, there's not much in the way of facilities here. There's a bathroom in the back of the bus if you need it."

Travis nodded and stepped off the bus.

As he looked around, he understood what the bus driver meant about the lack of facilities. The "station" was no more than a couple of benches under a tin roof. It was nothing like the station in Richmond. Another passenger got off the bus and hurried away leaving Travis alone to gather his thoughts.

He glanced back at the bus and noticed Nathan staring at him through the window. When their eyes met, Nathan quickly looked away, as though he hadn't been watching. Travis looked back at the bus again and, even though Nathan was no longer visible, he couldn't shake the feeling that he was being watched. As the bus idled, two more passengers got off the bus and were picked up by friends or family. A third man, who appeared to be in his mid-thirties, hopped off the bus, wearing a dingy white T-shirt, faded jeans, and scuffed work boots. He sat on the bench, pulled out a cell phone, and made a quick call before heading down the street.

Travis scanned the surrounding area, unsure of which way to go. The Washington Hotel was across from the bus stop, and beyond it were several other motels and businesses. Looking in the opposite direction, beyond where the bus remained idling, there seemed to be fewer businesses. Travis glanced at the bus again and spotted Nathan and another person watching him from the window. Nathan waved frantically in an attempt to get his attention. Ignoring Nathan, Travis began walking away from the bus.

As he continued down the street, he heard the bus driver honk his horn. In the distance, he spotted a Waffle House restaurant and headed toward it. After a few minutes, Travis looked back to confirm that the bus had gone. He stopped walking and twisted the wedding band off his finger. He held it in his palm for a moment, and then tossed it into some nearby bushes before continuing toward the Waffle House. He soon caught up with the young man who had gotten off the bus. When Travis tried to pass him, the man turned abruptly.

"You following me or something?" he asked, scowling.

"No," Travis replied, caught off guard. "No, I'm not."

Travis kept walking, but could feel the man's eyes on him.

"Hey, wait a minute. Didn't you just get off the bus?" the man called out, speeding up to close the distance between them. Travis ignored the man and kept walking.

"Hey. You hear me talking to you?" the man said, finally catching up to Travis. "You deaf or something?"

Travis stopped and turned to face him. "Look, man, I don't want any trouble. I'm just minding my business, okay?"

"Ain't no need to get snippy," the man said. "I'm just trying to be friendly, that's all."

"All right, I get it. But I really need to go." Travis sighed and started walking again, hoping to reach the Waffle House without further incident.

"Hey, man. Wait up. You're on your way to the Waffle House, right?"

Travis continued walking without responding.

"Yeah, you are," the man yelled, catching up with him again. "Look, you got a couple of dollars you can help me out with? My ride didn't pick me up back at the bus stop. All I need is enough to get something to eat and maybe catch an Uber. Hey, man. I'm talking to you."

Travis stopped walking. As an adult, he'd never had to defend himself against a physical attack, and wondered if he could now. Instead of considering the possibility further, he decided to avoid the likelihood of a confrontation by abandoning his plans to go to the Waffle House.

"Look, I can't help you," Travis said, raising his arms in mock surrender. But as he turned to walk away, the man grabbed his jacket and one of the packs of money dropped to the ground.

"Hey, what's that shit?" the man said, rushing toward the pack of cash tumbling across the sidewalk. A few of the bills spilled out of the pack as Travis rushed toward the man, shoving him out of the way. He snatched the pack of money from the ground and stuffed it back into his pocket. The man, now on his hands and knees, scrambled to grab the loose bills, then lunged in Travis's direction. They wrestled for a moment until Travis was able to free himself from the man's hold. The man rushed toward him again but stopped unexpectedly. In the distance, Travis heard someone yelling.

"Hey Floyd," the person yelled again. "I grabbed us some breakfast."

Travis turned to see a man running from the Waffle House carrying a large bag. He wore a loose-fitting white T-shirt, faded jeans, and a trucker's cap. He yelled out again.

"Floyd, what the hell's going on?"

"Ain't nothing going on, Troy," Floyd yelled. He glanced at Travis, then back toward the man heading in their direction, "We just having us a little misunderstanding, that's all."

While Floyd was distracted, Travis began walking away—but not quickly enough.

"Hey, where the hell you think you're going?" Floyd yelled loudly enough for anyone nearby to hear.

Travis began running. Behind him, he could hear the two men yelling. Once their voices faded into the sounds of Washington's morning traffic, Travis slowed down enough to check to see if he was being followed. Satisfied that he'd escaped the men, he patted his jacket pocket, confirming the money was still there and paused to catch his breath. The sound of an approaching car startled him, and he exchanged glances with a watchful driver. Once he was sure the driver wasn't a threat, he continued walking—without any idea where he was or where he was going.

* * *

It was the sound and smell of water that oriented Travis as he continued walking. Both reminded him of a simpler time and seemed to reduce the anxiety lingering after the confrontation with the two men. According to the street sign, he'd stumbled upon Washington's Main Street. The buildings, old but well-maintained, were reminiscent of an earlier time. On one side of the street was a boardwalk where boats of various sizes were secured to the dock and on the other side, a wide and uncluttered sidewalk lined with storefronts. Benches and chairs outside many of the businesses added to the relaxed, nostalgic feeling of Washington's Main Street. Only a few people were on the street. Some, loaded down with fishing gear, lounge chairs, and coolers, headed towards the boats while others strolled leisurely without apparent purpose or destination.

Travis enjoyed the feeling of detachment as he walked along the sidewalk, peeking into various storefront windows. Aside from a drugstore and a few restaurants, most of the businesses hadn't opened. With no destination in mind, it didn't take much more than the aroma of cooking food and his empty stomach to coax him into the Main Street Café. He paused and scanned the restaurant's spacious interior before taking a seat in the dining area.

As he looked around, Travis decided that although the café wasn't much larger than the Commonwealth Lounge, it was a lot more stylish. Marble-topped tables rested on polished wood floors that reflected the natural light streaming through the cafe's picture windows. On some of the tables were small vases filled with freshly cut flowers, their colors and scent adding to the room's coziness. A lone television hung above a bar that stretched along one wall.

Travis tried not to let his eyes linger too long on the large assortment of liquors neatly arranged on the shelves behind the bar. Instead, he looked out the window at the morning sun as it began filling the sky above Washington's Pamlico River and listened to the sound of light jazz floating in the air. A week ago, he would never have imagined himself sitting in a restaurant in a city he'd never heard of. He patted his jacket pocket and wondered if the money he had would last until it was safe to return to Richmond.

"Beautiful, isn't it?" Travis turned to face a tall, slender Black woman. She placed silverware and a menu on the table in front of him. "Oh, I'm sorry. I didn't mean to sneak up on you."

"I was just . . ." Travis paused, not sure how to respond.

"Oh, no need to explain," the woman continued. "There's nothing wrong with sometimes just taking it all in—and the view is beautiful especially this time of morning."

"Yes," Travis said finally. "Yes, it is."

"So, what can I start you with, dear? Coffee, maybe?"

"Yes, coffee would be fine," Travis said as the panic he initially felt because of the woman's sudden appearance began to subside. Her folksy demeanor was a welcome change from his previous encounters since leaving Richmond.

"By the way, my name is Jenna," she said. "Our special this morning is the Denver omelet. It comes with pancakes and beverage of choice, but take a look at the menu—everything's good. I'll be right back with that coffee."

A few minutes later, Jenna returned with his coffee. "So, are you ready to order, or do you need more time?"

"No, I'm ready," Travis said. "I think I will try the special with a glass of orange juice."

Jenna took his menu, topped off his coffee, and returned ten minutes later with his order.

"So, what brings you to Little Washington?" Jenna asked. Travis found it difficult to maintain eye contact as he considered the best way to respond.

"I was just asking because you're not one of our regulars," she continued without waiting for an answer. "We see a lot of folks on their way to Nags Head or Cape Hatteras. Thought you might be heading to one of those places."

"No, I'm just passing through," Travis finally replied. He poked at the omelet with his fork, hoping his brevity would discourage additional conversation. "I should be leaving later today or first thing tomorrow morning."

"It's too bad you're not planning a longer visit. Maybe you'll still have time to see some of the sites before you leave. Washington's a small place but there's lots to see and do."

"I really don't think I'll be around long enough to do much sightseeing," he said. "But if I did decide to stay overnight, is there a hotel or motel you would recommend?"

"You can pretty much take your pick. The Days Inn and Washington Hotel are the least expensive. They're about a mile away on Carolina Avenue. The Marriott and Hampton Inn out on 15th Street are probably nicer but cost a little more."

"About how far is the Marriott from here?" Travis asked. "Is it within walking distance?"

"Oh, no. It's too far to walk," she said as she laid his check on the table. "So, you're not driving?"

"No—I mean, yes," Travis stammered, pausing to come up with something other than the truth. "What I meant is my car broke down not too far from here. So, I'm not driving right now."

"Oh, dear. I'm sorry to hear that," Jenna said. "What did you say your name was, again?"

He paused for a moment before responding.

"Travis," he said, after deciding it was probably safe to use his real name so far from Richmond.

"Well, Travis. Maybe my husband, TJ, can help you find a mechanic. He knows all the local repair shops if you need help."

"Thanks, but it's already being taken care of. The mechanic I spoke to was pretty sure he could get the parts needed for the repair once their supplier opens later this morning," Travis said.

"I'm going to head back over to the repair shop and check on his progress once I leave here. I was just asking about a place to stay just in case it takes longer than expected to fix my car. I also wanted to clean up."

Travis watched Jenna's smile vanish and her forehead wrinkle with genuine concern.

"How about I call you an Uber?" she asked. "That way you can check on your car and have a ride to one of the hotels if you need one."

Travis accepted Jenna's offer and headed toward the register to pay for his meal. At the register, he was greeted by a short, stocky Black man who smiled as he handed him the check.

"Travis, right? I'm TJ, Jenna's husband," he said and shook Travis's hand. "Jenna's in the back calling that Uber for you. Shouldn't take long for one to get here this time of morning. She tells me you broke down nearby. Where about?"

"Over near the bus stop," Travis replied. "I'm not real sure of the street."

"Sounds like somewhere around Ninth or Carolina. There's a couple of decent repair shops over that way. You were pretty lucky to catch someone this early on a Saturday morning. Who's fixing it for you?"

Before Travis could answer, Jenna walked up. "This is the nice young man I was telling you about, TJ. Your ride should be here in about fifteen minutes."

"Excuse me for a minute, Travis," TJ said as another customer approached the register. Travis stepped out of the way but continued talking to Jenna. In the fifteen minutes he waited for the Uber, he found out Jenna and Thomas Johnson—or TJ, as everyone called her husband, had been married for forty years. They'd owned the Main Street Café for almost twenty. Travis was struck by their friendliness and openness toward a stranger. He was relieved when TJ rejoined the conversation and didn't inquire about the car's status again. They talked for a few minutes more before the Uber pulled up in front of the restaurant. Once he was in the car, he waved one last time before turning his attention to the driver.

"The caller said you were going to a hotel," the driver said. "Which one?"

"Actually, can you take me to a place where I can buy an inexpensive used car?"

"Yeah. There are a couple of places around town," the driver replied. "You looking for anything in particular?"

"Nah, just something clean with four wheels."

The driver nodded and smiled. "I know just the place."

As the car pulled away from the curb, Travis began to relax but couldn't help wondering how long he would have to live a lie before the truth finally caught up with him.

Chapter 17

Washington City Motors was a small lot located only a couple of blocks from the hotel where Travis had decided to stay. It seemed like the perfect place to find something that wouldn't stand out or attract attention. As he wandered through the rows of cars, a man stepped out of the office and headed in his direction.

"Welcome to Washington City Motors," the man said once he was close enough to shake Travis's hand. "Looking for anything in particular?"

"No, not really. Just something reliable," Travis replied.

"Well, look, my name's Bill. Take your time. We've got some nice ones on the lot. I'm pretty sure you'll find something you like," he said with a warm smile. "I'll be in my office if you have any questions. Just give me a holler."

Travis watched Bill walk back toward the office. Like TJ and Jenna, Bill had a friendly, folksy demeanor that was oddly comforting. It eased some of Travis's anxiety that something—or someone—might be lurking just around the corner. After a brief look around the lot, Travis decided on a 2013 Honda Accord EX-L. The car was clean, and despite having over 170,000 miles on the odometer, it was an upgrade from the Honda he'd lost in the wreck.

"Yes sir, that's a good choice," Bill said as he quietly reappeared. "Nothing like a Honda."

"How much?" Travis asked as he slid into the driver's seat of the Honda.

"I can't let it go for less than the sticker price."

Travis glanced at the price on the windshield and nodded. "Can I test-drive it?"

"Sure thing, let's go to my office. I'll need to see your license first."

As they walked to the office, Travis glanced back at the Honda. He'd already used his license when he checked into the hotel, and the thought of using it again made his stomach tighten. He began to wonder if buying the car might put his anonymity at risk. Despite his apprehension, he handed the license over.

Bill examined the license and raised an eyebrow. "You're a little ways from home," he said. "What made you travel so far to buy a car?"

"Just visiting some friends in the area," Travis said, pausing as he thought through what he was about to say. "I've been car shopping for a while, and when I passed your lot, I thought I'd stop and see what you had."

Bill picked up his phone and took a picture of the license before handing it back to Travis.

"Well, you came to the right place. Here are the keys. Just make a left on Carolina Avenue and follow the signs to 264 West. That'll give you a little over a mile before you hit the Hackney Avenue exit, and that'll bring you back here. You can push the speed limit a little, but not too much. Just pull back up to the office when you're done."

Travis took the keys and went back to the Honda. The car started smoothly, then settled into a quiet idle. As he drove off the lot it occurred to him that he should just keep driving. In a few hours he could be back in Richmond, pick up the rest of the money, and keep going—but where would he go? Unable to come up with a good answer, and with the reality that Bill had seen his license, Travis finished the test drive and returned to the lot.

Inside the office, Bill was scribbling on a sheet of paper. When Travis got closer, he saw it was a sales contract.

"So, is she a keeper?" Bill asked without looking up.

"Yes," Travis said. "I think I'll take her."

"Good choice," Bill said, finally looking up from the paperwork. "Should I use the address on your license?"

"Yeah, sure," Travis said, trying to suppress a growing sense of uneasiness.

"I'll need to take another look at it."

Travis laid his driver's license on the desk. Bill flipped it over a few times before jotting down the address.

"Will you be financing through your bank, or do you want to use our in-house financing? A decent credit score will get you a rate somewhere between six and nine percent."

"No, I'd like to pay cash," Travis said. "How much am I looking at?"

Bill paused, his eyebrows lifting slightly. "Cash? Well, we don't get many cash buyers, but we'll definitely take it."

He gave Travis another long look before returning his attention to the paperwork. He signed the form then slid it in Travis's direction.

"Just need your signature here," he said and pointed at the form. "Oh, and proof of insurance."

"Insurance?" Travis repeated, caught off guard. Until now, he hadn't considered that the insurance company might already be aware of his recent accident. "I don't have my insurance information with me."

"That's fine," Bill said. "Most folks just pull it up on their phone these days anyway. If you can't, I can give your insurance company a quick call to verify. Who are you insured with?"

"GEICO," Travis said, then quickly added, "Do you have a restroom?"

"GEICO," Bill repeated. "Great. I pretty much have their number on speed dial. Shouldn't take more than a couple of minutes."

"Do you have a restroom?" Travis asked again, this time louder, to get Bill's attention.

"It's the door over there to the left," Bill said. He pointed in the direction of the restroom before picking up his cell phone. "You go ahead while I make this call. I'll be just a minute."

By then, Travis had decided he'd had enough. The feeling of paranoia was more than he could bear. He slid his license off the table and stuffed it back in his wallet as Bill began dialing. He glanced at Bill one more time before standing and walking toward the restroom. Once he reached the restroom door, he rested his hand on the knob, then looked toward the exit door. Behind him he could hear Bill chattering away on the phone.

"Yeah, that's it right there," he heard Bill say, "I've got your insurance confirmed. All I need is your signature on these additional forms and she's yours."

Travis acknowledged Bill with a nod before entering the restroom. Once inside, he stared at his reflection. He splashed cold water on his face and wondered if this was how life was going to be from now on—constantly looking over his shoulder, always on edge. When he came out of the restroom, Travis signed the remaining documents, paid in cash, and drove away in the Honda.

* * *

Later that evening, Travis sat in his room at the Washington Hotel. The faint smell of stale carpet and disinfectant made him wonder if he should have treated himself to one of the more upscale places to stay. After leaving the car dealership, he had gone to a nearby Walmart to buy some clothes and a cell phone. He bought the clothes he wanted, but abandoned his plans to buy a phone when the sales associate insisted he provide a credit card for service activation. Not willing to take another chance with a credit card, he purchased a laptop to use as an alternate means of communication. The experience at Walmart, along with checking into the hotel and buying a car, made him realize how difficult it might be to remain anonymous.

Travis's concerns about remaining anonymous were lessened once he connected the laptop to the internet using the hotel's Wi-Fi. To his surprise, there was no mention of the accident on any of Richmond's news websites—despite it having occurred just two days ago. The absence of information made him realize that to the rest of the world, the accident may have been nothing more than a fleeting news story. Although he felt some relief, he couldn't help but wonder how those closest to him were coping with his presumed death.

He imagined Elana's grief, like their love for each other, would be short-lived. His insurance policies would ease the financial strain for a time, and he was sure Maurice would be around to satisfy Elana's other needs. Karen, on the other hand, would likely grieve longer. The bond they shared had been growing steadily over the years. His biggest regret was that he had not had the chance to tell Karen how much her friendship meant to him.

Travis thought about what might have happened if Karen had met him at the Commonwealth Lounge on the night of the accident. If she had, he was sure he wouldn't have crossed paths with Orlando or, even if he had, wouldn't have offered him a ride. But as Travis considered it further, he realized that avoiding

Orlando would not have spared him from the chaos his life had become. He would still have been out of a job, and his marriage to Elana still would have been irreparably damaged. Perhaps the only difference would have been the slim chance of preserving Karen's friendship—though now, even that seemed lost.

The more Travis thought about Karen, the harder it became to resist the urge to call her. Picking up the hotel phone, he listened for the dial tone and punched in the first few numbers. Then he paused. Memories of misplaced trust came to mind. Hadn't he trusted the management at Lucent Technologies? Hadn't he trusted Elana—and even Orlando? He tapped two more numbers, then stopped, and wondered if he was really ready to trust Karen too.

Travis placed the phone back on its cradle and lay on the bed. He tried to ignore the sounds of footsteps, doors opening and closing, occasional laughter—the sounds of life outside of his room. He decided that retrieving the money from the culvert as soon as possible should be his next priority. The money would allow him to find someplace where he could sort things out. He just needed to figure out where that place might be.

Energized by the idea of finding somewhere he could start over, Travis went back to the laptop and searched Google Maps for possible destinations. Eventually, his excitement gave way to fatigue. Shutting off the laptop, he considered the many uncertainties ahead. The only things he knew for sure were that tomorrow would be his last day in Washington, North Carolina, and his next destination would be Richmond, Virginia. What might come after that remained unclear.

Chapter 18

Sleep did not come easily for Travis that first night in Washington, North Carolina. Each time he drifted off to sleep, he was awakened by questions for which he had no answers. The last question that awakened him just before daybreak was about Orlando. Travis recalled how often Orlando was on the phone with a person he referred to as his boss. Certainly, this person would be concerned about Orlando's whereabouts. More than likely, this same person also knew about the large amount of money and drugs in Orlando's possession. The more Travis thought about it, the more he wondered how far a person would go to recover what he had hidden in a culvert in Richmond.

The next time Travis opened his eyes and squinted at the blurry red numbers on the clock beside his bed, it was almost ten o'clock. His thoughts about Orlando prompted him to turn on his laptop and take another look at Richmond's local news sites. He also did a Google search and found a Virginia State Police site that allowed users to perform an alphabetical search of people reported missing. When he found no mention of the accident or any missing person reports, Travis knew he had to recover the money from the culvert as soon as possible. The sooner he did, the sooner he could distance himself from the risk of anyone connected to Orlando tracking him down.

Once he had showered and shaved, Travis decided to find a place to grab something to eat before leaving Washington. Despite the many possibilities near the hotel, he found none of them appealing. Besides, the hotel was too close to the bus stop and he didn't want to risk running into Floyd or his friend again. Instead, he considered returning to the Main Street Café. The food had been delicious, and he enjoyed how comfortable the couple who owned the restaurant had made him feel. Even more so, returning to the restaurant would spare him the paranoia he experienced every time he entered someplace new and unfamiliar.

Out of curiosity, and because his laptop was still on, Travis decided to check the restaurant's meal hours before leaving the hotel. When he pulled up the Main Street Café's website, he noticed customers could order online for pickup. He decided that doing so would shorten his wait time and give him a chance to see Jenna and TJ one last time before leaving Washington. After placing his order, Travis checked out of the hotel and headed for the restaurant.

* * *

"Hey, look who's back," Jenna said when Travis entered the restaurant. "You're running a little bit later this morning. Go ahead and have a seat. I'll be right over."

Travis smiled and took a seat at the bar. TJ, at the register with a customer, greeted him with a friendly wave. The restaurant was much busier than it had been during his last visit. Each time another customer walked in, he was glad he'd already placed his order online.

J. Marcus Evins

"So, honey, did you get that car of yours fixed?" Jenna asked when she reappeared. She placed an empty coffee cup in front of Travis and began pouring.

"My car?" Travis asked, not immediately recalling the details of their conversation from the previous day. "Oh, my car is okay. It's running as good as new."

"Well, that's good to hear. I'm sure you're happy about that," she said. "So, besides coffee, what can we get for you today?"

"I've already ordered," Travis said.

"You've already ordered?" Jenna repeated slowly and looked around the room. "So, which one of our servers took your order?"

"I placed it on your website about thirty minutes ago," he said.

For a moment, Jenna's face went blank, as if processing what he'd just said. Then she turned toward the register.

"Hey, TJ, can you come over when you have a second?"

TJ finished ringing up a customer before walking over to where Travis and Jenna were standing.

"Travis says he placed an order on our website about thirty minutes ago, but I haven't seen any online orders come through since we opened this morning," Jenna said. "I thought you said the online order function had been fixed."

"As far as I know, it has been. Let me go back to the office and take a look," TJ said with a shrug and walked away.

"Sorry about that, Travis," Jenna said with a sigh. "It seems like every time we turn around, something's not working with that site. We should probably just take it offline until we're sure it's fixed," Jenna said. "So, what can I get you? It won't take long."

Travis gave Jenna his order, then moved from the counter to one of the booths. A few minutes later Jenna reappeared with his food.

"Here you are, dear. I want to apologize again for the problem we're having with our website. Even though taking it offline would be easy, I don't think that's the right thing to do. Most of the restaurants in Washington are doing business online. Some even offer home delivery."

"I agree with not taking it down. I can't think of many businesses that don't have a website," Travis said. "I'm sure there's someone around town who works on websites that can fix the problem you're having."

"Maybe," she admitted, "But a couple of years ago, we hired a company out of Greenville to upgrade the website. Even with the so-called professionals, we've run into problems. It was during the pandemic, and it wasn't always easy to get them to keep the website updated.

"Actually, they did a pretty good job. The rest of your website looks great. Fixing the order function shouldn't be too difficult for someone who does it for a living, and they can probably do the work remotely. It's usually just a plug-in configured to work with your existing website."

"So far, it's been easier said than done," Jenna said. She took a seat across from Travis. "Sounds like you know a little something about building websites."

"Well, honestly, I haven't messed around with any websites lately, but one of the first IT jobs I had was as a web developer," Travis said. "A few years ago, the company I worked for maintained its own website, but once they switched their focus to artificial intelligence-related projects, an outside company was hired to maintain it."

"Web development, IT, artificial intelligence, plug-ins. All of that stuff is way over our heads," Jenna said, then glanced toward the kitchen, "Look, Travis, I've got another order up. Don't you go anywhere until I come back."

Travis watched Jenna as she rushed toward the kitchen. Despite being one of the owners, and older than the other servers, she moved with more energy than anyone else. He felt comfortable around her and TJ despite everything that had occurred. As he watched Jenna make her way around the restaurant, he recalled the page on their website that shared how she and TJ relocated to Washington, North Carolina, twenty years ago to pursue the restaurant business. Travis was glad he'd had the good fortune to stumble upon the place and witness for himself how two people worked together to accomplish their dreams. He was just about finished eating when Jenna and TJ slid into the seat across from him.

"So, what do you think?" TJ asked.

"Think? think about what?" Travis's eyes remained on TJ for a moment before glancing at Jenna.

"Helping us out with our website," TJ said. "Jenna tells me you have a background in web development. The way she made it sound it wouldn't take you but a minute to fix ours."

"I didn't actually say a minute," Travis said with a smile. "Maybe more like two."

Everyone at the table laughed for a minute before becoming silent.

"Well, look, Travis, we could really use your help if you have the time," TJ said. "We know you said you were just passing through—but who knows? Your car breaking down might just have been a blessing in disguise."

"Tell Travis what we talked about, TJ," Jenna said and nudged TJ to prod him on.

"We were hoping if you have any flexibility in your schedule, you'd consider taking a look at the cafe's website and tell us how much it would take to repair the online order function," TJ said. "We'd really appreciate anything you could do to help, and we'd pay you for your time."

Travis wondered if TJ and Jenna could see the excitement he felt about doing something that reminded him of a time when he actually enjoyed the work he did at Lucent Technologies.

"I don't think I'll be able to," he said finally. "I was planning to leave Washington today, and I've already checked out of the hotel."

Travis looked from Jenna to TJ and could see the disappointment on their faces. He considered the website and the potential complexity of fixing the online order feature. From experience, he knew the simplest problems sometimes had the most complicated solutions—and he had no idea what tools the previous web developer had used to create the site.

"Well, look, we tried," TJ said, putting an end to the silence that had fallen between them. "I guess this is going to be goodbye, then. So, where are you headed?"

"I'll be returning home to Richmond," Travis replied, although he knew that beyond retrieving the money from the culvert, he had no idea where he was actually headed.

"Well, darling, you take care of yourself," Jenna said. She walked over and gave him a hug as though they'd known each other for years instead of barely more than twenty-four hours.

"Don't be a stranger, Travis. Maybe you can come back and plan to stay a little longer," TJ said while shaking Travis's hand. "You haven't seen much of Little Washington, and Richmond isn't really that far away."

"That's right," Jenna chimed in. "You're like family now. You ought to stay in touch. Who knows? Maybe we can still figure out a way for you to help us with the website remotely once you've gotten settled back home."

Travis watched as TJ walked back toward the register to take care of another customer. Jenna gave Travis another hug before heading toward the kitchen. The entire experience felt like he was leaving old friends. In recent years, he had not met anyone as down-to-earth and honest as TJ and Jenna seemed to be. His mind drifted back to the restaurant's website again and how much fun working on it could be. He wiped his mouth and stood to leave.

At the register, a young woman refused to let him pay for his meal. She returned his money and gestured toward TJ and Jenna, who were talking with a customer on the other side of the restaurant. They both stopped talking and waved. Travis waved and mouthed a silent thank you before walking toward the exit.

Once he was outside, Travis stood in front of the restaurant, shielding his eyes from the bright afternoon sun with the palm of his hand. He felt a cool breeze coming off the Pamlico River and could smell its brackish water. He thought about the drive to Richmond and the uncertainty that lay ahead. He looked at the long, seemingly unending street to his left, then looked to his right, and saw the same. He rocked forward as though to leave, then turned around to find Jenna and TJ standing behind him in the doorway of the restaurant.

"Let's take a look at that website. Bet it won't take two minutes," Travis said, and followed Jenna and TJ back into the restaurant.

Chapter 19

Detective Kelly scanned the room and noticed the office manager, Anne Holt, was still on the phone. When their eyes met, she smiled briefly before continuing her conversation, then returned her attention to the computer screen on her desk. Kelly liked Anne. She'd been with the department almost as long as he had. Over the years, he had watched her blonde hair become streaked with gray. She had put on a few pounds, but it didn't stop a good number of guys from hanging around her desk.

This morning, besides Anne, the office was empty. Most of the officers in the department were already out in the field doing police work. Aside from the occasional phone ringing and Anne's typing, the office was quiet. Kelly looked around the room again before squinting at the medical examiner's report. It had been three days since he'd accepted the case, and it finally felt like he was making some progress. In addition to preliminary DNA results from the medical examiner, he had received dental records for both the deceased and the registered owner of the vehicle.

J. Marcus Evins

The records revealed that the person removed from the wreckage had received extensive dental work, while the car's registered owner, Travis Pace, had hardly any. Forensics had also been able to obtain the owner's fingerprints, and when they were run through the local database, they confirmed that he wasn't driving. More telling still, when Travis Pace's wife came to the station to identify the body, she showed very little remorse, despite not having seen him since the afternoon before the accident.

These peculiarities confirmed what Kelly had already begun to suspect and piqued his interest enough to canvass the area where the wreck had occurred. His persistence paid off when he discovered that a person matching Travis Pace's description had checked into the Roadway Motel less than five miles from the accident site. He also hit pay dirt after following a hunch to investigate nearby travel services. An employee at the Greyhound Bus Station on Arthur Ashe, a few miles from the motel, confirmed that Travis Pace had been there on the evening of the accident.

Even more puzzling, their records indicated he had used the name Orlando Richardson and had exchanged his ticket the following morning for a bus headed to Wilmington, North Carolina. Kelly had already given Anne the name Orlando Richardson, along with other details he'd collected, to run through the NCIC database. Scratching his head, he jotted a few additional thoughts in his notepad. It was beginning to feel like only a matter of time before all the pieces came together.

"Hey, Kelly," Anne called out. "Your 10 o'clock is here. A Ms. Harris. You want her to come around to your desk?"

"Nah, take her to the conference room. Let her know I'll be there in a few minutes," he replied. "You mind asking her if she'd like some coffee or a Coke while she waits?"

"Sure, Kelly. I'll take care of it. I need to make another pot of coffee anyway."

"Thanks, Anne. Got anything back on the NCIC check yet?"

"Working on it," she replied. "You're not the only detective in the department, you know. I'll let you know as soon as I've got something."

Kelly thanked Anne again and returned his attention to the notes from the interviews he'd already conducted. A subsequent meeting with Travis Pace's wife had proven fruitless. She seemed unaware that her husband had been fired on the day of the accident. Almost his entire conversation with her had been more about when she could cash in his insurance policies than anything helpful to the case.

It was his visit to Travis Pace's former place of employment, Lucent Technologies, that had been more promising. Most of Travis's coworkers had little to offer in the way of useful information. However, they unanimously pointed to one person who they believed was closest to Travis and might have had a personal relationship with him outside of the office. Coincidentally, that person had made themself unavailable during his visit to Lucent Technologies. He knew he was grasping at straws, but if anyone at Lucent Technologies knew where Travis Pace might be, it was likely Karen Harris—and she was waiting for him in the conference room.

* * *

"Good morning, Ms. Harris," he said as he entered the conference room. "My name is Detective Phillip Kelly. I'm investigating the automobile accident involving Travis Pace. Thanks for coming in."

He took a seat across from the woman and placed his notepad on the table. She was dressed in business casual attire—black pants, a matching jacket, and a crisp white blouse. Most men would have considered her attractive, and he could hardly blame Travis Pace if they had been more than just coworkers.

"I just want to help as much as I can," she said slowly. "But I'm not sure if I can provide any more information than you've already received from my colleagues."

"Anything you can share will help, Ms. Harris," he said. "I'm just trying to tie up some loose ends and I spoke to everyone except you when I visited the office, so I'll be brief."

"Please call me Karen, Detective."

Kelly paused for a moment and flipped through several pages of his notepad. He wanted to give her the impression he might already have the answer to the questions he was going to ask.

"Well, Ms. Harris—I mean, Karen—I'm sure you're aware that I visited Lucent Technologies last Friday and spoke to your colleagues about Travis."

"Yes. I remember leaving early the day of your visit. The company leadership allowed employees flexible leave that day. I wasn't feeling well after hearing about the accident, so I left."

"I see. So, the news of Travis Pace's death hit you pretty hard?"

"Yes, of course. Travis and I have been in the same department for more than four years. He was the person who hired me."

"Well, Karen, when I spoke to your coworkers, I got the impression Travis had a closer relationship with you than with his other coworkers. As a matter of fact," Kelly said, then paused. He flipped through several pages of his notes before continuing. "A couple of your coworkers referred to you as his work wife."

"That's just office humor," she said. "They say that because Travis and I worked together on many of the same projects."

"Projects?" Kelly asked. "What kind of projects?"

"Well, I'm a software engineer at Lucent. We worked on artificial intelligence, cloud-based programming, and various other software development projects."

"Whew, that just went over my head," Kelly said. "So, you and Travis spent a lot of time working on different projects together. Sounds like a lot of work for two people."

"Most of the time, it wasn't just me and Travis working alone. We have a team of technicians who also take part in the projects. At one time, Travis was my direct supervisor, so we worked on many projects together."

"Just a supervisor? You know, one of the people I spoke to—" Kelly looked at his notes again—"Brad, or maybe it was Bradley, told me he was your supervisor. He also mentioned that you and Travis went to lunch together almost every day. So, I'm a little confused. How many supervisors do you have at Lucent Technologies?"

"I'm not sure what any of this has to do with Travis's death," Karen said, "but Bradley only recently became my direct supervisor a few months ago. After Bradley was hired, Travis became my indirect supervisor. And just so you know, Travis was more than just a supervisor. He was also a friend. So yes, we did occasionally go out to lunch together."

Detective Kelly watched Karen's eyes fill with tears. He pushed a box of Kleenex toward her and waited until she looked in his direction.

"I know this is hard, Ms. Harris. Like I said, I'm just trying to tie up some loose ends so I can close my report," he said. "Now, considering the relationship you and Travis had, would he tell you if he had been dealing with some sort of problem or was in some kind of trouble? Do you think he would have shared something like that with you?"

Karen dabbed her eyes with the tissue again and stared at Detective Kelly for a moment. She appeared to scan the room, as though looking for somewhere to discard the tissue, before finally stuffing it into her handbag.

"Look, detective, I'm not sure how much Travis would share with me," she said. "We talked about a lot of things."

"Yes, but did you two ever talk about problems he might have been having at work or at home?" he asked. "Or maybe something financial?"

"You do know Travis was married, don't you?" she asked. "I'd think his wife would be the person he'd do most of his sharing with."

Detective Kelly looked into Karen's eyes. She returned his stare for a moment, then looked down at her handbag and removed the tissue. She dabbed her eyes, then looked back at him. He diverted his attention to his notes before allowing their eyes to meet.

"If that's all of your questions, Detective Kelly, I'd like to leave now," Karen said, standing. "I'm still not sure what any of this has to do with Travis's death."

"Actually, I do have one more question, Ms. Harris," Detective Kelly flipped through some of the pages on the notepad he'd been scribbling on. "When was the last time you spoke to Travis? Was it before or after?"

"Before or after?" she repeated. "I'm not sure I understand your question. Before or after what?"

Kelly could tell by the look on Karen's face that she was probably unsure of how to respond, so he let her off the hook.

"According to your company's leadership, Travis was terminated from Lucent Technologies on the afternoon of Thursday, August 17."

"Yes, but—"

"So, was the last time you communicated with him before or after he was terminated?"

"I think it was before. Or maybe it was after," she said. "I guess I'm not sure. We talked several times that day."

"Then it could definitely have been afterwards."

"I guess so."

"If so, what did you talk about?"

"I don't know—I mean, I don't remember. There was so much going on. As you said, he had just been terminated."

"I see. Well, that's all I have for now, Ms. Harris," said Detective Kelly. "I'm sorry if I've upset you in any way."

Karen looked at Detective Kelly, then turned to leave the conference room. She stopped at the door, just as he looked up from his notepad.

"I'm not sure I understand why you asked me to come here, Detective. Travis was a decent man," she said. "I guess being decent doesn't matter these days. None of your questions are going to bring him back."

Kelly watched Karen as she disappeared down the hallway. When he could no longer hear the tapping sound of her heels on the wood floors, he clicked his BIC pen and reviewed his notes. Although he couldn't put his finger on it, there was something Karen Harris wasn't telling him. Now, after speaking with her, he was certain she was worth keeping an eye on.

When Kelly returned to his desk, the two junior detectives who had been initially assigned to the case, Tyler Beiring and Victoria Lazaro, were seated at their desks. He hesitated for a moment to prepare himself for the usual load of shit they tried to give him.

"So, how's the big case coming?" Lazaro asked. "You actually interviewing witnesses about the wreck last Thursday involving the drunk driver?"

Kelly nodded without commenting and decided to ignore the detective's sarcasm.

"Yeah, but wasn't the victim the only person in the car?" Beiring chimed in. "What possible evidence are you hoping to get from witnesses that weren't even at the scene?"

"And he spent the entire weekend looking for leads," Lazaro laughed. "Hey, Kelly let us know if you need our help on your big case."

"I think I can handle this one," Kelly said and grabbed the sports jacket hanging on the back of his chair. "Just doing my due diligence."

Kelly decided he'd already had enough of the two rookie detectives. He remembered a time, not too long ago, when a junior detective would never have questioned the actions of someone more senior. It was yet another reason to dig as deeply as possible into this case. There were too many unanswered questions to write it off as simply a drunk driver incident. Anyway, he figured time would tell. He headed for the exit not sure where he would end up, but the office was definitely not where he needed or wanted to be at that moment.

"Hey, Kelly," he heard Anne say just as he reached the exit. "Got something for you."

Kelly looked over his shoulder to see Anne waving a sheet of paper. It was obvious she was excited about what she'd received. He walked back toward her desk, and she handed him the paper. The sheet contained a photo of a serious-looking Black man, a physical description, and the person's last known address in Elizabeth City, North Carolina. An additional page listed a handful of charges. It looked like he'd done a little jail time too.

"Looks like we got a match from NCIC. Are you familiar with the name Roy Patterson?"

"Doesn't ring a bell," he said, continuing to look over the report.

"Well, the name you gave me, Orlando Richardson, is one of his aliases," Anne said. "You might want to check with the Special Investigation Section in Elizabeth City, North Carolina. Looks like this person is someone that's been on their watch list for some time."

"Thanks, Anne. I'll do that," he said. "Good work. I owe you lunch or something."

"Yeah, sure, Kelly. Promises, promises," Anne said with a wave, walking back to her desk to answer the phone.

Detective Kelly looked back at the office before continuing toward the exit. The two detectives were still at their desks. Lazaro had her feet propped up on the desk as she talked on the phone. Beiring was playing basketball with wadded paper he tossed in the direction of a nearby trash can. Kelly shook his head and took another look at the NCIC report Anne had given him. He took a picture of Travis Pace out of his pocket and attached it to the report beside the mugshot of Roy Patterson, a.k.a Orlando Richardson. Now, with pictures of both Travis Pace and Orlando Richardson in hand, he decided it might be a good idea to visit the bus station again. It was time to positively ID who had gotten on the bus the morning after the wreck and confirm whether or not his suspicions were correct.

Chapter 20

Travis sat up abruptly and realized the soft thumping sound wasn't part of the dream he was having. His heart pounded as he slowly peeled the sweat-soaked sheet from his body. He looked around and took in the unfamiliarity of the room. He inhaled deeply and held it for a moment before exhaling. Behind him, the mid-morning sun had begun to bleed through the window blinds, making the contents of the room appear less foreign. Then, he heard a slightly louder thump. He remained frozen, listening to the sound reverberate through the tiny space.

"Hey, Travis. You up, man?"

Relieved, Travis opened the door to find TJ smiling. He had a covered plate in one hand and a cup of coffee in the other.

"Good morning," TJ said. He stepped into the room and set the plate and cup on the table. "I remember you said you wanted to get an early start this morning, so Jenna and I thought you might like breakfast. Hope I'm not too early."

"No, no, you're all right," Travis replied, still trying to shake off the dream he'd just had. "What time is it anyway?"

"Almost eleven. Nothing wrong with sleeping in. After all, you're supposed to be on vacation."

"You know you didn't have to do this," Travis said, taking a sip of the coffee and peeking under the lid of the covered plate. "I was planning to go out and get something later."

"Wanted to—after all, you're doing us a big favor," TJ said, frowning as he put his hands on his hips and leaned toward Travis. "And I know you weren't thinking about eating somewhere other than the Main Street Café."

Travis tried to read TJ's expression, unsure if he was serious.

"I'm just kidding, Travis," TJ said, letting him off the hook. "One thing you'll find out about Little Washington is that there are a lot of places around town where you can get a good meal. Besides, you ought to get out and see some of Little Washington. Anyway, how's the room?"

"I like it," Travis said. "I really do appreciate you and Jenna letting me crash here."

"No problem at all. Believe it or not, Jenna and I lived in this little room for a few years after we bought the restaurant," TJ said. "Back then, it was our entire world."

"So, are either of you originally from Washington?" Travis asked.

"No, we're both actually from Charlotte."

"What made you decide to open a restaurant here?"

"Well, both Jenna and I were experiencing career burnout and always talked about trying something different. She was a marketing manager, and I worked in human resources at the same company," TJ said. "We'd visited Little Washington a few times and always enjoyed it. The people were so nice. One of those people was the previous owner of this restaurant. During one of our visits, he told us he was ready to retire and wanted to move to Florida, so we made him an offer."

"Looks like things worked out," Travis said.

"Yep, sure did. I couldn't have done it without Jenna, though. You see, there weren't many Black-owned businesses in Washington back then, and in the beginning, things were tough for a while. I had some serious reservations at first, but Jenna was confident we could do it. Twenty years later, here we are. Anyway, I didn't come up here to reminisce. I just wanted to bring you something to eat and make sure the room is somewhere you can relax while working on the website."

"The room's great. By the way, I was just about to take a look at the website. I think I'm going to make a copy and play with it offline. Sometime today, I can let you and Jenna know how long it'll take to repair the online order function."

"Sounds good, Travis. But, look, I'm going to get out of here so you can get back to what you were doing. Let us know if you need anything," TJ said and headed for the door.

"Hey, TJ," Travis said.

"Yeah?" TJ stopped and faced him.

"I just want to let you know how much I appreciate you and Jenna," Travis said.

"Well, hey, man. We appreciate you too," he said as he started back toward the door, then stopped. "By the way, Jenna and I are planning to eat dinner at six if you'd like to join us."

"Sure thing," Travis said. He waited for the door to close before returning to the desk and turning on the laptop.

After the computer booted up, Travis clicked on the link to the restaurant's website and reviewed its current design and structure. Then he searched the web, found the software he needed, and started the download. As Travis watched the progress of the software download, he could hear the low murmur of activity coming from downstairs. The aroma of cooking food wafted through the air, reminding him of the plate TJ had left. He ate a forkful of scrambled eggs and looked around the room again. It was small and inexpensively furnished, with a bathroom and a private entrance accessible by a stairwell located in the rear of the restaurant. By accepting the room, Travis had finally discouraged TJ and Jenna's attempts to pay him for his work on the website. It also gave him a more secluded place to figure out what to do next.

His thoughts returned to the dream he'd had that morning. It hadn't been the first time the accident had come back to haunt him. The recurring dreams and his inability to sleep made him wonder if he was experiencing withdrawal. After all, he hadn't had a drink since the accident and felt no desire for it. Before the accident, drinking had become the only way he could escape what his life had become. Now, the money he'd hidden back in Richmond promised all the escape he needed. The money made it easier to accept Orlando's death and even Elana's infidelity, but so far it hadn't brought him peace.

After showering, Travis returned to the laptop and checked the progress of the software download. While the download continued, he decided to check the Richmond news sites again to see if anything related to the accident was being reported. Finding nothing, he began to relax. He thought about Karen and was certain she would have heard about the accident by now. He wondered how she was handling the news of his death or if she was thinking about him at all. Travis recalled the feeling of her body against his and the warmth of her kiss when they'd met for drinks at the lounge. After considering it further, he opened the email program and stared at the blank page. He thought about what TJ had said about having Jenna by his side. He began typing, and after a quick review, he hit send.

Chapter 21

After visiting the Greyhound Bus Station for a second time, Detective Kelly decided it was time to find out more about Roy Patterson, a.k.a. Orlando Richardson. He wasn't surprised to confirm that the person who boarded the bus a couple of days after the accident was Travis Pace and not Roy Patterson. What he couldn't figure out was the relationship between the two. From what he could tell, Travis Pace was as average as they come: married, working a nine-to-five, and without even a speeding ticket. Roy Patterson was the complete opposite. According to the NCIC report, Roy had a history of criminal activity ranging from possession with intent to distribute to illegal gun charges.

Kelly figured whatever the two men had in common might give him the answers he was looking for. The report also confirmed that Roy Patterson had been one of the people arrested in Elizabeth City, NC, back in 2020 during Task Force Rock Bottom. More than a dozen gang members were arrested and given hefty prison sentences. Unlike the others, Roy had somehow received a lighter sentence and had disappeared off everyone's radar—except for the Elizabeth City Police Department.

When Kelly contacted the Special Investigation Section in Elizabeth City about Roy Patterson, they wanted to meet as soon as possible. Apparently, they felt several of those arrested during the feds' sweep had escaped justice and still owed a debt to society. The officer he'd spoken to was clearly interested when he told him Roy Patterson was under surveillance in Richmond and there was evidence he might still be involved in trafficking drugs to and from Elizabeth City. As far as Kelly was concerned, the opportunity to talk to someone on the phone would have been good enough, but the officer's insistence that they meet Tuesday afternoon with one of his confidential informants was even better.

The CI lived in Richmond, and it was the officer's idea that they meet there. Kelly first suggested the lounge located across the street from the Greyhound Bus Station on Arthur Ashe Boulevard, but the CI refused to meet in a place that was so public. Finally, they agreed to meet at the motel where Travis Pace had stayed the night before leaving for Wilmington, North Carolina.

It wasn't difficult for Kelly to determine who the two were when he entered the motel lobby. Both were Black men. One man, probably in his mid-thirties, wore a tracksuit. He had dreads tied into a bun. The other man, probably in his late thirties or early forties, wore a military high-and-tight. As he got closer to the table, Kelly could tell by High-and-Tight's serious demeanor that he was no-nonsense.

"Officer Jenkins?" Kelly asked, extending his hand to the man with the high and tight. "I'm Detective Phillip Kelly. Thanks for meeting with me."

Both men stared at Kelly as he slid into one of the chairs on the opposite side of the table until he pulled out his badge and flashed it. Officer Jenkins did the same.

"So, what do you have for me, Detective?" Officer Jenkins asked. "On the phone you said something about having Roy Patterson under surveillance."

"Sure, like I told you, we've determined Roy has been making several trips each week by bus between here and North Carolina," Kelly said. "We suspect he's back in the same business he was in before."

"Any idea where he might be now?" asked Officer Jenkins. "When was the last time he made one of his bus trips?"

"That's just it. We've been able to monitor his activity up to a certain point, but we didn't want to jump to any conclusions without probable cause. I was hoping you could tell me more about what he might be up to."

The officer looked over at the CI who seemed not to be a part of the conversation. He continued tapping on his cell phone unaware that both men were now staring at him.

"Ronald. Tell the detective what you told me," Officer Jenkins said, motioning toward the CI to get his attention, then looked at Kelly. "Ronald Jones used to do some business with Roy back in the day. They're still friends but he hasn't talked to him in a few days."

The CI tapped on his cell phone a couple more times before looking up at Officer Jenkins.

"First of all, y'all need to stop using my government so freely. I'm not the one under investigation. You know I go by RJ. Who the fuck is this Roy person anyway?"

"Orlando Richardson is who we're talking about, but Roy Patterson is his government name," Kelly said.

"I don't know nothing about that shit," RJ said. "Me and Orlando go way back. I'm not doing any business with him now, but whenever he comes to Richmond, we still hang out. He's a pretty cool dude."

"Yeah, but tell Detective Kelly what you told me when we talked earlier," said Officer Jenkins.

"Well, last Thursday I got a text from Orlando. He said he was on his way to North Carolina, and would be back in Richmond on Friday," RJ said. "Like I said, when he comes to Richmond, we normally hang out. I thought it was strange when he didn't check in with me by the weekend, so I started checking around. Turns out nobody's seen Orlando. Not even the people he's working for. It's like he disappeared off the face of the earth."

Kelly listened to RJ and wondered if he should reveal any more information than he already had. Apparently, there was more to the story and he didn't want the free flow of information to stop.

"Yeah, nobody's seen Orlando in over a week. Word on the street is he disappeared with cash and dope worth over a million dollars but I think different."

"What do you mean?" asked Kelly. "That's a lot of money. A lot of people would skip town with less."

"That ain't Orlando, man," RJ said. "He wouldn't do no shit like that knowing how crazy the people he deals with are. Stealing from them would be the last thing he'd do. Nah, something's happened to Orlando. I don't know what, but that's not him."

"So, Detective Kelly—here's the million-dollar question. When was the last time anyone saw Orlando?" Officer Jenkins said. "Have your people been talking to anyone at the bus station?"

"Sure. One of the employees on duty last Thursday said Orlando purchased a ticket to Elizabeth City that evening but exchanged it a couple of days later for one to Wilmington," Kelly said. "Maybe the people he works for diverted him to Wilmington instead."

"Y'all don't know," RJ said. "This shit Orlando is into runs like clockwork. Besides, his people are looking for him too. Nah, something else has gone down."

As RJ and Officer Jenkins continued talking, Kelly thought about what RJ had said about the kind of business Orlando was into. He also thought about what the bus employee said about possibly seeing Orlando and Travis together the night of the accident. He was still puzzled about how two men who were complete opposites ended up in a car together. Either Travis Pace was completely clueless or knew exactly what he was doing when he and Roy Patterson got into his car the night of the accident.

"So, why am I here?" Officer Jenkins' question brought Kelly's attention back to the conversation. "What's your department's next move?"

Kelly realized he wasn't going to get much more from the men. Besides, he certainly knew where Orlando was. What he didn't know was where Orlando's money and drugs were, but he had an idea who might. For the time being he needed to make Officer Jenkins feel like he wasn't going back to North Carolina empty-handed.

"I think if Orlando has disappeared all we can do is continue monitoring the situation to see what his next move will be. Maybe he's working out of another location, or maybe he got wind of our surveillance. He'll pop back up soon enough."

"So right now what you're telling me is we don't have anything. I was hoping for a little more, Detective Kelly," Officer Jenkins said. His voice had begun to reflect the weariness that was already on his face. "How about your surveillance reports. Can I get a look at those?"

"Sure thing," Kelly lied. "Where do you want me to send them?"

"Couldn't you just give me an unofficial copy," Officer Jenkins said. "It would help me to justify the trip I made up here."

"Sorry, man. No can do," Kelly said. "My captain would have my ass if word got out I distributed department information before getting it cleared."

"Okay," the officer said and slid his business card toward Kelly, "You can use the fax number on the card."

"So, are we finished?" RJ said. He bumped fists with Officer Jenkins and ignored Detective Kelly's attempt to do the same. "I've got some other business to take care of. Besides, if somebody sees me sitting around with you two official looking motherfuckers, I might be the next one that come up missing."

"Here's one of my cards just in case you think of something else," Kelly said, sliding one of his business cards toward RJ.

"Is he for real?" RJ asked. He looked at Officer Jenkins, picked up the card, flipped it over a couple of times, and then pushed it back toward Kelly. "Nah man, I'll pass. I know how to reach out if need be."

RJ left the table and headed for the motel exit. Both men remained silent as they watched him leave.

"He's not as hard as he likes people to think he is," said Officer Jenkins, "Lived in North Carolina for a while until he got into some trouble down there. He moved here to live with relatives once he was released from probation."

"Do you believe what he said about Roy disappearing with over a million dollars in drugs and cash?" Kelly asked.

"No reason not to believe him," Officer Jenkins said. "He hasn't steered me wrong yet. Besides, I think he's trying to use us as much as we're trying to use him. I really think he wants to find Roy too."

"I sort of had the same feeling," Kelly said. "Hey look, the motel bar's open. You want to grab a drink before you leave?"

"Nah, I've got to head back," Officer Jenkins said. "I sure wish we had more to go on. Don't forget the surveillance reports. There might be something in them that will give us a clue as to why Orlando is no longer coming to the bus station."

"Yeah, right, man," Kelly said. "I'll get them to you as soon as possible. They just might be there waiting for you by the time you get back to North Carolina."

The men shook hands. Kelly watched Officer Jenkins as he left the motel before walking over to the bar. He ordered a beer and thought about the over one million dollars in cash and drugs that was missing. He regretted misleading a fellow officer about having surveillance reports, but he had to give him something, even if it was a lie. He recalled the conversation with the two young detectives back at the office. He bet they would shit themselves if they knew how big this case really was. All he had to do now, was find Travis Pace. Doing so might just be the final piece of a very lucrative puzzle.

Chapter 22

Kelly had to admit he was surprised to get a call from Officer Jenkins's CI, Ronald Jackson—or RJ, as he preferred to be called—less than twenty-four hours after they'd met. He had pretty much written RJ off as someone who would be of no value to the case. But it turned out that now RJ wanted to set up a meeting between him and a friend of Orlando's who might have additional information about his whereabouts.

At first, Kelly didn't like RJ's suggestion that they meet at the Roadway Motel again, but he also didn't want to raise any suspicions by conducting witness interviews at the precinct on a case that should have already been closed. Besides, there was some comfort in knowing the motel's restaurant was seldom busy yet public enough to prevent the meeting from getting out of control.

Kelly had just pulled into one of the parking spots near the entrance to the motel when he heard the rumble of bass from a black Range Rover that drove past him toward the motel lobby entrance. Two men jumped out of the car—one of them was RJ.

Unlike RJ, who was dressed similarly to the day before, the person with him wore a sports jacket, slacks, and an intense expression. The man scanned the area before waving to the driver of the car, then walked up the stairs, followed by RJ.

The car drove away and rolled to a stop a couple of parking spaces from where Kelly was parked. He tried to see who was driving the car without being too obvious, but its tinted windows made it impossible to see anything but the sun's reflection. Kelly waited for a few minutes before getting out of his car and walking toward the motel entrance. Immediately upon entering the motel's restaurant, he spotted RJ and the other man. RJ motioned for him to come over to the booth where they were seated.

"I told you I knew how to reach out if I had something," RJ said.

"So, what do you have, RJ?" Kelly asked, taking a seat. "Interesting choice of meeting locations, by the way."

"Well, I figured if it was all right for your official meeting, it would be all right for mine. But look here, this is the friend of Orlando's I told you about, Willie—I mean, Mr. Smith."

"So, what can you help me with, Mr. Smith?" Kelly asked. Up until now, the man had remained quiet. His demeanor was the extreme opposite of RJ's. While RJ was animated and talkative, Mr. Smith sat motionlessly, as though absorbing everything around him. He hadn't taken his eyes off Kelly since he'd sat down across from him. Mr. Smith waited until RJ left the booth before speaking.

"Thanks for meeting with me, Detective Kelly," he said finally. "I'm hoping we can do something to help each other."

"RJ said you were friends with Orlando and I'm pretty sure he's told you we've been trying to find out his whereabouts. Is that something you can help me with?"

"First of all, let me be clear, detective. Orlando is not my friend. He is my employee. Someone who works for me."

"Works for you?" Kelly said. "So, what sort of business are you in, Mr. Smith?"

Mr. Smith did not respond, but instead stared at Detective Kelly as though he had asked a question for which he might already know the answer.

"The details of my business are not important. What's important is that one of my employees is missing. I was hoping if I provided you with the information I have, you'd be willing to do the same."

"Need I remind you the information I have is part of a police investigation? If you think he's missing, why not file a missing persons report? Why come to me?"

"RJ tells me you're also looking for Orlando and that you've had him under surveillance for some time at the bus station."

"Once again, Mr. Smith, police business," Kelly said. "Unless you've got something else, this meeting is over."

"As I've said, Orlando is an employee of mine. As an employee, he had a company phone and credit card. Both were very trackable. After numerous attempts to contact him, I was able to track his phone to this motel. Coincidentally, he also used his credit card here as well."

Kelly thought about what Mr. Smith said. He'd already confirmed the person who checked into the motel was Travis Pace. Now, Mr. Smith was telling him the person who stayed there was Orlando. He was beginning to wonder if the information the man had would be of any value.

"So, you have the phone?" Kelly asked.

"Yes. It was found in the room by housekeeping and turned into the motel's lost and found," Mr. Smith said. "They also found some of Orlando's other belongings in the room—some clothing and a duffel bag."

"Since it sounds like you've already conducted your own investigation," Kelly said, "what else can I tell you that you don't already know?"

"One thing puzzles me, detective," Mr. Smith said. "The duffel bag found in the room was cut open. What I can't figure out is, why would Orlando cut open a bag he has a key to?"

"Okay, I guess I don't follow."

"The motel staff I spoke to were very cooperative when I told them I was worried something might have happened to my employee. They said the police came by with a couple of pictures asking questions, and even took a look at the room."

"So, Mr. Smith, let me see if I'm getting this. You've tracked Orlando to this motel. He checked in. He checked out. What I still don't get is where do I fit in?

"The description of the police that went to the room sounded a lot like you, detective."

"So, what? It's called conducting an investigation, looking for evidence. It's called police business."

"Well, let me ask you this last question, detective. Was anything confiscated from the room when you were conducting your investigation?"

"Okay, already. I've had enough of this bullshit. If that's all you've got, this meeting is over," Kelly said. He stood as if to leave but continued staring at Mr. Smith. "I'm not about to have you interrogate me. Who the hell do you think you are?"

"You should have a seat, Detective Kelly. You're making a scene."

"Making a scene?" he said. "Look, you little shit, I can arrest you right now on two or maybe three charges."

"Go ahead, detective. Make your arrest," he said. "And when you do, I'll be sure to inquire why you were at the motel asking about the whereabouts of a dead man."

"A dead man?" Kelly repeated.

"Yes, a dead man. You see, detective, the desk clerk remembered one of the pictures you showed him. One of the pictures looked familiar to him and at first he couldn't figure it out, but it finally came to him. The reason is because it was of a person he remembered seeing on the news—a person who was killed in an accident not too far from here. His name was Travis Pace."

Detective Kelly slowly lowered himself back into the seat. He stared at Mr. Smith for a moment, not sure what to say next. All he knew was he didn't need the department knowing he was still working on a traffic accident that had occurred over a week ago and was supposed to be closed.

"Okay, so maybe you have my attention. Now what?"

"Let me just cut to the chase, detective. The contents of the empty duffel bag left in the room belonged to me and represent a substantial loss to my business. I don't give a shit that you're looking for a dead man or a live one. All I want is what belongs to me."

"Well, I don't know how I can help you with that," Kelly said, "I'm basically at the same dead end as you seem to be. The case is pretty much closed."

"Come on, detective. I know you're sitting over there trying to figure a way out of this shit. Case closed, my ass. I also know you showed those same two pictures to the employees at the bus station. So, I have to ask myself, why would you put so much effort into a case you claim is now closed."

"I'm listening, Mr. Smith. You seem to have all of the answers."

"Let me tell you what I think, detective. What are you, nearly sixty years old and at the end of your career? You're probably wishing you'd saved more or invested more over the years, but you didn't. Now, you're closing in on retirement and wondering how you're going to make it on your pension until you're old enough to draw social security. Even then, you're not sure how you're going to make it. You feel me?"

"I hear you."

"A man in your position might be thinking he's found a way to supplement his retirement income.

"I think you got me all wrong," Kelly said. "I don't know anything about any supplemental income or whatever the hell else you're talking about."

"Okay, detective. Let me put it to you like this. For whatever reasons, I think we're trying to find the same person. All I need you to do is keep me in the loop about the progress of your investigation."

"You serious?" Kelly asked. "And why in the hell would I do that?"

"You'll do it because, despite the fact that you may be at the end of your career, you still value that pension, and I'm going to let you keep it."

"Keep what? My pension?"

"Yeah, your pension. It seems to me there is a lot more going on here than meets the eye. Can you imagine what would happen if your department found out you have been conducting an investigation to find a dead man while withholding evidence? Of course, if you work with me, there could be a different outcome."

Kelly watched Mr. Smith pull out his cell phone and respond to a text. He couldn't help but despise the man. The entire conversation up to now made him feel dirty.

"So, detective," Mr. Smith said after he put his phone back in his pocket. "Where are we with our case as of today?"

"Our case? Look, if you think you can come in here and make me your bitch you're —"

"Careful, detective. Is that any way to talk to your partner?" Mr. Smith interrupted. "Just give me a little something to make me feel like you want to keep this between us."

Kelly sank back into the cushion of the chair. For a second, he had the strange feeling of vertigo. When it stopped, all he knew was that he wanted the conversation to end and needed to figure out a way to get out of the trap he had somehow fallen into.

"The only lead I'm working right now is a friend of the person I've been looking for."

"The person you've been looking for?" Mr. Smith repeated.

"You did say we were looking for the same person, didn't you?"

"So, who are you looking for, detective—Orlando or Travis Pace?"

"Let's just say for now I have reason to believe Travis is the person of interest, not Orlando."

"How can you be sure, detective? I mean..."

Mr. Smith's voice trailed off. He stared at Kelly for a moment, then slowly nodded his head before speaking.

"And this friend of Travis Pace?"

"Just someone I've got a hunch he might eventually get in touch with."

"How can you be sure? Who is it?"

Kelly exhaled deeply. He pulled out a pad from his pocket and thumbed through the pages. When he found the one he was looking for, he tore it out and slid it across the table toward Mr. Smith.

"What is this?" Mr. Smith asked. He flipped the paper over before looking back at Kelly. "Are you sure she can help us find who we're looking for?"

"I met with her a few days after our man went missing. I think she knows more than she's letting on."

"This better not be some bullshit," Mr. Smith said as he looked at the paper.

"Like I said, it's just a hunch."

"So, if that's all you have, it doesn't seem like much."

"Look, we're stuck in the same place, and she's a loose end I haven't been able to tie up."

"So, maybe if we put a little pressure on her, she might —"

"No, no, I wouldn't do that. At least not until we're sure our person has made contact," Kelly said. "Let me keep an eye on her. If anything comes of it I'll let you know."

"Fine, no pressure for now, but I think we'll plan to keep an eye on her too," Mr. Smith said. Kelly heard Mr. Smith's phone vibrate.

"Yeah, I'm ready," Mr. Smith said into the phone. "I'll be out in a minute,"

He turned back to Kelly.

"Like I said, we'll keep an eye out too, but don't think for a minute you're off the hook, detective. Let me get one of your cards."

Kelly handed Mr. Smith one of his business cards and watched him input his number. A second later, his phone vibrated and displayed a phone number. Looking up, he noticed RJ had reappeared and was now standing at the entrance to the restaurant. Mr. Smith stood and motioned to Detective Kelly.

"That's my number," Mr. Smith said. "Keep in touch, partner."

Kelly watched as Mr. Smith left with RJ. He wondered if he'd gone too far by giving him Karen Harris's information. He felt like a man grabbing at anything to keep from falling into a bottomless pit. Despite his concerns for her safety, he hoped it would buy him some time to come up with another angle. Maybe by then, he could salvage not only the case but what was left of his career.

Chapter 23

Karen's alarm was rarely set for 8:30 on a Thursday morning. Normally, it was set for 6:30, but this Thursday she decided to take the day off, which allowed her to toss and turn a little longer. Today, there would be no demands from Lucent Technologies to distract her from thinking about the inevitable. The only possible diversion was Craig, whose snoring she could hear outside her closed and locked bedroom door. Reluctantly, she got out of bed and made her way to the shower. Afterward, she slipped into panties and a bra, then sat on the edge of the bed, staring in disbelief at the details of Travis's memorial service.

It was still too early to dress for the 11 a.m. service, and she hoped to avoid interacting with Craig until absolutely necessary. Karen had told Craig she was taking the day off but hadn't mentioned the memorial service. What she didn't realize, until she was dressed and finally opened her bedroom door, was that he had done her the favor of leaving while she was in the shower. At least, that's what she initially felt—until she looked out the window.

Not only was Craig gone, but so was her car. Furious now, Karen snatched up her phone and dialed Craig's number. Since she hadn't paid his phone bill last month, it was no surprise when a message played indicating his phone service had been suspended. Karen was about to call for an Uber when she remembered that Natalie Nguyen had mentioned attending the service and might be able to give her a ride. After a couple of rings, Natalie answered.

"Hello, this is Natalie."

"Hey, Natalie. This is Karen. I hope I'm not catching you at a bad time."

"Oh no, you're fine," Natalie replied. "What's going on?"

"I was wondering if you could do me a favor," Karen said. "Are you still going to Travis's memorial service? I'm having car trouble and wondered if I could catch a ride with you?"

The line went quiet and Karen initially thought the call might have dropped.

"Hello, Natalie? Are you still there?"

"Yes, I'm still here, Karen. Of course I can give you a ride," Natalie said. "I'm running a little late, but I can pick you up. Just text me your address."

"I really appreciate this, Natalie," Karen said, and after sending Natalie her address, she put down the phone and finished dressing.

About twenty minutes later, she heard a car horn blow outside. After they'd driven about a mile, Natalie finally spoke.

"You know something, Karen," she said. "I really appreciate you reaching out to me about attending the service."

"No, I appreciate you giving me a ride," Karen said. "I know I live a little out of your way."

"Oh, that's okay. But what I want to thank you for is helping me to make up my mind," Natalie said. "Honestly, I was feeling a little uncomfortable about attending the service."

"Why is that? You worked with Travis, and I'm sure his family would appreciate you being there," Karen assured her. "Besides, I don't think we're going to be the only Lucent employees attending."

"It's not that. It just didn't seem right that I attend," Natalie said.

"Is it because Travis is Black?" Karen asked, trying to understand. "I don't think that's something—"

"No, that's not it," Natalie interrupted and glanced at Karen, "That's not it at all."

"I'm sorry Natalie. I guess I don't understand then," Karen said. "I hope I'm not pressuring you to do something you hadn't planned to do."

"No, I feel much better about it now," Natalie said. "It's just that Travis was no longer an employee at Lucent Technologies when he died. He had been fired, and I didn't know how his family would feel."

Karen thought about what Natalie had said. She had never considered that Travis's family might not want anything to do with Lucent Technologies. She had been so preoccupied with her own grief and her relationship with Travis that she had neglected to think about how others might feel.

"Natalie, if you aren't sure about attending, I wouldn't mind if you just dropped me off. I can pay you for gas."

"No, maybe I shouldn't have mentioned it. I guess I can sometimes talk too much," she said. "I've just felt so terrible about Travis getting fired and then the accident."

"Me too, Natalie," Karen said softly. "Me too."

* * *

The service was held at Grace Baptist Church on Richmond's Northside. A tall Black man wearing dreads was speaking when Karen and Natalie entered the chapel. He offered condolences to the family and ended with a short prayer. Karen was surprised by the large turnout which included a few familiar faces from Lucent Technologies. The CEO, Patrick Oberman, was seated near the front of the chapel and so was Ben Williams. Despite having tendered his resignation, Ben had decided to delay his departure from Lucent Technologies because of Travis's death. Karen and Natalie decided to sit in the rear of the chapel to prevent causing any distractions. Karen listened as several more speakers rose to share memories and condolences.

Once the service ended, she and Natalie made their way to the front of the chapel to express condolences to the family. She was surprised to see Detective Kelly leaning against a wall with his notepad in hand. Karen tried to avoid making eye contact with him but couldn't help wondering what possible motivation he had for attending Travis's memorial service. He nodded in her direction when they passed but otherwise remained motionless.

Now, only a few feet away, Karen could see why Travis had once fallen in love with his wife. She and Elana were about the same height. Elana's shoulder-length hair matched her dark brown eyes, and her caramel complexion was accentuated by the black attire she wore. No one could say she wasn't pretty—or even beautiful. Beside her stood a handsome Black man who shook hands and smiled politely. At times, they moved in unison, as though connected by an invisible thread that kept him within inches of her as they greeted attendees.

As Karen moved closer to Elana she could hear her interaction with other sympathizers. She did not detect the bottomless grief in Elana's tone or expression that she had been experiencing ever since hearing of Travis's death. When they were finally in front of Elana, she smiled and shook Natalie's hand, then Karen's.

"Hello, Mrs. Pace. I am so sorry for your loss," Karen said, "I worked with Travis at Lucent Technologies. He will truly be missed."

"Thank you so much. We do appreciate that so many of his coworkers came to pay their respects. It's comforting to know that Travis was well-liked at Lucent," Elana said.

Elana's use of the word "we" caused Karen to wonder if other members of Travis's family were present.

"So, does Travis have other family members here that I can also express my condolences to?" Karen said, allowing her eyes to scan the room.

"No, Travis was an only child and both of his parents are deceased," Elana said, then motioned toward the man standing beside her, "but this is Maurice. He's one of Travis's closest friends."

Maurice shook hands with Karen and Natalie but didn't comment. Instead, he continued smiling and scanning the room.

"And what did you say your name was again?" Elana asked Karen.

"Oh, I'm sorry," Karen said, nodding toward Natalie. "This is Natalie Nguyen and my name is Karen. Karen Harris. Travis was our supervisor at Lucent."

The moment she said her name, Karen felt Elana's hand relax. Her face wrinkled into a frown, and her seemingly frozen smile melted.

"Karen Harris," Elana repeated, glancing at Maurice, who looked at Karen and then averted his eyes. He also stopped smiling.

For a moment both Karen and Elana stared at each other until another mourner stepped forward, diverting Elana's attention. As Karen walked away, Natalie commented on the obvious tension.

"Do you mind telling me what just happened?" Natalie asked as they walked toward the exit. "His wife seemed so friendly at first."

"I don't know what to tell you Natalie," Karen said, "but I think I'm ready to leave now."

* * *

When Natalie dropped Karen off at her apartment, she noticed that Craig had not returned with her car. Once she was inside, it was obvious that he had been back in the apartment. The remainder of a joint was smoldering in the ashtray, and two empty beer bottles were on the coffee table. Seeing the clutter made her even more certain it was time for Craig to go, and the end of the month was not soon enough. After she changed clothes, Karen decided to boot up her laptop and check email. Doing so would give her something else to focus on, besides wondering where Craig had taken her car.

The emails from work were the usual stuff. Most of them were from Bradley who liked to comment on every project detail. That was one other thing she missed about Travis. The office was no longer as laid-back as it used to be. Travis's relaxed management style promoted creative freethinking and every analyst willingly contributed their ideas. Now, thanks to Bradley's micromanagement, the team was afraid to move in any innovative way.

Reflecting on the past, Karen couldn't help thinking about her relationship with Travis. Despite his marriage, she believed their connection had grown beyond its professional and platonic boundaries. She would have called it love if the term could fully capture the depth of their bond and the longing she felt when he wasn't around. Even now, as she slowly rubbed between her thighs—first unconsciously, then deliberately—a warm feeling began to consume her. Soon her moans mixed with tears and she began to sob until she heard a knock at the bedroom door.

"Hey, Karen. You in there?"

She didn't respond immediately. Instead, Karen walked over to the mirror and stared at her tear-streaked face and attempted to compose herself. Her eyes were puffy and red, still glistening with tears. When she finally opened the bedroom door she couldn't conceal her anger.

"Craig, where have you been with my fucking car?" she demanded, quickly stepping toward Craig, who took a few steps back as he patted his pockets. "You know what, I don't even want to know. Just give me my keys."

"Wait a minute, Karen," he said and handed her the key fob. "I just borrowed your car for a few minutes. When I came back you were gone."

"Craig, I don't want to hear it. You almost made me miss an important appointment."

"Important appointment," he repeated. "I don't know when you're going to stop treating me like I'm stupid. So, was your appointment at the Commonwealth Lounge?"

Karen could tell by Craig's slurred speech and heavy eyelids that he was high as usual. She tried to understand what he was talking about but it wasn't making any sense.

"Yeah. That's right. I saw the email from—let me get this right—a friend."

"So, now you've been messing with my laptop, Craig?"

"I guess you need a stronger password than your birthdate. Especially if you're going to be fucking around on me."

"I don't have any idea what you're talking about and I'm too tired to deal with this right now," she said heading toward the bedroom. "You know what? I don't want to be here with you right now. I think I'm going to spend the night at Kiara's. I need to pack."

"See, this is the kind of shit I'm tired of," Craig yelled. "You're always running to your sister's house whenever you don't want to deal with what's going on here."

"Deal with what's going on here, Craig. What are you talking about?" Karen stopped and looked at Craig. "When are you going to get it through your thick skull that there's nothing going on here. Nothing!"

"You know what Karen, don't think I didn't know you're fucking around with that dude at work. What's his name? Travis?"

Karen stopped and looked at Craig. Tears blurred her vision. "Well, you don't have to worry about Travis anymore, Craig."

"So what, you and your boyfriend break up or something?"

"Travis is dead, Craig. He died in an automobile accident last Thursday. This morning I attended his memorial service," Karen said and continued toward the bedroom.

"Well, I can't say I'm sorry," Craig said following behind her. "So what, now you mourning this niggah or something? I don't see why you even went to his fucking memorial service."

"Fuck you, Craig," she said. "I hate you so much."

Karen pulled two suitcases and a garment bag from her closet. She began throwing clothes in the bags, unaware Craig was now standing behind her.

"Hey look baby. You know you don't really mean that. Now that he's gone why can't we just put all of this behind us?"

Karen remained silent. She moved from closet to drawer choosing what she wanted to take with her. Soon she had one of the suitcases and the garment bag packed. She stomped past Craig, taking both to the car and returning to finish packing the last suitcase. She could feel Craig's eyes on her as she moved around the room but refused to acknowledge his presence until she felt his hand on her arm pulling it with enough force to turn her in his direction.

"You must be out of your damn mind!" she screamed. "Get your fucking hands off of me, Craig."

"No, Karen. You're going to stop and listen to me," Craig said. He shoved Karen causing her to stumble backwards onto the bed. "You're not going anywhere."

Craig grabbed Karen's wrists and climbed on top of her. She twisted beneath his weight, but could barely move.

"Get off of me, Craig," Karen yelled. "I'm not playing with your ass. Let me up."

"Nah, babe. I'm not letting you up until you promise to listen to what I have to say."

Karen continued struggling under Craig's weight. When he tried to kiss her she turned her head so the attempt landed on her cheek, then she looked into Craig's eyes and spit in his face.

"You bitch. I can't believe you spit on me," he said. "You're gonna make me fuck you up in here."

When Craig released Karen's wrists to wipe his face she shoved him away just far enough to knee him in the groin. She got up from the bed and looked at Craig twisting in pain on the floor.

"So, is this the kind of love you want, Craig," she screamed and went back to packing her suitcase. "You need to get some help."

"Karen, please don't leave. We can still make this work," Craig pleaded. He struggled to his knees but collapsed into a seated position on the floor. "Just tell me what you want me to do."

Karen paused as though unsure what to say or do next before turning toward the man on the floor and slowly shaking her head. She realized words had become useless but wanted to try one more time to make her intentions clear.

"Craig, you can do whatever you feel you need to do as long as it doesn't involve me," she said, snapping the last suitcase closed. "Rent is paid through the end of the month. After I leave here tonight, when I come back it will be with a U-Haul to move the rest of my stuff."

"But, Karen," Craig moaned. "Just one more chance. That's all I'm asking. Just one more chance."

Karen did not respond to Craig's pleas. Instead, she walked past him carrying her suitcase. She paused after opening the front door and looked around the dimly lit apartment. She recalled how it felt when she first moved in and how much things had changed. She smiled, closed the door, got into her car and drove off into the darkness.

Chapter 24

When Travis agreed to work on the restaurant's website, he hadn't planned to be in Washington for more than a day or two. However, after reviewing the website's current design and functionality, he decided it would be better to rebuild the site from scratch. Doing so would allow him to use software tools he was familiar with but meant it would take longer. He didn't mind delaying his plans to return to Richmond. It had been easy to become comfortable with Washington's slow pace and with people who felt more like family than friends.

Travis enjoyed working on the website so much that by Thursday morning, a working prototype was completed, and he sat down with Jenna and TJ that afternoon to share his progress.

"Well guys, I really do appreciate the opportunity you've given me to work on your website. I only hope it lives up to your expectations. Once you're okay with its appearance and functionality, we can talk about when you want to go live."

"So, let's see what you've done so far," TJ said. "I'm sure it will be an improvement over what we had."

Travis booted up his laptop and turned it around so that everyone could see the screen. He was probably more excited about the website redesign than both TJ or Jenna. It wasn't just that he enjoyed doing something he was actually good at—unlike his time at Lucent Technologies, here he knew his efforts were appreciated.

"I transferred a lot of the graphics from the original site and added the new stuff you gave me, so the site now reflects the current menu."

"Looks good, Travis," Jenna said. "It's definitely an upgrade."

"Well, let's see just how user-friendly it is," Travis said. "Jenna, how about submitting an order?"

Travis and TJ watched as Jenna poked around the website. She selected several menu items, added them to the order, then clicked submit. A payment page immediately displayed.

"Okay, Jenna, at this point, customers can use their bank cards, PayPal, Venmo, or even their checking accounts as the payment method. I haven't activated payments yet, so you can go ahead and click through it."

Jenna completed the order, and a message appeared on the screen indicating an order was waiting. Travis went to his email and retrieved Jenna's order.

"Later, I'll set up your office computer to display these pending orders. That way, they can be processed by anyone given access to the order function. Customers will also receive an order confirmation via email and text once the website goes live. And, in case you're both on the floor, a text message will also be sent to your phones so you don't need to monitor the computer constantly."

"Wow, Travis, I really like the way this has turned out," TJ said. "What do you think, Jenna?"

"I think we have a new website thanks to our webmaster here," she said. "Travis, how can we ever repay you?"

"You're kidding, right? I should pay you guys. I'd forgotten how much fun this could be," Travis said. "Besides, your friendship is more than payment enough."

Travis noticed a concerned expression on Jenna's face as he spoke. TJ had also become quiet.

"Something wrong?" he asked. "I realize there are a few things I need to do so it has all the functionality we talked about. Is there something you two think I need to add?"

"That's not it, Travis," Jenna began, "I think TJ would agree the website is perfect even if you didn't do another thing to it. I was just thinking about how you're going to be leaving us soon now that you're close to finishing."

"So, when are you planning to leave Washington, Travis?" TJ asked. "I know we've already asked you to stay longer than you planned. When does your vacation end anyway?"

"I have a few more days," Travis lied. "So, you guys are going to be stuck with me at least until I get the home delivery feature configured and tested."

"How long do you think that will take?" Jenna asked.

"I should have everything completed and ready for testing sometime later today or first thing tomorrow morning. If everything is working as expected, it should be ready to go live before the restaurant opens on Saturday morning."

For a moment, the room became quiet again. It was TJ who finally spoke.

"Sounds like your last day with us might be Friday or Saturday," he said, as though not speaking to anyone in particular.

"I guess we couldn't expect your vacation to last forever," Jenna said. "Let alone wanting to spend all of it with us."

Travis hated to keep lying to TJ and Jenna. From the beginning, both had shown him nothing but kindness, and all he had given them were lies. Temporarily freed from the catastrophe his life had become, his time in Washington working on the website had been the closest thing to a vacation he'd experienced in a very long time. As he looked at TJ and Jenna, Travis decided that no matter what happened once he left Washington, he would find some way to show them how much their friendship was appreciated.

* * *

Following the meeting, Travis remained in the office, working on the website until after the restaurant closed at ten. He was hoping to finish the home delivery feature so he could demonstrate it to TJ and Jenna in the morning. Once it was completed, he tested the function by creating a fake order that appeared on the restaurant's computer screen. Satisfied that the restaurant had received the order, Travis checked his email account, which he used as if he were a customer, to verify receipt of confirmation emails.

Despite his excitement at having successfully configured the function, his mind remained preoccupied with thoughts of his impending departure from Washington. His decision about when to leave had become further complicated by the promise he'd made to the Johnsons to finish the restaurant's website. It had been a little over a week since the accident, and he could feel the clock ticking on how much time he had left to return to Richmond to retrieve the money left in the culvert. The more he thought about it, the more he realized that if the money was gone, he had no Plan B.

He was also bothered by the lack of response from Karen, despite several attempts to contact her via email. At first, he'd convinced himself that his motivations for contacting her were simply to let her know he was okay, but each day that passed without a response, his heart told him something different.

Travis returned his attention to his computer display and submitted another order. Once the order detail displayed on the restaurant's computer, he clicked his inbox to review the confirmation email. It was then that he noticed Karen's email. He opened the message and looked at the clock. It had been sent at 10:30 p.m., and now it was almost eleven. He reached for the phone but immediately thought it might be too late to call her—especially if she and Craig were still living together. He placed the phone back on the desk and tried to focus on the website but couldn't. He picked up the phone again and entered Karen's number.

"Karen?" he texted, unsure of what else to say. A sudden wave of paranoia made him wonder if it was really Karen who had responded to his email after all. The phone vibrated—displaying the text: "Travis, is that you?"

Still unconvinced, Travis wondered if the police were somehow monitoring the communications of someone he might contact. He immediately dismissed the possibility but still decided to be careful. Before he could think of what to do next, he heard the phone vibrate again, saw Karen's number displayed and this time answered.

"Hello," he said. The caller remained quiet before finally speaking.

"Travis. Is that you?"

"Yes, Karen," he said, "It's me."

"Oh my god, Travis," Karen screamed. "You mean that wasn't you in the car? Travis, please tell me what's going on."

"I can't say too much right now," Travis began, pausing to collect his thoughts. "I just wanted to let you know I'm okay."

"Oh, Travis," she said. "Where are you? Are you in Richmond? Can I meet you somewhere?"

"No, wait, Karen. Let me think this through," he said. "We've got to be careful. I don't want you getting mixed up in this."

"Travis, I'm already mixed up in whatever is going on," she said, then became quiet. "I attended a memorial service for you today."

"Memorial service?" Travis repeated.

"Yes. I even gave my condolences to your wife. She's very pretty."

"Elana?" he said. "Did she know you?"

"No, I don't think so. How would she? Besides, I wasn't the only one there from Lucent. The CEO and Ben were also there. Natalie and I rode to the service together."

Travis remained silent as he listened to Karen. He tried to imagine the service.

"Travis, you still there?"

"Yes. I'm here. I'm sorry anyone had to go through that— especially you," he said.

"So, where are you Travis? I want to see you right now."

"What about Craig?" Travis asked, hoping it might discourage her. "What's he going to think if you just up and leave?"

"Travis, I decided to move in with Kiara until I figure out what I want to do next." Karen became silent, and Travis heard her sniffle, "I decided I couldn't live like that anymore."

"Karen, you don't know how much I've missed you," he said.

"I miss you too, Travis. So, where are you? Is there anything you need?"

"No, Karen, I don't need anything."

"So, what happened Travis? Why does everyone think you were killed in the accident?"

"I promise to explain everything."

"When Travis?"

"Soon. For now, just know that I'm okay. Things got complicated after the accident. I just need time to figure it all out."

"Travis. Travis, I —"

"Karen. I've got to go. I'll be in touch." He abruptly ended the call.

"I thought I heard someone in here," TJ said as he entered the office.

"Yeah, I was making sure the update I posted earlier was working. As a matter of fact, I just tested the delivery order function, and it's ready to go live as soon as tomorrow."

"Travis, Jenna and I can't thank you enough for what you've done with the restaurant's website. I guess we'll have to hire a couple of drivers pretty soon to make deliveries."

"Well, everything's configured. The home delivery feature can be activated once you're ready."

"That's good, Travis. Real good," TJ said. "By the way, I didn't mean to interrupt your phone call."

"Phone call?" repeated Travis. "Oh, I was—"

"Look man, you don't have to explain. I know you have a life outside of this restaurant."

"I was just checking on a friend," Travis said. "I hadn't talked to her for a while."

"One day, you and your friend ought to come down here for a visit. Who knows, you've found something to like about Little Washington, maybe your friend will too."

Travis smiled at TJ but remained silent. He was thinking about the conversation with Karen. It felt good to hear her voice and he could tell, despite circumstances, she still had feelings for him too.

"So how long are you going to work tonight?" he heard TJ say, "Jenna's already left, and I've shut down everything out front."

"Only a little while longer," Travis said. "I've got a couple of things I want to tweak before turning in."

"Okay. Sure. I didn't realize you were such a workaholic," TJ said, starting for the door, then stopping abruptly. "By the way, Jenna and I were talking earlier. We'd still like to pay you something for the work you've been doing. Maybe it'll make up for you spending your vacation with us."

"TJ, you and Jenna have done more than enough already. Trust me. This has been one of the best vacations I've ever had."

"Yeah, but," TJ said, "who can't use a few extra dollars in their pocket?"

"I'm good," Travis said. "You guys have provided me with a room and all the food I can eat. I can't think of anything else I could possibly need."

"Okay, I get it," TJ said. "Just can't tell you enough how much we appreciate you sticking around to help us out."

"And I appreciate both of you," he said. "Now, get out of here so I can finish up. I'll see you bright and early tomorrow morning."

TJ pulled the office door closed, and Travis listened for the front door of the restaurant to lock. As soon as the restaurant became quiet again, he went back to his laptop. He clicked on his inbox and saw a new email from Karen. In it, she mentioned meeting with the police. Travis immediately dialed her number.

"You talked to the police?" he asked as soon as she answered. "I don't understand."

"Honestly, Travis, I don't either," she said. "A detective stopped by Lucent Technologies on Friday, the day after the accident. He talked to our team, the CEO, and maybe a couple of other employees. I was so stressed when I heard about the accident that I left the office before he arrived. I met with him Monday at the precinct on Grace Street. He said it was just standard procedure."

"I don't understand why the police would question anyone at Lucent if they thought I was killed in a car accident," he said.

"I don't either but when I met with him he was giving me this weird vibe. He was even at your memorial service. Seeing him there is what made me respond to the email you sent. I thought I was being silly thinking it was you—especially after attending your memorial service. I know it might sound crazy, Travis, but I think that detective knows more than what he told me."

"I don't know what he knows, Karen, but there's a lot more to this," Travis said, mostly to himself.

"Then talk to me, Travis. Tell me what's going on."

Travis considered what he should tell Karen about what had happened. He thought about what had occurred leading up to the accident and afterwards. He also wondered if the police had determined that he was still alive—and even worse, that he was in Washington, North Carolina.

"Travis, you still there?"

"I'm sorry, Karen. What were you saying?"

"I asked you to tell me what's going on."

"I really don't know where to begin."

"How about from the beginning?"

And that's what Travis did. He took Karen back to when he thought his life was perfect. He'd married a woman he thought was his soulmate and believed he had the perfect job—until he found out neither was true. He told Karen how, for a while drinking had taken the edge off both. He told her how the Commonwealth Lounge had become a safe haven between a job he didn't like and a house that was no longer a home. Then, he finally told Karen about the night he'd had drinks with Orlando at the lounge and the accident that occurred afterwards. He left out almost nothing—not even the drugs or the money. He told her everything except where he was.

"Hey, you still there?" he added finally. Travis looked at the clock and realized they had been on the phone for almost two hours.

"Yes, I'm still here, Travis," she said. He heard what he hoped was only fatigue in her voice.

"Look, I'd better let you get some sleep. You're going to have to get up in a few more hours to get ready for work."

J. Marcus Evins

"I'm not worried about that right now, Travis. I'm more worried about you."

"I'm okay, Karen," he said. "I've met some really nice people. They've even given me a place to stay temporarily. I've told them about you."

"And what did you tell them?"

"Everything, Karen. Especially how much I enjoy being with you and how much I miss you."

"So, why can't I come to see you?"

"I don't know. There's so much I need to figure out—and even more so now that you've told me you think the police might be on to something."

"I don't care. We can figure out whatever needs to be figured out together."

"I just don't know if that's a good idea right now."

"Travis, I've told you before. You're not in this alone. I'm here, and I'm not the kind of person who turns their back on someone they care about."

Travis listened to Karen. He thought but could not say the words he felt. All he knew at the moment was that he couldn't imagine a future that didn't include her.

"Hey you," she said.

"Hey," he said.

"You certainly are quiet," she said.

"Just thinking, that's all," he said.

"About what?"

"Everything. What's happened so far—but mostly about the things you've said."

"Did I say something wrong?"

"No, not at all. I just need to figure some things out."

"Travis, we can figure this out together. I just need to know where you are. What if something happens and—"

"And what?" Travis asked. He could hear what sounded like a muffled sob, then silence. "Karen, you okay?"

"I'm okay. This is just so much to take in all at once. Travis, I really need to see you."

"Look, let me think about it," he said. "But right now I think we both need some sleep. I didn't realize it was almost three o'clock."

Travis and Karen said their goodbyes and ended the conversation. For the next few minutes, Travis remained seated at the desk, staring at the computer screen. He knew he wouldn't be able to go to sleep now. He wished he could tell Karen more about the safe refuge he'd found in Little Washington. Just before he powered down his laptop, he noticed another email from Karen. After reading the email, he typed.

"I love you too, Karen. I promise we'll see each other soon."

Travis pushed send thinking he'd feel a little less burdened after doing so. Instead, he headed upstairs to his room almost certain he'd told Karen too much.

Chapter 25

After shutting off her computer, Karen lay on the bed, thinking about the conversation with Travis. She'd held back a scream she might have let loose if her sister hadn't been sleeping in a bedroom only a few steps away. During the call, there had been so much more to say than she had time or words to express. Already, she knew the email she'd sent after hanging up would fall short of expressing what she wanted Travis to feel. Words, she finally decided, would never be enough. Knowing Travis was alive was the only thing that really mattered.

For the next thirty minutes, Karen remained wide awake until curiosity drove her to turn her computer back on. As the home screen loaded, she felt more confused, especially about the detective's interview and his presence at the memorial service, now that she knew Travis was alive. When Karen logged into her computer, she noticed a new email from Travis. She clicked on it, read his words, and exhaled. Momentarily relieved, she lay back on the bed. Then she immediately sat up, glanced at her cell phone, and knew what she had to do.

Changing Pace

Karen checked the time before clicking on the phone number displayed on her cell. She hoped Travis was still awake and would answer. Knowing he was alive without knowing where he was staying was just too much for her to bear. She was certain, with a little more effort, she could convince him to tell her. Karen's excitement faded as she listened to the phone ring several times before a greeting began playing. Once the phone went to voicemail, she grabbed a pencil, scribbled a note, and ended the call. Then Karen tapped the Google icon, entered "Main Street Café, Washington, North Carolina," and began packing.

* * *

"What the hell's going on in here, Karen?"

Karen turned to see Kiara standing in the doorway. She knew her sister wouldn't understand if she told her the truth.

"I'm just putting some stuff away," Karen said. "Sorry to wake you. Go back to bed."

"Putting some stuff away?" Kiara frowned. "Come on, Karen. You need to do better than that. It's after three in the morning. Is something wrong?"

"No, nothing's wrong. I couldn't sleep, so I figured I'd unpack a few more of the boxes I brought with me. That's all. I didn't mean to wake you."

Karen glanced at the open suitcase on the floor, certain Kiara could see it. She watched her sister sit in the chair near the door.

"So, what's with the suitcase, Karen?" Kiara asked. "I'm not going anywhere until you tell me what's really going on. You doing a booty call or something?"

"No, girl. Ain't nobody doing any booty calls," Karen said, though she couldn't help but smile at the thought. "There's just something I have to do."

"Karen, you're scaring me. I don't understand. What is it that you think you have to do?"

"He's alive, Kiara, and I think he's in trouble."

Karen sat on the edge of the bed and began crying.

"Who's alive, Karen? Who are you talking about?"

"Travis. Travis is alive."

Karen watched her sister's eyes widen in confusion. Kiara placed the palms of her hands on the sides of her face and let out a low moan.

"No, Karen. Travis is dead. Didn't you just go to his memorial service?"

"Yes. I know, but he called me a couple of hours ago. He called and—"

"And what? So, what are you going to do, Karen?" Kiara glanced at her sister and then at the suitcase. "Oh, hell no, Karen. Not over my dead body."

"I'm going to see what I can do to help, Kiara. I can't imagine what he's going through."

"Help, Karen. How? What can you possibly do to help him?" Kiara's voice rose. "You need to think this through. Keep in mind, if he wasn't the person killed in that accident, someone else was. What if he had something to do with it?"

"Don't be silly, Kiara. I know Travis. He'd never hurt anyone."

"So, where is he anyway?"

"Washington, North Carolina."

"Washington, North Carolina? I've never heard of a city called Washington in North Carolina."

"I'm just going to see how he's doing," Karen said, placing a few more items in her suitcase. "I should be back by Sunday."

"Come on, Karen. Have you lost your damn mind? What about work?"

"Kiara, work is the least of my worries," Karen said, then walked over to the suitcase and continued packing. "Don't worry. I'll send Bradley an email to let him know I won't be coming in."

"Karen, please don't do this. If you leave, I swear I'll call the police," Kiara said. "I'll call the police and tell them everything."

Karen loved her sister but knew Kiara would never understand how she felt about Travis. She also knew Kiara would do exactly as she threatened. Reluctantly, Karen agreed to wait until later that morning before deciding what to do. Hoping her sister would return to her room, Karen lay down. Instead of leaving, Kiara lay beside her and soon fell asleep.

Karen remained awake, listening to the rhythmic sound of Kiara's snoring. It reminded her how, as a child, Kiara could sleep through anything. Back then, a hurricane could have blown their house away, and Kiara would have remained asleep. With that in mind, Karen quietly slid from under the sheets. Picking up her suitcase, she tiptoed toward the bedroom door. She paused to listen for Kiara's snoring before quietly crossing the hall into the bathroom.

Once she was inside the bathroom, Karen gently pushed the door closed and turned on the light. She made sure she had enough packed for at least a couple of days. Then, as quietly as she'd entered, she turned off the bathroom light and headed for the kitchen. Leaving a note, Karen hoped Kiara would give her the twenty-four hours she asked for before going through with her threat to call the police. Once she was in the car, Karen relaxed. She pulled out her phone and entered the address for the Main Street Café into Google Maps. Starting the engine, she let the car roll slowly onto the street before accelerating.

* * *

There was very little traffic when Karen decided to stop at an ATM to withdraw some cash. That's why she was startled when a black Range Rover with tinted windows pulled in behind her. Karen hurried to finish her transaction and quickly drove off. A few miles later, her car's low fuel light blinked on. She passed several gas stations before finding one that was brightly lit. After pumping gas, she went inside the store for coffee.

"Good morning, ma'am," the cheerful cashier greeted her immediately. "What can I help you with?"

"Good morning," Karen said, motioning toward her car at the pumps, "I already got gas. I was just hoping to get a cup of coffee."

"Sure thing. There's fresh coffee right over there," he said, pointing in the direction of the urns a few feet away. "Around here, the early bird doesn't just get the worm, they also get the freshest coffee."

Karen smiled at the man's corny attempt at humor and headed toward the coffee urns. She listened to the cashier as he continued talking. She poured coffee into one of the paper cups, added cream and sugar, then snapped on a plastic lid. By the time Karen returned to the register and handed the cashier her debit card, his nonstop chatter was beginning to give her the creeps. Even creepier was the next customer who walked into the store. He ignored the cashier's cheerful greeting and continued toward the coffee urns. At the urns, he poured two cups of coffee, then sipped from one while staring in her direction.

Karen averted her eyes, paid quickly, and hurried out of the store, ignoring the cashier's attempt to give her a receipt. Once she was in her car, Karen looked back in the direction of the store. The man was at the register and still watching her. As she shifted the car into reverse, the man exited the store and walked over to a Range Rover identical to the one that had been behind her at the bank. Karen was unable to shake the slight chill she felt until she was finally on I-95 South and the gas station was miles away.

* * *

An hour or so later, Karen was finally able to stop thinking about the strange encounter at the gas station and focus on Travis. She thought about calling the Main Street Café again, but decided not to. Instead, she hoped her presence would be enough to convince Travis how much she cared. Karen also thought about Kiara and knew she had to call her soon. She'd already ignored several of Kiara's texts and had decided she would respond once she was far enough from Richmond that she couldn't be persuaded to turn back. Karen figured she was just about at that point when she noticed the exit sign for the North Carolina Rest Stop. She took the exit and found a place to park close to the visitor center's entrance.

After responding to Kiara's texts, she went inside the center to use the restroom. The large number of people streaming in and out of the building reminded her that not only was the end of summer approaching, but also the end of her lease. She made a mental note to reserve a U-Haul when she returned to Richmond so she could move the remainder of her belongings out of the apartment.

When she walked out of the restroom, Karen paused at one of the center's huge windows. She stared out into the parking lot and imagined a life less complicated. Perhaps that was why she didn't notice the man who walked up behind her.

"Excuse me, miss," he said. "Are you Karen Harris?"

Hearing her name spoken in a place where she was certain of anonymity startled Karen, almost as much as the man's sudden appearance.

"I'm sorry," Karen said. She could feel her voice tremble as she looked for someone who might help. "I don't think I know you."

J. Marcus Evins

"No, you don't. We've never met. I'm an associate of Detective Kelly," he said. "I believe you've spoken to him about a case he's working on."

"Yes, but I'm afraid I don't understand," she said. "What do you want from me?"

"You know it's difficult to talk in here. So much noise," he said. "Why don't we step outside?"

"I'm not ready to go outside just yet. I was going to use one of the phones before I leave."

"Would you be calling your sister? What's her name, Kiara?" he asked. "Perhaps you should call her. Maybe she can help persuade you to be more cooperative."

The man's mention of Kiara's name frightened Karen. Reluctantly, she followed him toward the exit. Outside the building, she stopped and faced him.

"Okay, we're outside now. How can I help you?"

Karen looked around to make sure they were standing where the other people streaming in and out of the welcome center could see them.

"Just keep walking toward your car," he said.

Karen remained silent. She looked around to see if anyone was noticing their interaction. Once she was a few steps ahead of the man, Karen screamed and ran toward her car. Unfortunately, the few people who glanced in her direction quickly looked away.

Shaken, Karen continued running down the walkway, but the possibility of escape disappeared when she noticed the man she'd seen at the gas station standing beside her car. Next to her car was the black Range Rover. The man's mouth broke into a crooked smile as she came closer. He opened the front passenger door of Karen's car and motioned for her to get in. He slid in the back seat behind her and the other man got in the driver's seat.

"Try something like that again and we're going to stop being nice," the man in the driver's seat said.

"Please don't hurt me," she said. "What do you want?"

"I think you know what we want," the man seated behind her said. "Where are you headed?"

"I think there's some sort of mistake," she said. "I don't have anything of value. Look, you can take my car, but please let me go."

"Don't nobody want your damn car," the man in the front seat said. "Now, answer the man. Where are you headed?"

"To a friend's house," she said. "Please let me go. I'm already late."

"So, where does this friend live, Karen?"

"You said you were an associate of Detective Kelly," she said. "Did he tell you to follow me?"

"Look, we're asking the questions," the man beside her said. He was so close she could smell the odor of coffee and cigarettes on his breath. "So, where does your friend live?"

"Nearby," she said. "Not too far from here."

"Nearby where? Here in Nash County? Is that what you're telling us?" he said, then glanced at the man in the back seat.

"Would your friend's name be Travis Pace?" he asked.

Karen looked toward the man in the driver's seat. She was sure he could see the answer to the question on her face without her saying anything.

"No, I knew Travis, but he's dead," she said, and watched the expression on the man's face. He glanced at the man in the back seat again.

"Hey man, what's her sister's name again? Kiara, right? Doesn't she still work at St. Mary's Hospital?"

"Why are you doing this?" Karen asked. "My sister doesn't have anything to do with Travis."

"So, one more time, Karen. Is the friend you're going to see Travis Pace?"

"Yes, but he doesn't know I'm coming."

"Where is he?"

J. Marcus Evins

"I don't know for sure. I think a place called Washington."

"I swear, Karen, if you're lying you're going to be sorry.

"I'm telling the truth," she said. "I was using Google Maps. The address is on my phone."

The man sitting beside Karen snatched her handbag and located the phone. He handed the phone to Karen and ordered her to unlock it. Once the phone was unlocked, he looked toward the man in the back seat.

"Got it," he said. "That's all we need."

Karen struggled for a moment when the man in the back seat covered her face and nose with what felt like a damp cloth. She gasped for air but could only smell and taste a mild sweetness before succumbing to the darkness that followed.

Chapter 26

Anyone could tell that the man wasn't one of Main Street Café's regular customers. Most of the locals who patronized the café wore attire suited to the late summer heat. Tourists typically dressed as if they had spent most of their day along Washington's Pamlico River. In contrast, the stranger wore a blue windbreaker and khaki pants that were too conservative for the restaurant's relaxed ambience.

Travis watched as the man made his way to a seat at the bar and began scanning the dining area. The only change in his expression was the obvious interest he showed when their eyes met.

"Have you decided yet?" TJ asked.

"Decided? Decided what?" Travis responded. TJ's voice sounded distant, even though he was seated only a few feet away.

"You said you might leave for Richmond tomorrow," TJ said. "I asked if you'd decided what time. You seem a little distracted, Travis. Everything okay?"

"Yeah, I'm fine. I guess I was just trying to decide if there was anything I needed to finish on the website before I leave."

"So, do you think you'll ever come back this way? You never did get a chance to see much of Little Washington."

"Honestly, I haven't thought that far ahead, TJ. But who knows? It's definitely worth considering. I've never been any place this friendly."

Travis glanced again toward the bar, trying to ignore the paranoia building inside him. After all, nothing about the stranger posed a threat. Maybe he was just waiting for a table. Besides, he didn't look like someone who would have a connection with Orlando or the money left back in Richmond.

Travis kept listening to TJ, but his eyes eventually drifted back toward the bar. He watched the man place an order with one of the servers, then pull a cell phone from his jacket pocket.

"I bet one of the first things you'll take care of when you get back to Richmond is that lady friend of yours," TJ said. "What's her name again?"

"Oh, you mean Karen. She's definitely the first person I'll want to see."

"Like I've told you before, you two should come back here for a visit. Who knows? Maybe she'll fall in love with Little Washington too."

"We'll see, TJ," Travis said with a smile. "We'll see."

He considered the idea of visiting Washington with Karen, but was distracted again by the man at the bar. Travis watched him take a sip of beer, then tap on his phone for a few minutes before glancing back in Travis's direction. This time, Travis was sure he saw a faint—almost imperceptible—smile on the man's face when their eyes met.

"Hey, look, TJ, I'll be right back," Travis said, standing. He looked toward the rear of the restaurant, then back at the man at the bar.

"You sure everything's okay, Travis? You don't look so good."

"I'm fine. I just think something didn't agree with me."

"It's probably all that spicy food you eat," TJ chuckled. "You know you can't put hot sauce on everything. How about I get you a Sprite or a ginger ale while you're gone?"

Travis nodded in agreement with TJ's suggestion before heading in the direction of the restrooms. The restrooms were located down a short hallway at the rear of the restaurant. The hallway was also used by restaurant staff rushing in and out of the kitchen with customer orders. But at that moment, Travis was more concerned with the exit door at the end of the hallway than either the kitchen or the restrooms. As he made his way through the dining area, he resisted the urge to determine the source of the commotion behind him. Once he entered the hallway, Travis nearly collided with a server coming out of the kitchen. The server was followed by Jenna, who stopped and turned in his direction.

"Travis, I thought I saw you rush by. Where are you going in such a hurry?"

"To the restroom," he said, and patted his stomach. Over Jenna's shoulder, he could see the man from the bar heading in his direction.

"Well, don't let me hold you up," Jenna said, as though understanding his abruptness.

Travis backpedaled a few steps before waving at Jenna. She smiled, shook her head, and went back into the kitchen.

Now only a few steps from the exit, Travis glanced over his shoulder and saw the man entering the hallway. He pushed the exit door handle. It swung open and triggered the deafening sound of an alarm—though not loud enough to prevent Travis from hearing his name being called. Outside, the warm air filled Travis's lungs and seemed to add weight to his footsteps as he ran through the parking lot.

Before crossing the street, Travis paused long enough to observe customers streaming out of the restaurant, but was unable to determine if the stranger was among them. Continuing across the street, he pushed through a group of people coming out of a store. Past the storefronts, Travis noticed a cluster of storage sheds surrounded by a chain-link fence and ran toward them. With some effort, he climbed over the fence and tried the door of each shed until one finally opened. Once inside, he pulled the shed's squeaky door shut. He could hear footsteps ending abruptly nearby, followed by the metallic jangle of someone climbing the fence. Shortly afterward, a light flickered through the shed's crevices.

"Hey, Travis Pace. Come on out. I know you're in here somewhere. My name is Kelly. Detective Kelly," he said, sounding out of breath. "I'm with the Richmond Police Department. I just want to talk."

Travis remained frozen. He was able to control his breathing but not his heart's rapid pace. He heard the stranger yanking on the door of one shed and then another. The sound of additional footsteps approaching the sheds could also be heard, followed by an unfamiliar voice.

"Hey, what are you doing in there? This is private property," Travis heard the voice say. "Come on out, or I'm calling the police."

"I am the police," Kelly said. "I saw him run in this direction. I know he's in one of these sheds."

"You saw who? Who'd you see run over here?" the voice asked. "I didn't see anybody."

"He climbed over the fence. He's in one of the sheds."

"What did this person do?" Travis heard TJ's voice.

"Did you actually see him go in one of the sheds?" the other voice asked. "Those sheds are padlocked. Nobody can get into them without the key, and I keep them in my office."

"Look, folks, this is police business. My name is Kelly. Detective Kelly. I'm with the Richmond Police Department. I need to take a look in those sheds."

"Richmond Police Department? You mean Richmond, Virginia?" the voice asked. "Aren't you a little out of your jurisdiction?"

"The man's a fugitive." Travis could hear the exasperation in the stranger's voice. "He's wanted for questioning."

"You have a badge?" Travis heard TJ's voice again. "And a warrant?"

For a moment, Travis could hear the low murmur of voices and assumed a number of other people had gathered at the fence.

"Okay, so you have a badge," Travis heard TJ say. "Do you have something to show why you're after him? How about a warrant? Isn't this something that should be cleared through our local police department?"

"Look, I don't have time for this. I saw you sitting in the restaurant with him. I could arrest you as an accessory."

"Officer, I'm going to have to ask you to leave the premises. Like I said, this is private property," the other voice said. "Whoever you're looking for could be anywhere, and unless you have a warrant, I'm going to have to insist that you leave."

"You people don't know what you're doing," Kelly said. "You're harboring a possible criminal."

"You people, huh? Okay, look, officer, you need to come on out of there and come back when you have a warrant. Otherwise, I'm asking you for the last time to leave."

"I just want to ask him a few questions, and I'll be on my way."

"Maybe we should call our police to help sort this out," TJ said.

"Now wait a damn minute. I'm coming out."

"Not over the fence, man. I'll unlock the gate."

Travis could hear the jangle of the chain being removed from the fence and the clang of the gate when it closed. A low murmur of conversation continued for some time, followed by what sounded like footsteps leaving the area. Then it became quiet, and although it was hot inside the shed, Travis found himself shivering. His sweat-soaked clothing clung to his body like a second skin. As he crouched, straining to hear what he could not see, Travis was certain that at least one other person knew he'd survived the crash that had killed Orlando—and that was one person too many. Now, more than ever, he knew it was time to leave Little Washington as soon as possible.

Chapter 27

A few hours later, Travis approached the rear of the Main Street Café. He saw that the inside lights were off, which usually meant TJ and Jenna had locked up for the night and gone home. Moving as quietly as possible, he climbed the stairs leading to his room above the restaurant. Upon entering the dark hallway, Travis paused when he noticed his door was slightly ajar. He strained to hear any sounds before slowly pushing the door the rest of the way open. After a few seconds, he stepped inside and gently closed the door behind him. He considered himself lucky—until he turned on the light and saw the room was in shambles. Everything that could be opened had been opened, and anything that couldn't was overturned. As he sifted through the ransacked room, Travis was relieved he had hidden his remaining cash in the car.

A low moan coming from the restaurant downstairs caused him to freeze. At first, he thought it was his imagination. His first instinct was to leave the same way he had come in, but instead, he decided to determine its source. Creeping through the dark hallway, he reached the top of the stairs leading to the restaurant. It was darker than usual because the dining room lights, normally kept on for security purposes, had been turned off. Travis remained still and searched the darkness again before placing his foot on the first step. Each creaky step heightened his anxiety.

He heard the moan again. This time, Travis noticed the door to the office was open, allowing a sliver of light to spill out. Once he was closer, he saw what appeared to be someone's legs positioned as if the person were lying or sitting on the floor. An overturned chair was also visible. Taking a deep breath, Travis pushed the door open wider. Inside, he found TJ sitting on the floor. His eyes were closed while he rubbed the back of his head. When Travis stepped into the room, their eyes met, and they stared at each other without saying anything.

"Are you okay?" Travis rushed over and helped TJ to a nearby chair. He picked up the chair that had been knocked over and sat down. He watched TJ touch a spot on the back of his head and wince.

"I'll be all right," TJ said finally. He shook his head as though doing so would relieve the pain he was feeling. "Two guys forced their way in after we closed and asked where you were. When I told them I didn't know, they shoved me around a little. I guess one of those bastards hit me in the head hard enough to knock me out before they left."

"Where's Jenna?" Travis asked suddenly. "Was she here? Is she okay?"

"Jenna's fine," TJ assured him. "She went home right after we closed at ten. This didn't happen until much later, closer to midnight."

"Did they say why they were looking for me?" Travis asked.

"No. They didn't say much. Just showed me your picture and asked where you were. When I told them a detective had been looking for you earlier, they went upstairs to your room. It sounded like they went through it pretty good too."

"Are you going to call the police?" Travis asked.

"I don't know, man," TJ said, still rubbing his head. "But tell me something. Is what that detective said true? I mean, about what happened in Richmond."

"What did he say happened in Richmond?" Travis asked.

"Something about you leaving the scene of an accident and somebody dying," TJ said. "He said you owed some bad people a lot of money, and they'll do whatever it takes to get it back."

"It's more complicated than that," Travis said, slowly shaking his head. "All I know is I need to leave Washington as soon as possible. I just wish I hadn't gotten you and Jenna mixed up in this."

"But where will you go?" TJ asked. "If these people can find you here, they can probably find you anywhere."

"I'll figure it out," Travis said. "But look, whatever happens, I appreciate everything you and Jenna have done for me."

"Well, let me do one more thing for you, Travis," TJ said, pulling a business card out of his shirt pocket. "Take this. Call the detective. He said he was with the Richmond Police Department. If what he says is true, the most you would be charged with is leaving the scene of an accident. Who knows, maybe he can even prevent those other guys from catching up with you."

"So, this detective, was he the same person who came to the restaurant earlier?" Travis asked, although he was pretty sure he already knew the answer.

"Yeah, that's him," TJ said and managed a smile. "You should have seen how he tore out of here after you. I tried to slow him down a little until you could put some distance between you two. Once things settled down, I talked to the detective. That's when he told me what had happened and showed me his badge. Honestly, Travis, I think he's legit."

Travis accepted the card, studying it for a moment before sliding it into his pocket. Over the next hour, he and TJ discussed what had happened. Travis apologized for his dishonesty, and in an attempt to make amends, revealed everything to TJ about how his life had, in one day, seemed to have spiraled out of control. He told TJ about losing his job, Elana's infidelity, and his fear of calling what he shared with Karen "love" because of the marriage vows he had tried to uphold. When he finished, the office remained quiet for some time until it was disturbed by the sound of the office phone vibrating.

"Hey, honey," TJ said after answering. He glanced at Travis before averting his eyes. "Sorry I didn't call you earlier. No, I'm okay. Travis is here. He and I were talking, and I guess I just lost track of time. Yeah, he's fine. I'll fill you in on what's going on when I get home. No, really, everything's okay. I'll let him know. Love you too."

TJ hung up the phone and returned his attention to Travis.

"So, what are you going to tell her about what happened?" Travis asked.

"Not sure, but it'll be as close to the truth as possible," TJ said. "We don't have many secrets."

"Well, whatever you tell Jenna, please also let her know I appreciate everything you two have done for me since I've been here," Travis said. "Let her know I wish I could have hung around to see her before I left."

"Don't worry. I'll explain why you had to leave. She'll understand."

Travis glanced around the office.

"I guess I'd better get going then," he said. He was going to miss the restaurant and knew he might never return, even if the police cleared him of any responsibility for the wreck or Orlando's death. "If it's okay, I'd like to get a few things from upstairs before I leave."

"Sure," TJ said. "Take your time and don't worry about the mess."

The two men said their final goodbyes, but not before agreeing that TJ would contact the local police. He would report the incident as an attempted robbery, leaving out any mention of Travis. Both men decided that the police's presence in the area might discourage anyone who might be lurking around. TJ would just have to convince Jenna that he hadn't told her about the attempted robbery because he didn't want to worry her. When Jenna called again, Travis gave TJ a final wave before heading back upstairs.

* * *

Later that morning, Travis left Washington and drove east on I-264 toward Bethel, North Carolina. He figured it was the quickest route to I-95 North and the money he hoped was still safely hidden in the culvert. He figured the small town would be the only stop he'd make for gas and coffee before heading north. As Travis drove along the nearly empty highway, he thought about how just a week ago he had been on a bus heading for Wilmington. He wondered what would have happened if he'd decided to stay on the bus instead of getting off in Washington. One thing was for certain, meeting TJ and Jenna had been a stroke of luck and he wondered how much TJ would actually tell Jenna about why he had to leave without saying goodbye.

As Travis considered what lay ahead, he realized there were only two options, and weighed the pros and cons of each. He didn't like the first option, which was to turn himself in to the police. He wasn't sure what they might charge him with, and he questioned whether or not they could provide protection from the people who might be looking for him. He also realized that turning himself in to the police meant he would be back in Richmond, at the same point in life he'd been at before leaving. The other option—recovering the money and doing a better job of disappearing—appealed to him more. The only problem was, it meant he might continue to be pursued by whoever the money belonged to, and also possibly by the police. By the time he reached Bethel, he remained uncertain of the best option.

The early morning traffic was just as sparse on the streets of Bethel as it had been on the highway when Travis drove into the small town. A handful of service vehicles were making early deliveries. Perhaps that's why the black Range Rover that pulled up next to him at the light seemed odd. Its oversized wheels and tinted windows seemed out of place in the quiet town of Bethel. Travis tried to ignore its presence until the driver revved the SUV's powerful engine, causing him to glance at the car again. This time, the passenger window slid down, revealing a face devoid of expression, eyes hidden behind dark sunglasses. As soon as the light turned green, Travis pressed the Honda's accelerator pedal to the floor, hoping to shake off the eerie feeling he had.

About a half mile later, he pulled into the parking lot of a convenience store and parked next to the pumps. As he sat in the car, the Range Rover crept to a stop at the pump behind him. The sight of the car startled Travis. He stared in his rearview mirror, and a moment later, the driver's door swung open. A Black man in his mid-thirties—tall and lanky—stepped out and looked in Travis's direction. At first glance, Travis felt something about the man seemed oddly familiar but dismissed the idea just as quickly. He continued watching as the man moved toward the rear of the Range Rover and disappeared behind the car's open hatch. He kept his eyes on the man at the rear of the car until the passenger door opened and the man he'd seen earlier stepped out. As soon as the man reached for the gas hose, Travis started his car, steered away from the pumps, and continued down the street.

He'd only driven about a mile when he noticed the Range Rover in his rearview mirror again. Travis glanced at the Honda's fuel gauge and then at the rearview mirror. The needle was now hovering above E and the low fuel indicator was flashing red. Despite his unfamiliarity with Bethel, he continued driving. After several turns, Travis was certain he'd lost the Range Rover—but as soon as he began to relax, it reappeared in his rearview again. Up ahead, he noticed a sign for I-64 which would take him to I-95 North. Unfortunately, he was unable to change lanes and was forced to continue past the exit. Seizing the next opportunity to U-turn, Travis headed back toward the exit. This time, as he approached the exit he made a sharp turn, cutting in front of several cars to make it onto the ramp and pressing the gas pedal to the floor.

Despite the quick maneuver, the Range Rover appeared behind him again—this time, nearly on his bumper. Now, as he continued down the highway, the Honda's low fuel indicator became a steady bright red. Once he was in heavier traffic, his panic began to subside when he could no longer see the Range Rover. Convinced that he'd finally lost the car, Travis exited the highway just as the Honda's sluggishness made it clear he was almost out of gas. Not wanting to tempt fate any further, he pulled into the first gas station he saw. Travis scanned the area before stepping out of the Honda. Once he was confident that he had finally lost the Range Rover, he headed toward the store.

As he neared the store's entrance, Travis noticed the cashier waving at him. He returned the wave as he entered.

"Hey, man, you know those guys?" the cashier asked as Travis approached the register.

Travis froze and slowly turned his head in the direction of the pumps. The Range Rover was now parked beside his car. One of the men was peering through the Honda's driver-side window, while the other stared at the store.

J. Marcus Evins

"They just opened your car door," the cashier said. "You think I should call the police?"

"That'd be a good idea," Travis said, trying to appear calm. "Where's your restroom?"

"Back there," the cashier said, nodding in the direction of the restrooms. "Shouldn't we let them know we're calling the cops?"

Travis ignored the cashier's suggestion and hurried toward the restrooms. As he walked away from the cashier, he couldn't ignore the EXIT sign pointing toward the opposite end of the store—or the feeling of déjà vu. He paused, listened to the cashier on the phone, then rushed toward the exit door. He pushed the handle, setting off the alarm, but panicked and ran instead toward the women's restroom. Inside, Travis pushed and pulled on the windows to see if they might offer a way to escape. Unable to open a window he climbed into the nearest stall, and locked the door.

Almost immediately he heard one of the men questioning the cashier. The cashier was saying a guy came in but had run out through the emergency exit. As the questioning continued, Travis could hear the sound of someone running—then it became quiet. Travis relaxed slightly, assuming the men believed he'd gone out of the exit, until he heard a nearby door slam. One of the men was across the hall in the men's bathroom.

As the sound of kicking and slamming doors reverberated throughout the building, Travis peeked over the top of stall door, searching for another way to escape. Seeing none, he lowered himself back into the stall. The slamming stopped and Travis could hear one of the men yelling at the cashier. Suddenly, the women's restroom door burst open.

Feeling his situation hopeless, Travis remained crouched with his feet on the toilet seat and waited. He reassured himself that the men probably wouldn't kill him because he was the only person who knew the location of the drugs and money. Nearby, he could hear the man's heavy breathing as he kicked open the door to the first stall. A second door slammed loudly. Travis moved as far into the stall as possible but heard the restroom door open again.

"Hey, man, you find anything?" Travis heard one of the men say.

"Nah, man," the other man said. "I've been in both bathrooms. I think the cashier was telling the truth when he said that motherfucker ran out the exit."

"Look, we need to bounce anyway," the man said. "That fuckin' cashier kept running his mouth about calling the cops, so he had to be handled."

"Fuck, man. You always shooting some shit up," the other man said. "Let's get the hell out of here."

Travis could hear the men still in the store. He heard the sound of the cash register.

"What are you doing?" one of the men asked.

"Might as well get something out of it," the other said, "This way it'll look like a robbery."

"C'mon, man, we don't have time for that shit. Which car are you going to drive?"

"I'll drive the clunker," the other man said. "Once we check it out, we'll ditch it someplace."

Travis listened until it became quiet before climbing out of the stall. When he stepped out of the restroom, both men were gone and he saw no sign of the cashier. Travis assumed the clerk must have escaped when the men were distracted. He looked out the window toward the pumps. The Range Rover and Honda were gone, along with what little money he had left. Travis thought about the cash register, but as he neared the counter, he discovered the clerk lying in a pool of blood on the other side. In the distance, Travis heard the wail of sirens becoming louder. He backed away from the register and ran toward the emergency exit. Unsure of which direction to go, he paused a second before stepping out. As he walked quickly away from the gas station, his only option had now become clear.

Chapter 28

Travis watched as the server topped off his coffee cup before placing the check on the table. He thanked her, then went back to staring out the window at the cars coming in and out of the restaurant's parking lot. He picked up the check and searched his pockets to make sure he had enough money for the coffee and a tip. The crumpled bills he spread out on the table added up to just under fifty dollars. He laid a five-dollar bill on top of the check, stuffed the remaining money back into his pocket, and returned his attention to the restaurant's parking lot. It was almost 1 p.m., but he figured he'd wait a little longer before giving up on the idea of meeting with Detective Kelly.

Travis picked up the detective's business card from the table. Detective Kelly had said he would be at the restaurant within the hour. He checked the clock on the wall again and flipped the card over several times before studying the information on the front. Travis hoped he and TJ had come to the right conclusion. TJ had talked to the detective and felt sure that contacting him might be the only way for Travis to clear his name. Travis also hoped the detective had been honest with TJ when he told him the most he would be charged with was leaving the scene of an accident. He decided he'd just tell the man the truth. He had been frightened when he made the decision to leave Richmond. Surely a reasonable person would understand. Travis only hoped it wouldn't take too long to complete a police report, collect the rest of the money, and leave Richmond, Virginia, for good.

It wasn't too much longer before Travis watched a tan, late-model Pontiac pull slowly into the restaurant parking lot. The car circled the lot once before drifting into one of the available spaces. The driver exited the car, paused a moment, and scanned the area before slipping a baseball cap over his thinning blonde hair. Although dressed differently, he was definitely the man Travis had seen the previous evening at the Main Street Café. This afternoon, he was dressed more casually in jeans with the same windbreaker jacket over a T-shirt. Once Detective Kelly was inside the restaurant, he pulled off his baseball cap and headed in Travis's direction.

"Mr. Pace," he said, extending his hand before taking a seat. "I'm sure glad you called me."

Travis shook the detective's hand but remained silent. He had already decided to let the detective do most of the talking. Almost on cue, the server came to the table with an empty coffee cup and carafe.

"Coffee, sir?" she asked, first looking in the detective's direction and then topped off Travis's cup again before looking back at the detective.

"Yeah, I'll take a cup," he said. "That's not some of that decaffeinated crap, is it?"

"No, sir," she said, and set a cup in front of the detective. "Sugar and creamer are on the table. We're serving lunch. Can I put in an order for you?"

"You eating anything?" the detective asked, looking at Travis.

Travis shook his head, and the server disappeared with the detective's order. He had too much on his mind to have an appetite. He was more interested in hearing what the detective had to say about the accident and heading back to Virginia as soon as possible.

"Oh yeah. You probably need to see this," Detective Kelly said, sliding his wallet on the table. He unfolded it to reveal a badge and picture ID. "I want you to be sure I'm someone you can feel comfortable talking to."

Travis listened as Detective Kelly continued making small talk.

"You did the right thing to call me," he continued. "You've got some dangerous people after you. Any idea why?"

"No, I don't," Travis said. "Maybe they think I had something to do with Orlando's death."

"Orlando," Detective Kelly repeated. "Oh, you mean Roy Patterson. The guy that died in the wreck. So how'd you meet Roy anyhow?"

"First of all, I didn't really know Roy at all," Travis said. "He introduced himself as Orlando. He was just a guy I had a drink with at the Commonwealth Lounge."

"So, how'd you two end up on that road the night of the accident?" Detective Kelly asked.

Both men paused while the server carefully placed a plate in front of the detective. She topped off their coffee cups before leaving the table.

"He was waiting for a bus that got cancelled because of the weather, so I offered him a ride," Travis said.

"Where to?"

"He was headed to Elizabeth City, North Carolina. I figured I'd help him out since he couldn't catch his bus."

"So, let me get this straight. You were willing to give a ride to someone who you hardly knew over a hundred miles away in some of the worst weather we've had this summer," Detective Kelly said. "Any idea why he needed to get to Elizabeth City so badly that he couldn't wait for the next bus?"

"I don't know," Travis said. He was beginning to feel uncomfortable with the questions the detective was asking. "All I know is it was probably not the best thing to have done considering how things turned out."

"So, tell me, Travis, why did you leave Virginia without reporting the accident to the police?"

"I was afraid." Travis paused and looked out the window toward the parking lot to avoid looking into the detective's face. "I was afraid there might be some confusion about what really happened that night. So, I panicked."

"I can see that," Detective Kelly said. "Now, that's where I can help. We'll just head on back to Richmond and clear up some loose ends." He gobbled down the last piece of his sandwich and wiped his mouth. "We can talk more during the drive back."

Detective Kelly waved at the server, who promptly responded with his check. He looked at the check, then laid a twenty-dollar bill on top of it.

"That ought to cover it," Kelly finger-combed his hair back and slid on his cap. "By the way, do you remember if Orlando had any luggage?"

"Luggage?" Travis repeated. "I don't know. I think all he had was a small duffel. Why do you ask?"

"Just a question," the detective said. "Let's get going. Once we get back to Richmond, we can wrap things up before it gets too late."

* * *

As expected, the mid-afternoon traffic on I-95 North was thick with semis and cars weaving in and out of the three-lane highway. Travis focused on the scenery outside his window as it whizzed by while he tried to imagine what the future could be like once he gave his statement to the police. He had hoped the more than two-hour drive would be an opportunity to consider his options, but he spent most of the time responding to Detective Kelly's constant barrage of questions.

"So, let's start from the beginning one more time," said Detective Kelly. "You first met Roy Patterson at the Commonwealth Lounge across from the bus station."

"Yes," Travis said, "just like I told you before. I'd seen him at the lounge a couple of times and one day just offered him a drink. That's all. I don't know much else about him."

"Did he ever tell you why he was catching a bus to Elizabeth City so often?" he asked.

"No, like I've said, I didn't know him that well and we never discussed anything personal. All I basically knew was his name."

"Well, not even that really," Detective Kelly chuckled. "After all, his name isn't really Orlando."

Travis stared at the detective for a moment before returning his gaze toward the traffic outside the passenger window. He tried to ignore the feeling that it had not been a good idea to accept the detective's assistance.

"Now, walk me through the night you decided to give Roy, I mean Orlando, a ride," said Detective Kelly. "Hadn't you two been drinking that night?"

"Yes, that's why I let him drive. I'd had a couple of drinks before I ran into him that night," he said. "At the time, letting him drive seemed like a good idea."

"So, you let Roy, who you really didn't know, drive your car while intoxicated? That doesn't sound too smart."

Travis couldn't ignore how Detective Kelly's demeanor had shifted from empathy to sarcasm since leaving the restaurant. The change added to his feelings of discomfort, as did the pistol attached to Detective Kelly's belt, and he began to wonder if the detective knew more than he was letting on.

"How'd you two end up on that back road where the accident occurred anyway? Was it Orlando who decided on the route?"

"No, I'm the one who suggested we take the shortcut," Travis said. He was sure by now the detective could hear the annoyance in his voice. "So, where did you say your precinct was located, Detective?"

Travis waited for Detective Kelly to answer. When he didn't, he asked the question again.

"So, which precinct are we going to?" Travis asked again, raising his voice slightly. "I didn't think it would take this long."

"Precinct? Well, the one on Grace Street, of course," Detective Kelly said. "And don't worry about the time. We're open twenty-four-seven. We'll get there soon enough."

Travis glanced at Detective Kelly but looked away when their eyes met.

"Hey, do me a favor and pop open the glove compartment," he said suddenly.

Travis slowly twisted the latch to the glove compartment, and the door fell open revealing its cluttered contents. A pint bottle of brown-colored liquor rested on top.

"Yeah, that right there," Detective Kelly said, pointing at the bottle. "Go ahead and get yourself a taste."

"No, thanks. I'm straight," Travis said. He started to push the glove compartment closed.

"Hey, wait a minute. Hand that over. I think I'll take one."

Travis handed Detective Kelly the bottle of liquor and watched as he unscrewed the top while holding the steering wheel steady with his knees.

"You sure you don't want one?" he asked, offering the bottle to Travis.

"No, I'm sure," Travis said. "Should you be drinking right now?"

"Look, Travis. Don't get all sanctified with me. I already know you liked to have a few yourself. Isn't that why you lost your job at —"

"No, I didn't lose my job because of drinking," Travis snapped. He had become fed up with the detective's questions and now just wanted to get to the precinct to give his statement.

"Oh, I'm sorry. I guess your boss lied when I asked him if he knew if you had a history of drug or alcohol use. Or, was it your wife who was mistaken? She seemed to think you liked a taste now and then too."

"I don't know what anyone told you, but it's not true," Travis said. He watched the detective take another sip from the bottle.

"Here, it'll make things go a whole lot smoother," he said, and offered the bottle to Travis again.

Instead of responding, Travis returned his gaze out of the window. He was relieved to see the downtown exits for Richmond were just a couple of miles away. It meant the ride would soon be over. He thought about what he'd say to Elana when he saw her again but immediately decided that even if she knew he was alive, and on his way back to Richmond, it wouldn't matter. He'd already made up his mind to contact only Karen once he'd given his statement to the police.

"Hey, you still with me?" Detective Kelly said.

"What?" Travis said.

"I asked you where is the shortcut you and Orlando took the night of the accident?"

"Don't you know? It's not too far from the lounge on Arthur Ashe Boulevard where we had drinks."

J. Marcus Evins

"Just making sure. Tell you what, why don't we make a quick detour and swing by the accident site. Just want to make sure I have all the facts."

"But I've told you everything. I don't think going there will make any difference."

"Just bear with me. I'm thinking going to where everything took place can be a good way to remember any details you or I may have missed."

"There are no additional details," Travis said. "I've told you everything that happened."

Detective Kelly took the Hermitage Road exit off of I-95 North and shortly afterwards they were driving down Arthur Ashe Boulevard in the direction of the Commonwealth Lounge. To Travis, it felt like a very long time had passed since his last visit to the lounge, although it had only been a little more than a week. As they neared the lounge, Travis struggled to suppress the panic he was feeling as he recalled the last night he had been there.

"I bet it's all coming back to you now," Detective Kelly said, as he pulled the car into the lounge's parking lot.

Travis looked at the entrance to the lounge then over toward the bus station. Both felt strangely foreign to him.

"I still don't understand why this is necessary," Travis said, "I thought all I needed to do was make a statement."

"Oh, you'll make a statement all right," the detective said and smiled. "Now, just show me the route you and Orlando took the night of the wreck."

Travis looked at Detective Kelly. The alcohol he'd consumed had not only begun to affect his speech but also his demeanor. Travis could tell he was beyond reasoning with. He eyed the pistol on the detective's belt and wondered how hard it would be to grab it if needed."

"Keep straight for about a mile. You'll see a Rodeway Motel on the right. Just past the motel is a gas station," Travis said. "The road we took that night is the next right after the station."

The detective pulled the car back onto Arthur Ashe Boulevard and followed the route Travis described. Once they passed the gas station, he made a right and continued down the road. Like the night of the accident, there was not much traffic.

"Okay, so on that night you and Orlando are on this road. It's raining. You've both had a few. What did you talk about?"

"It's like I've already told you," Travis said. "We didn't talk about anything. We were too busy trying to maneuver in the storm."

"So Orlando didn't say anything about why his trip to Elizabeth City was so urgent?"

"No, we'd only been driving a short time when a deer came from nowhere and —"

Detective Kelly turned sharply off the road and the car jerked to a stop.

"Go ahead. A deer came out of nowhere and what?"

"He lost control of the car. We slid off an embankment and hit a tree."

"So, does this look about right?" the detective asked as he pulled further onto the shoulder of the road and put the car into park. "Let's get out and take a closer look."

Travis scanned the area. He was beginning to wonder if the detective really intended to clear him of any wrongdoing. It was obvious he was looking for more than just additional details and Travis wondered if he might know about what was in Orlando's duffel.

"Come on, Travis. Let's hurry this up. It'll only take a few minutes and we'll be on our way to the precinct."

Travis followed the detective down the embankment. From a distance, he could see the tree the car would have hit. It was a large oak which was now permanently disfigured. Travis looked up toward the embankment to see if any other vehicles were on the road. Everything he felt told him something wasn't right. He scanned the area for a possible escape route.

"So, Orlando's trapped in the car and it's on fire. What happened next?"

"I tried to get him out of the car but his foot was stuck," Travis said. "I tried until the car was completely covered with fire."

"You left him?" Detective Kelly asked. He pulled the bottle of liquor out of his jacket pocket and took another sip. "You left him here to die?"

"No, that's not what happened at all. His foot was stuck and I went up to the road to see if I could flag somebody down. But, when I came back to the car it was already covered by fire. That's when I decided to hike back to the motel."

"Okay, Travis. I get it. Orlando was trapped in the car, but when you made it to the motel you didn't tell anyone about the accident. Did you?"

"I wanted to," Travis said, "but by the time I reached the motel I saw emergency vehicles already heading toward the accident."

"You could have still called the police to let them know what happened."

"Like I told you before, I panicked."

"So, what happened to Orlando's luggage?"

"Luggage, what luggage?"

"Back at the restaurant, when I asked you if Orlando had any luggage you said he had a duffel. So, what happened to it?"

It was then that Travis knew. Detective Kelly had no intention of taking him to the police station and his only interest was recovering Orlando's drugs and the money.

"I don't know anything about his duffel," he said. "Maybe it burned up in the fire or was thrown out of the car during the wreck."

"Let me ask you something, Travis," Detective Kelly said. He pulled open his windbreaker jacket and rested a hand on the butt of his pistol. "Do I look stupid to you?"

"Look, man. I don't know what you're talking about," Travis said, as he backed away from the detective.

"Oh, you don't know what I'm talking about. Your wife had your credit cards frozen so your dumb ass used Orlando's credit card when you checked into the motel we passed on the way here. You spent the night at the motel then jumped on a bus to Washington, North Carolina the next morning. So, again, where's the fuckin' duffel, Travis?"

"I don't know what you're talking about," Travis said. He looked around to see if there was a possible way past the detective. Worst-case, he figured there was a chance he could rush the man and subdue him if necessary. But, before Travis could decide on the best course of action, Detective Kelly pulled out his pistol and pointed it in his face.

"Look, you dumb fuck. I'm tired of this game you're playing. I know you took the duffel with you because it had Orlando's phone in it. I bet it rang nonstop until you ditched it at the motel where we found it."

Now, Travis was sure he'd run out of options. He rushed the detective, causing him to stumble backwards. The detective's pistol went off, causing a ringing sensation in Travis's ears. At first, Travis felt he had underestimated the detective's strength after receiving several punches in the face. Yet, he was eventually able to wrestle the detective to the ground, where they rolled around for what seemed like minutes. With some effort, he finally straddled the man. As he struggled to restrain the detective, Travis noticed the pistol lying a few feet away. He reached out to grab the pistol but froze when the sound of gunfire came from somewhere behind him.

Chapter 29

Get up, both of you," a man said as he made his way down the embankment.

He was followed by a younger man who seemed familiar to Travis. Another man stayed at the top of the embankment.

"So, Detective Kelly, is this the person who has my property?" the man asked. He looked at Detective Kelly then Travis.

"He said he doesn't know about the duffel bag." Detective Kelly stooped to retrieve his pistol and returned it to its holster. "At least, that's been his story—so far."

"I see. So, do you believe him?" the man asked, speaking very deliberately, as though he were scolding a misbehaving child.

"No," Detective Kelly said, "I don't, Mr. Smith. But I think he was just about to let me know what happened to Orlando's duffel bag when you showed up."

"I'm sorry, Detective Kelly, but it didn't look that way to me," Mr. Smith said. "Is that the way it looked to you, Lamar?"

Lamar looked at Detective Kelly, shook his head, but remained silent.

"What I think, Detective Kelly," Mr. Smith said, "is that if I want something done right, I have to do it myself. And if that's the case, why do I need you?"

"Look, Smith, I did what I promised," Detective Kelly said. "I used my resources to track him down, and here he is—just like we agreed."

"Yes, but we also agreed we would meet at the motel," Mr. Smith said. "Yet I find you and Mr. Pace here. Why is that, Detective Kelly?"

"I thought it would be a good idea to bring him to the scene of the wreck, just in case he had difficulty remembering what happened that night."

"And so far it hasn't worked," Mr. Smith said, cutting off the detective. He then turned toward Travis. "Where is my property, Mr. Pace?"

Travis could feel his heart racing as the men waited for an answer. He felt a sense of hopelessness and wished he'd been less gullible when the opportunity to escape had been possible. Now, he was unsure what he should do. All he did know was that he wasn't ready to die for any amount of money, and he needed time to figure out what to do next.

"I'll have to take you to it," he said finally. "I hid it in a culvert not too far from here."

"Wait a minute. You put over a million dollars' worth of fentanyl and cash in a culvert somewhere?" Detective Kelly asked, shaking his head. "Are you fuckin' nuts?"

"That's enough, detective," Mr. Smith said. "What's it near, Mr. Pace?"

"Not sure how to describe it to you exactly," Travis said. "But once I'm in the area I'm pretty sure I can find it."

"Good. So, take us to it," he said.

"It's not too far from the motel where I stayed," Travis said. He could tell the man was becoming impatient.

"Okay, tell you what—let's all head back to the motel. And this time, make sure that's where you take him, detective. Lamar, you hop in the back seat with them. RJ and I will follow you there."

Travis followed Mr. Smith and Lamar up the embankment, with Detective Kelly behind him. Once they reached the road, Travis saw a black Range Rover and knew why Lamar and RJ looked so familiar. Both men had followed him out of Little Washington and he had met RJ at the Commonwealth Lounge a couple of days prior to the accident. It also dawned on him that the bus RJ was waiting for that evening was probably Orlando's. Travis shuddered as he recalled how Lamar and RJ had left the service station attendant lying in a pool of blood in Bethel, North Carolina.

"Kelly, you head out first," Mr. Smith said as he walked over to where the Range Rover remained idling. "We'll follow you there."

Travis could feel the increased tension once he was back in the detective's car. He could also tell that Detective Kelly was not happy with the way things had turned out. It was also obvious he didn't like taking orders from the apparent leader of the group, but Travis assumed he accepted the man's arrogance because of the money involved.

"Travis, you know you really fucked up," Detective Kelly said. He started the car and pulled out onto the road. "Whatever made a person like you think for a minute that they could take a million dollars' worth of dope and cash and just disappear?"

"You need to shut the fuck up and drive," Lamar said from the back seat.

"Look, buddy, I don't have to listen to you." Detective Kelly tilted the rearview mirror so that he could see Lamar in the back seat. "I don't know who in the hell you think you are. I'm police."

"Yeah, policeman," Lamar said. "Anybody can see you're a regular serve-and-protect kind of guy."

"Oh, you think that shit's funny?" Detective Kelly said. "It was you and your compadre that let Travis here get away when he was in North Carolina. If it weren't for me, you'd still be chasing your tails."

"Sure you're right, Mr. Policeman," Lamar said. "Just fuckin' drive."

Travis ignored the men as they continued to argue. He looked out of the passenger window and was reminded of the night of the wreck. As they drove toward the motel, he wondered what was in store for him once they reached their destination. One thing was certain, Detective Kelly was no longer in charge and perhaps never was. He figured the detective was in just as much danger as he was if things didn't turn out the way the men wanted. It had also occurred to him that the money might no longer be in the culvert and he wondered what would happen to him if it wasn't.

It didn't take them long to reach the motel. Once there, the Range Rover pulled in behind the detective's car. Mr. Smith got out and approached the passenger side.

"Let's go, Mr. Pace," Mr. Smith said as he pulled the door open. "Where's that culvert from here?"

Travis got out of the car. He looked around the area. On the night he left the motel, he would have been traveling down the road in the direction of the bus station.

"I walked that way," Travis said, pointing down the road he had taken when he left the motel. "I figure the culvert can't be much more than a mile from here."

"Okay, so this is what we're going to do," Mr. Smith said. "Detective Kelly, I want you to drive down the road about a mile and pull over. Lamar and I are going to walk with Travis to see if we can find this culvert."

"Wait a minute there, Smith. What happens if you find it before you reach me? What kind of shit are you trying to pull?"

"Don't worry, detective. You'll get the finder's fee we agreed on," Mr. Smith said. "Nothing's changed. We just need to make sure the area is secured. Can I count on you to do that, detective?"

"Okay, already, I'm going," Detective Kelly said, and got back into his car.

Once the detective disappeared down the road, Mr. Smith turned toward Lamar and Travis. He motioned for Travis to begin walking. He then looked back at the Range Rover and made a circular motion with his hand above his head, and Travis could hear the engine start. For a while, all he could hear were the men's footsteps behind him as he walked along the gravel shoulder of the road.

"So, Mr. Pace," Mr. Smith said, after they had walked for about twenty minutes, "is any of this looking familiar yet?"

Travis paused for a moment to get his bearings. Across the road he could see the power lines running neatly along the tree line. He recalled how the utility pole across from the culvert was in a clearing. He began to worry that the tree line might look different.

"Sort of," he said finally. "It was pretty dark the night I left the motel, but it can't be too far because I hadn't been walking long."

"You know, Mr. Pace, I don't understand guys like you. What did you think would happen after you took what was in Orlando's duffel bag?"

"I guess I didn't give it a lot of thought," Travis said. "Like I told the detective, I panicked."

"But why? It seems like you had a nice, quiet life—a good job, a pretty wife," Mr. Smith paused before continuing "You even had a pretty side chick."

Travis stopped walking and turned to face him. He wondered if the side chick he was referring to could be Karen.

"What side chick?" Travis asked. "I don't have any side chick."

"Hey, don't worry, Mr. Pace. Your secret's safe with us," Mr. Smith said. Both he and Lamar laughed.

"You need to keep walking Mr. Pace. We're going to lose daylight soon." Mr. Smith said before turning back to Lamar. "I've got to give it to Detective Kelly. He's thorough, if nothing else."

Travis started walking again. He thought about what the man said about his nice quiet life. As far as he was concerned it had been a life that was not so quiet and was what he had, in desperation, run away from. The money had seemed like an opportunity to leave it all behind, but his desperation had kept him from thinking things through. It occurred to him that not doing so had put him, and possibly others, in danger. Now, Travis realized he needed to figure out how to escape from these men—not just for himself, but also for Karen.

"You sure about how long you walked that night, Mr. Pace?" Mr. Smith asked. "Seems like we've been walking for a while now."

"It's got to be close," Travis said, allowing his eyes to travel down the row of power lines again. In the distance he could just barely make out Detective Kelly's car parked on the shoulder. At a lesser distance, Travis also saw what could be a utility pole standing out from the tree line. He felt his heart racing.

"So, what happens once you get your money?" Travis asked without turning around.

"What did you say, Mr. Pace?"

"I said, what happens once you get your money?" he repeated. "You know, once you get your money, you won't have to worry about me. I can just disappear again."

"That's certainly an option, Mr. Pace," Mr. Smith said. "But honestly, you're not very good at disappearing now are you?"

The man's response troubled Travis as he continued scanning the tree line. He was now certain they were not too far from the utility pole he'd used to mark the location of the culvert. The closer they got to the pole, the greater the feeling of dread grew. It was then that he decided to throw caution to the wind.

"I think the culvert is just up ahead," he said.

"Where?" Mr. Smith asked. The excitement could be heard in his voice. "Show me."

"It's in there," Travis said, and pointed at the entrance to a metal culvert poking out of the bottom of the slope. "I'll slide down and make sure the bag is still there."

"Wait a minute," Mr. Smith peered over the edge of the embankment. He tilted his head slowly from side to side before continuing. "You sure you put it in there? It looks like water might be running through it."

"I'm sure it's the one. Either Lamar or I can slide down and get the bag." Travis said, starting down the embankment.

"No, wait. Both of you go down the embankment. Lamar, go with him and check it out."

At first, the loose gravel made it difficult for Travis to do more than slide a couple of feet at a time before having to stop and regain his footing. Each time he slid to a stop, he checked to see how far Lamar had made it down the slope. Once he was sure Lamar was experiencing the same difficulty navigating the slope, and he had lost sight of Mr. Smith on the road, Travis ran down the remainder of the slope to its bottom. Instead of stopping at the culvert, he ran into the woods beyond it.

Behind him, Travis could hear Lamar and Mr. Smith shouting. Minutes later, he heard the rustling sound of someone coming through the brush behind him. At first, Travis continued running with no real destination in mind. He just wanted to put some distance between himself and the two men. As Travis continued through the densely wooded area, he felt that if he followed a path along the road, he would be able to find the culvert where he'd actually left the money. He figured it was worth the risk to find out if it was still there. Once he recovered the money, he'd contact

Karen, and convince her they needed to get as far away from Richmond as possible.

In the distance, Travis could hear Lamar calling his name. He also heard what sounded like the detective's voice, whom he assumed had been made aware of his escape. Travis rested his back against the trunk of a large tree and allowed himself to sink to the ground. He tried to reorient himself to the location of the culvert. While the darkening sky provided him with some concealment, it was also beginning to make it difficult to navigate through the thick brush and remain oriented on the road.

After resting a moment longer, he continued through the woods, certain of the direction to the culvert. Up ahead, he could hear the sound of movement. He assumed at least Lamar and the detective were somewhere in the wooded area near him. He paused to determine their location before moving any further.

"Hey, dumb shit," he heard the detective yell. "Where are you?"

"I think I heard him over this way," Lamar said. "He couldn't have gotten that far."

"Where's your boss?" Detective Kelly asked. "How long is it going to take him?"

"Don't worry about where he is," Lamar said. "Let's just find this fucker."

"What do you think I'm trying to do?" the detective asked. "This wouldn't have happened if I hadn't been sent down the road."

"Just shut the fuck up and keep looking," Lamar said. "Let's look near the road."

Travis could tell by the men's voices that they were close. He was beginning to feel that trying to get to the backpack was too risky. Before he could take another step, he heard Mr. Smith.

"Hey, Mr. Pace, I've got a surprise for you," he said. "Someone you'll want to see."

Except for the sound of an occasional car driving by, it became very quiet. In the near distance, Travis could hear footsteps moving in his direction. An immediate feeling of dread washed over him as he wondered who the "someone" could be. He remained frozen in place, waiting for the man to say more.

"Hey, Mr. Pace," Mr. Smith began again, "if you don't come out, I assure you things are not going to end well."

"Take the tape off her mouth," Travis heard Mr. Smith say before continuing. "Mr. Pace, why don't you come out and say hello."

"Travis!" Karen shouted, her voice strained. "Are you alright?"

"Hey, check that out, Mr. Pace," Mr. Smith said. "She cares more about you than she does about herself."

"Yeah, Travis," Detective Kelly said. "Let's get this shit over with."

"Karen," Travis said. "Are you all right?"

Travis stepped out from behind the tree, hoping to determine Karen's location. The flicker of flashlights was the last thing he saw before feeling a painful blow to his head, followed by darkness.

* * *

When he awoke, Travis was seated against the trunk of a tree. Karen was seated to his left. Although her mouth was covered with tape, Karen's eyes told him all he needed to know.

"Please let her go," he said to no one in particular. "She doesn't have anything to do with this."

"She does now, Mr. Pace," Mr. Smith said. "What happens to her depends on what you do next."

"Look, I'll take you to where I put your money," he said. "Just let her go."

"First, take me to my property, Mr. Pace," Mr. Smith said, "then maybe there'll be some room for negotiation."

Travis searched the men's faces as they waited for his response. He knew if he gave them the backpack, both Karen's and his life would be in jeopardy. Travis had never prayed before, but he felt the need to do so now.

"Let's go, Mr. Pace," Mr. Smith said. "Time's wasting."

"We need to head toward the road. The backpack is in a culvert near the road," Travis said.

"Don't let this be some more bullshit, Mr. Pace. I've already run out of patience, and believe me, you've run out of chances."

"No, I'm telling you the truth. That's where it is," Travis said. "I just need a flashlight."

Lamar stepped forward and handed him his flashlight. Travis started walking toward the road. Behind him, he could hear the footsteps of Karen and the men as they followed him through the wooded area.

Once he arrived at the culvert, Travis got down on his hands and knees. He shined the flashlight into the dark tunnel.

"So, is this the one?" Mr. Smith asked.

"Yes, I think I can see the backpack from here," Travis said. "I'll crawl in and get it."

"No, wait," Mr. Smith said, then turned to the detective. "You and RJ go across the road to the other side of this thing, just in case our man here decides to abandon his girlfriend and escape through the other side."

Travis watched as Detective Kelly and RJ made their way up the embankment. A few minutes later, he heard their voices coming from the other end of the culvert. Mr. Smith motioned to Travis to continue. Travis crawled into the culvert. Once he was a few feet inside, Travis panicked when he initially didn't see the backpack, until he realized it was covered with dirt and leaves.

"What's taking so long? I thought you said you could see the bag." The excitement in Mr. Smith's voice was apparent. "Should I send Lamar in to assist you?"

"No. Give me a minute," Travis said. "It's covered with dirt and leaves. I almost have it."

When Travis reached the backpack, he remembered the pistol inside. He removed the pistol from the backpack and slid it down the front of his pants. He covered the bulge it caused with his T-shirt and began backing out of the culvert while dragging the backpack. Once outside, he was immediately surrounded by Mr. Smith and Lamar.

"Go ahead. Open it," Mr. Smith said while pointing his gun at Travis.

Travis unzipped the backpack and tilted the opening toward the man. Several banded packets of cash fell to the ground.

"Careful, Mr. Pace. Put those back in the backpack and zip it up," Mr. Smith said.

Travis knelt and picked up the packets of cash that lay at his feet. He stuffed them back into the backpack and stood.

"So, what now, Mr. Smith?"

"What now, Mr. Pace? I'll tell you what now. Zip the backpack closed and toss my property over here."

Instead of doing as instructed, Travis tossed the partially unzipped backpack beyond where the men were standing. Several more banded packs of cash bounced out when the backpack hit the ground. Both men lunged for the bag, and when they did Travis pulled the pistol from his pants and ran up behind Mr. Smith. He pressed the barrel against the back of the man's head and motioned toward Lamar.

"Now, toss your gun, Lamar," Travis said, motioning in the direction of Karen. "and untie her."

"Fuck you," Lamar said. He pointed his pistol at Travis. "You're going to have to just shoot me."

"I said untie her," Travis repeated and shoved the gun into the back of Mr. Smith's head again.

"Don't do anything stupid, Mr. Pace. Lamar, go ahead and untie that bitch."

Lamar looked at Travis for a moment before pulling out a knife and cutting the rope that held Karen's hands together. He then removed the tape from her mouth.

"Run, Karen," Travis yelled once she was free. "Run into the woods and stay away from the road."

"But Travis, I—"

"Please, Karen. Please just go. It'll be okay."

Karen stared at Travis for a moment before running into the woods.

"This shit's not over, motherfucker," Mr. Smith said. "How far do you think she's going to get before one of my men catches up with her?"

Before Travis could consider what to do next Lamar yelled to the two men on the other side of the road. In the distance, Travis heard gunfire. He pushed the barrel of his pistol into the back of Mr. Smith's head again.

"You see, I told you things would end badly," Mr. Smith growled. "Now her blood is on your hands."

"You motherfuckers," Travis shouted. "She didn't have anything to do with this."

"It doesn't matter now, Mr. Pace," Mr. Smith said. "You should have considered the consequences when you decided to take another man's shit. Now, drop that fuckin' gun so we can get this over with."

"Get this over with," Travis repeated. He could feel tears burning his eyes. "One way or another, you're going to pay for what you've done. Move over there."

Travis shoved Mr. Smith toward Lamar. At the same time, Lamar rushed toward Travis in an attempt to grab his gun.

Instead, the pistol fired unexpectedly. The bullet hit Lamar in the face, propelling him backward. As Lamar fell to the ground, Mr. Smith grabbed Travis and began wrestling with him in an attempt to take the pistol. Behind him, Travis heard the sound of footsteps. In his peripheral vision, he saw Detective Kelly running through the woods with his pistol drawn.

"Okay, Travis, let him go," the detective said. "And drop that fuckin' gun."

Detective Kelly kept the gun pointed at Travis's head until he reluctantly complied.

"It took you long enough to get over here," Mr. Smith said. "Where's my other guy?"

"You mean, what's his name—RJ?" asked Detective Kelly. "He won't be joining us."

He then aimed his gun at Mr. Smith and glanced at Travis.

"Where's the backpack, Travis?" he said, then looked back at Mr. Smith. "Don't even think about making a move."

"Over there," Travis said, looking in the direction where Lamar had fallen but noticing the man's body was no longer there.

"Over where?" Detective Kelly asked. "Look, Travis, I'm tired of your fucking games. Where's the bag?"

When Detective Kelly stepped in the direction Travis had indicated, Mr. Smith grabbed for the detective's gun. As the two men struggled, the gun went off and Mr. Smith fell to the ground, dead. The detective quickly turned and pointed the gun at Travis.

"Look, I'm going to ask you one more time. Where's the backpack?"

"I'm telling you," Travis said. "I tossed it over there."

Detective Kelly walked over to where the bag was thrown while keeping his pistol pointed at Travis. He pulled out a flashlight and shined it around the area.

"So, where is it, Travis?" he asked again. He searched the area again with his flashlight. "Hey, wait a minute. Where's your girl?"

Changing Pace

"Where's my girl?" Travis yelled. "I should be asking you."

"Now, how in the fuck would I know?" he asked. "She was here when I left."

Travis remained silent. The detective's response gave him some hope that Karen might still alive.

"Travis, I'm going to ask you one more fucking time," he said. "Now, where's the damn backpack?"

Detective Kelly took a step forward and pointed his gun at Travis. Behind the detective, a gun went off, and Travis saw Lamar crawling toward them. Blood streamed down one side of his face, covering his right eye. He squinted out of the other and seemed barely able to steady his pistol. Lamar fired at Detective Kelly again, and the detective immediately returned fire, hitting Lamar in the head. Lamar collapsed as the detective turned toward Travis and tried to speak. He gasped once more before falling to the ground.

Travis looked around at the bodies, then walked over to where Lamar must have crawled from and saw the backpack. He unzipped the bag and dumped everything out except the money. After zipping it back up, the only thing he could think of was Karen, and he headed in the direction she had gone earlier. In the distance, he heard sirens and knew he had to hurry before the woods filled with police.

As Travis made his way through the trees, he paused for a moment and looked toward the road. Already, the lights of emergency vehicles were visible. He continued through the woods but was startled by a shadow crossing his path. Moving toward it, he realized it was Karen. She appeared to be heading back in the direction of the sirens.

"Karen?" Travis whispered loudly, but she kept walking toward the road. "Karen."

"Travis?" she said, stopping. "Travis, is that you?"

J. Marcus Evins

Travis ran toward Karen's voice. She stepped out of the shadows, her hair matted and her face glistening with perspiration. She smiled wearily when their eyes met. Travis hurried to her just as she collapsed in his arms.

"Oh, Travis. I didn't know what to think. I thought you were—"

"I know, I know," Travis said, lifting her in his arms and kissing her deeply. "I'm so sorry. Did they hurt you?"

"No, I'm okay," she said. "What happened to those men? How did you get away?"

"I'll tell you everything later," he said. "Right now, we need to get out of these woods."

"I know. I heard the sirens—I was trying to get to the police to tell them what happened. Aren't you coming?" she asked, pulling Travis toward the flashing lights.

"Wait, Karen," he said. "Let's think about this."

"Think about what, Travis? After what those men did, what's there to think about?"

"They're dead, Karen," he said. "All of them are dead."

"But how?" she asked, then pointed at the backpack hanging from his shoulder, "What's that?"

"It's the money, Karen," he said. "I figured, why leave it there?"

"Travis, we've got to go to the police," Karen said. "Once we tell them what happened and turn in the money, your life can return to normal."

"Normal, Karen?" Travis shook his head. "Are you kidding? I have no job, no wife—and don't forget, I'm already dead. All I have is you. That is, if you'll still have me."

Karen turned toward Travis and looked into his eyes. She leaned into him again and pressed her lips against his. Travis held her tightly before letting go. He could hear vehicles arriving on the road near the culvert.

"We've got to go," he said, grabbing Karen's hand.

"Go where, Travis?" she asked.

"I don't know, Karen," Travis said as they hurried back through the woods, away from the road and the sound of sirens, "We'll just have to figure it out when we get there."

To Be Continued . . .

About the Author

J. Marcus Evins is a retired U.S. Army veteran and storyteller whose fiction blends romance, crime drama, and suspense. His debut novel, *Changing Pace*, explores the complexities of human relationships—how we love, how we struggle, and how we find our way when life forces us to change.

In addition to *Changing Pace*, J. Marcus is the author of several short stories, including *Flip-Flop, Cappuccino, Soul Mate*, and *The Truth About Love*. Each reflects his dedication to crafting narratives that balance emotional intensity with page-turning suspense.

When he isn't writing, J Marcus enjoys reading across genres, exploring new ideas, and connecting with readers who appreciate stories that are as emotionally engaging as they are gripping. Originally from Baltimore, Maryland, he currently resides in Virginia with his wife, Theresa.

A Special Message from J. Marcus

Hi everyone! I'm thrilled to share my first novel with you. For as long as I can remember, I've been fascinated by the complexities of human relationships—how we love, how we struggle, and how we find our way when life forces us to change course. *Changing Pace* is a story that explores exactly that, and I'm excited to share it with you.

If you enjoyed *Changing Pace*, I'd love to hear your thoughts. Please consider leaving a review on Amazon—it helps more than you know. You can also follow me on Facebook to learn about upcoming projects: https://www.facebook.com/JMarcusE.

For now, thank you—and please enjoy my short story, "*Soul Mate*." It's part of a short story collection I plan to publish in the near future. Thanks again!

Soul Mate

Her mother was the last person Rosalyn needed to think about—at least right now. Things hadn't been this bad when she'd moved to Atlanta to complete her MBA. Back then, the two-hour drive from Columbus, Georgia, hadn't been far enough to discourage her mother's frequent visits to preach the virtues of keeping her books open and her legs closed. Marriage and children hadn't factored into the equation yet. But now, since her thirty-first birthday, Rosalyn's conversations with her mother strayed predictably to those subjects. Part—but not all—of the problem had been resolved when she'd found a job in Richmond, Virginia—outside of Momma's "just stopping by" range.

For a moment, she recalled the frozen faces when Allen Dunn, one of the company's CEOs, had introduced her as a new member of their executive team. The company's old guard had some difficulty accepting the idea that a black woman could be smart enough to do what they did for a living. Rosalyn had shown them though—shown them that intelligence had nothing to do with skin color or gender. In time, doubts regarding her qualifications served more to illuminate strengths than expose weaknesses.

Despite a decidedly smooth transition into Corporate America, Rosalyn wasn't sure what prevented her from achieving the same level of success in her relationships with men. She'd just about convinced herself that she didn't need a man. Besides, every talk show, magazine and girlfriend confirmed there weren't enough "good men" to go around anyway.

Rosalyn never told Momma about the guys at the office who had asked her out and how she'd declined their invitations. For her, a romantic interest had to be a man who she shared more in common than work. It would have to be someone with whom she could hum Al Greene, Luther Vandross or Maxwell. Most of all, the person would have to be someone whom could replace Ramón.

Ramón rocked her to sleep on those nights when she'd given into one of Zane's steamy erotic novels or become too cozy with a Lifetime movie. He was a safe, undemanding alternative to taking chances. Best of all, there was no smelly breath, no long or short goodbyes, and no regrets. Ramón never cheated and was always just where she left him. All Ramón ever wanted was enough energy to satisfy—and she kept an ample supply of C batteries.

Rosalyn guessed that's why Tyree Johnson captured her attention. At least, that's why she'd started thinking about Ramón. Tyree was someone Momma would certainly approve of. It wasn't that he was particularly handsome—nor was he unattractive. He wasn't even as tall as the men she normally dated. But Tyree possessed the kind of head-turning symmetry that beckoned a second look. Along with his athletic appearance, there was a confidence in Tyree's voice that added to his attractiveness.

She glanced at him again and recalled his presentation to the group. He'd spoken intelligently about the advantages of e-marketing without resorting to that annoying, nasal way of talking as did so many professional brothers. She'd vowed never to date that type again. Besides, professional or not, a dog—even one with a pedigree—was still a dog.

Once the presentations ended for the day, Rosalyn mingled with the other conference attendees. Over a hundred sales and marketing representatives from around the country filled the Renaissance Hotel's brightly lit banquet room. She watched as they helped themselves to trays of assorted cold cuts, cheeses and vegetables. Waiters weaved intricate patterns through the crowd, serving drinks that quenched both thirst and inhibition.

Rosalyn chewed on celery and carrot sticks, listened to chatty reps, and wondered if she sounded as desperate as they did. She caught a glimpse, now and then, of Tyree. Although they hadn't spoken, Rosalyn was convinced she'd caught him sneaking a peek at her a few times. At least, that's what she told herself.

The crowd began to thin as the evening waned. Rosalyn assumed that many of the reps were booked on early morning flights. These days, the smaller the company, the shorter the turnaround time for business travel. She had just about decided to go upstairs to her room when she noticed Tyree. He was sitting alone at a table littered with the beer bottles and wine glasses of his departed colleagues. When she made eye contact, he smiled.

"Long day?" she asked after finally mustering enough courage to approach the table.

"What?" Tyree looked up slowly, as though seeing Rosalyn for the first time.

"I...I didn't mean to disturb you." Rosalyn felt awkward.

A smile crept across Tyree's handsome face, "You're not disturbing me. I was just sort of lost in my thoughts."

"I wanted to congratulate you on your presentation. You might get a couple of accounts out of this group," she said.

"You weren't so bad yourself," Tyree motioned towards the chair closest to Rosalyn. "Why don't you have a seat?"

"Well, I was on my way up...."

"So, you're booked on a red-eye too?"

"Not this time," Rosalyn hesitated, then sat in the chair across from him. "I fly out tomorrow at noon."

Tyree's easy manner relaxed her. After a second drink, he knew she was from Columbus, Georgia, what schools she'd attended, and the details of her five-year plan. She'd even loosened up enough to tell him how difficult it was to find a good man since moving to Virginia.

In contrast, Rosalyn barely knew any more about Tyree than when she'd sat down. She did know he'd graduated from the University of Virginia with a degree in engineering and had bounced around the job market before finding his niche in online sales.

She'd noticed the wedding band shortly after they'd begun talking. At least Tyree hadn't tried to hide the fact that he was married—he just hadn't mentioned it. The ring's presence answered the question of his availability.

"You know, Rosalyn," he said, his voice deep and melodic, "I just can't imagine a woman with your personality not being involved with someone..."

She wasn't sure what he meant by "woman with your personality." It reminded her about a too-smart little girl with horn-rimmed glasses, oxford shoes, and crooked teeth—the kind of girl that boys didn't look at twice. Rosalyn frowned, resisting the long-abandoned habit of running the tip of her tongue across her front teeth to confirm their straightness. Instead, she smiled and decided the man's opinion didn't count. After all, he was married.

"...and you're a very attractive woman with a lot of brains."

She blinked.

"Did I say something wrong?" Tyree's smile faded into a look of concern.

"Oh, no. I guess I'm the one who's lost...in my thoughts, that is."

"Well, it's probably time for both of us to call it a night," Tyree glanced at the silver Bulova dangling loosely from his wrist. "Want to share an elevator?"

"Sure, I—" she stood and stumbled slightly.

Tyree stood quickly and helped Rosalyn steady herself.

"I...I'm so embarrassed. That's never happened before. I actually feel fine."

"Maybe, but let's not take any chances. What floor are you on?"

"Look, I'm okay, Tyree...really."

Rosalyn dug into her handbag, pulling out a key card to verify the room number and realized no number was on the card. She continued sifting through the handbag without looking up, felt his eyes on her. Just before reaching the point of frustration, she remembered her room number. A feeling of vulnerability overshadowed the one of control she'd felt two or three drinks ago. They rode up to the third floor in silence until the elevator bumped softly to a stop.

"Which way?"

"It's at the end of the hall, room 315," Rosalyn nodded in the direction of the room.

She followed Tyree down the empty hallway. A small light glowed above the number of each room. Tyree whispered room numbers and paused once or twice along the way. An occasional muffled sound escaped into the hallway.

"Well, here you are," Tyree said once they stood in front of 315.

Rosalyn slid the key card in the slot. The door clicked and the light above the door handle changed from red to green.

"So, Tyree, it was nice talking to you," she said averting her eyes. "Thanks for walking me to my room."

The hallway became too quiet. There was a metallic click as the door returned to its locked position.

"So, where's your room?" Rosalyn ignored the sound.

J. Marcus Evins

"Let's see." Tyree looked away, dug deeply into his left pocket, then the right. He finally pulled a key card from his shirt pocket.

"Three," he hesitated, shoved the card back into his pocket then continued, "forty-two. I think that's back the way we came."

Rosalyn glanced down the hallway in the direction Tyree pointed then back at the door to her room. She inserted the key card again before turning toward Tyree. His brown eyes searched hers. She opened the door and looked into the dark room.

"Looks kind of scary in there," Tyree said. "I'll wait here until you turn on a light."

Rosalyn walked towards the nightstand and fumbled with the light switch. A pale amber glow exposed two undisturbed beds. She thought about how nice it would be to talk to Tyree a little longer—at least until the room became a more familiar place to spend the night.

"Hey, Rosalyn! You all right in there?"

"Everything's fine." She turned and walked back towards Tyree. Her lips curled into a smile that felt too suggestive.

"So, I guess this is good night," he said.

"Yes," Rosalyn paused and looked up at Tyree. "I mean, I really enjoyed talking to you."

"Me too. We should stay in touch," he said and handed her a card.

Rosalyn held the card at arm's length for a moment as though trying to see it better in the scant light of the hallway. She exhaled perhaps too loudly.

"It's my business card," Tyree continued. "I really enjoyed tonight and I wouldn't mind – maybe, you know, seeing you again."

Rosalyn did not know how she looked at that moment but was sure it was reflected in Tyree's face.

"Tyree, I'm a little surprised that you're giving me this. Aren't you..."

"I know what you're thinking, Rosalyn. I really enjoyed our conversation and just thought you might agree that it would be nice to talk again too."

Rosalyn felt a sudden and unexpected awkwardness when she finally said good night to Tyree. She could not deny her attraction. After the sound of Tyree's footsteps faded into silence, she felt the weight of the business card in her hand. Rosalyn could not help thinking of Ramón.

* * *

The Monday morning following the conference was typical in almost every way as Rosalyn hurried through the crowded lobby. Instead of waiting for the elevator, she decided to take the stairs to her fifth floor office. She was anxious to get to work. It would distract her from thinking about Tyree. He'd been on her mind all weekend. Even though she had already played the fantasy out with Ramon, Rosalyn couldn't help but wonder what would have happened if he'd been the least bit aggressive at the hotel.

On the fifth floor, she stopped at her assistant's desk to pick up messages.

"Good morning, Anne," she said with a smile. "How was your weekend?"

"Oh, Ms. Ross, good morning," the young woman said. She appeared to search for somewhere to stuff the Essence magazine she was reading. "I really didn't do much... you know, with finals next week."

"Nothing wrong with having priorities," Rosalyn said, ignoring Anne's attempts to conceal the magazine. "It'll all pay off. By the way, I thought you were going to call me Rosalyn. You're making me feel old."

"Well, Ms. Ros...I mean, Rosalyn, I'm sorry. I guess it's something I'll have to get used to."

Rosalyn liked Anne. She'd known during the interview that the attractive woman would be her choice—even before interviewing the other applicants. She was smart and ambitious. In many ways, Anne reminded Rosalyn of herself. Anne was currently taking classes at J.S. Community College and would be attending Virginia Unity University next fall. Rosalyn silently flipped through a handful of messages before picking up her briefcase. She noticed a large vase containing at least two dozen red roses on Anne's desk.

"Look at you," Rosalyn said. Her voice rose slightly, almost playfully. "Aren't you the lucky one?"

Anne's smile faded slightly as she followed Rosalyn's eyes to the desk.

"Oh, the flowers. They're not for me. They're for you. I was just about to put them in your office when the phone rang and I . . ."

"Well, I wonder who...," Rosalyn returned her briefcase to the floor, leaned close enough to smell the bouquet's perfume, and fought the urge to smile.

"They were delivered shortly after I arrived this morning," Anne said. "There's a card."

Rosalyn removed the small, ivory-colored envelop poking out from the vase. Inside was a note from Tyree. He would be in Richmond Friday and wanted to see her. She recognized the number. It was the one she'd decided not to call. The excitement she felt reminded her of dimly lit hallways, undisturbed beds—of fantasy.

"Ms. Ross, you have an appointment at nine..."

"You mean Rosalyn," she said warmly to Anne. "Thanks. I'll take a look at my calendar once I turn on my computer."

Rosalyn, juggling flowers, messages, and briefcase headed for her office. The flowers had thrown off her rhythm. Work was no longer the escape she desired. It was now something that would force her to mark time until Friday. Yet, she had not decided whether to meet Tyree or not. Why should she? After all, he was married. She sat down at the desk—noticed her distorted reflection in the blank monitor. She looked around at the office's bright décor and plush furnishings that normally cheered her— reassured her. Now they felt unfamiliar—distant.

The roses' perfume reminded her that she needed to call Tyree. No, she didn't have to call—she could ignore the flowers, the dinner invitation. Nevertheless, Rosalyn knew she'd call—if only to let Tyree know that there could be nothing between them. Perhaps she was making too much of the whole thing. Meeting Tyree could be perfectly innocent. After all, it was only dinner— dinner with a nice man, a nice married man. The thought of seeing Tyree made her tingle. The buzz from the phone penetrated.

"Hello. This is Rosalyn Ross," she answered the phone. "Yes, that's correct. I'll send you the contract by tomorrow morning."

She hung up and scribbled a reminder on a yellow Post-it. The feeling of control slowly returned. Rosalyn smiled. She loved her office with its plush furniture—its bright décor. The monitor glowed as the computer booted. Rosalyn punched in her login ID and password. She would face this thing with Tyree on her own terms—just as she did everything else. Anne's voice rattled over the intercom reminding her of the nine o'clock appointment. The women exchanged smiles as Rosalyn hurried for the meeting.

* * *

Rosalyn had not recalled Ma-Musu's cozy atmosphere when she recommended the restaurant to Tyree. The restaurant, specializing in West African cuisine, was located in one of the easily missed storefronts that blurred by the uninformed Broad

Street traveler. To the knowing, the restaurant's ambiance provided a comfortable nook to escape the daily hustle and bustle. Today was no exception. A smiling middle-aged woman dressed in traditional Ghanaian attire greeted her as she walked in the restaurant. Rosalyn could immediately tell dinner was clearly more popular than the lunch she remembered.

She followed the host to a table in the dining area. Tropical plants in large, colorful ceramic pots separated each table. The muted blues, reds and greens of the pots matched the tastefully arranged wall hangings around the room. The tempo of the music mixed easily with the steady chatter of the busy restaurant and the spicy aroma stirred her appetite. Rosalyn was unconsciously swaying to the reggae music when the server approached the table.

"Welcome to Ma-Musu's, Ma'am. Can I get you something from the bar?" the woman asked in a thick West African accent.

"Not just yet. I'm waiting for...for my party to arrive," Rosalyn said. She hadn't meant to say "party." It sounded too formal for the cozy restaurant.

The woman smiled, raised an eyebrow, and then spoke.

"Have you been to Ma-Musu's before? I could bring more menus for you . . . and your party."

"No. Two are enough. My guest is...I mean my friend should be here shortly."

"I will come back then—once you and your friend have gotten settled," the server said with a smile, then seemed to wink. "I've got to hurry now. I want to make sure the handsome gentleman who just walked in is seated in my section."

Rosalyn looked towards the entrance where Tyree stood. She watched him share a laugh with the host while glancing around the restaurant. He smiled when their eyes finally met then headed towards the table.

"Hi, Roz. Sorry I'm late. I got tied up at the meeting." Tyree sat down without breaking eye contact. "You are beautiful, you know."

The words sounded stolen to Rosalyn. She forced a smile.

Almost immediately, the server appeared at the table. Rosalyn suspected her hasty return was because she wanted to get a closer look at Tyree. He exchanged smiles with the server. Then, to Rosalyn's surprise, Tyree greeted the woman in her native Akan language. They both laughed. Tyree ordered the house draft. Rosalyn ordered wine.

"So, where did you learn to speak the language?" asked Rosalyn.

"I picked up a little when I was in college."

"Sounds like you had an interesting curriculum for an engineering major."

"Oh, no. I didn't take classes or anything. My roommate, Ashon, was a native of Ghana and used to talk about home all the time. He'd go on and on about how there was nothing like authentic West African cuisine and how amazing his mom's kelewele and seafood were. I had to admit, the brother could throw down on some collards and okra too."

Rosalyn smiled. "So, how did your meeting go?"

"It went okay. Although I must admit I was a little distracted."

"Why was that?" Rosalyn asked.

Tyree's face took on an exaggerated look of disbelief. He touched her hand, and she noticed that he did not have on his ring. Rosalyn resisted the urge to pull her hand away.

"So, are you incognito today?" she asked.

"Incognito?" Tyree repeated the word as though puzzling over its meaning.

The server placed a silver finger bowl in front of Rosalyn, then another in front of Tyree. She placed silverware, tightly wrapped in white cloth napkins, beside each bowl. She smiled broadly at Tyree again, then glanced at Rosalyn appraisingly.

"I can't believe this," Tyree said as he closed the menu. "No kenkey?"

"Kenkey? Oh, I should have known that you would know tradition." The server smiled again, then turned towards Rosalyn as she retrieved their menus. "You are so lucky to have such a worldly man. I will bring kenkey with your meal."

Rosalyn watched the server disappear into the kitchen then turned to Tyree.

"Well, so much for my special dinner. I thought I was bringing you somewhere different. I didn't know you were such a worldly man."

"No. This is special. It's exactly the kind of place I would have chosen for our first date too."

The word "date" made Rosalyn look at Tyree's hand. "You never did answer my question."

"Question?"

"You know—incognito?"

Tyree looked at his hand. He massaged the empty ring finger as though the slow manipulation would soothe its irritation.

"I guess I owe you an explanation," he said, frowning and twisting his lips.

"No, you don't owe me anything, Tyree. After all, it's just dinner. It's not as though we're really on a date. With or without the ring, you're still married."

Tyree continued massaging the empty ring finger.

The server quietly set their meals in front of them.

"We had the worst fight the other day and..."

"Tyree, let's just eat. Tell me more about your roommate. Are you still in touch with him?"

Tyree accepted Rosalyn's decision to change the subject. Their conversation started off mechanical, then slowly began to relax.

Soul Mate

Tyree talked about expanding his business by finding more suppliers. That was why he was in Richmond. He knew just the right words to say. He made Rosalyn laugh. She wished, just for a moment, that the missing ring was a sign that something miraculous had happened.

The table became quiet after the check was paid.

"Well, I guess I'd better get on the road. Charlottesville's almost two hours away," Tyree said, ending the silence.

"I've had a good time Tyree," Rosalyn said, knowing she needed to tell him she couldn't see him again.

"So, how far do you live from here?" he asked.

"Fifteen minutes—once I get on 64."

"East or west?"

"West."

"Sounds like we're going in the same direction again."

"Again?"

"Like at the hotel."

"I see."

"Look, I'm not that familiar with Richmond. Mind if I follow you to 64?"

"Sure."

Outside the restaurant, headlights were now more visible than the cars whose paths they illuminated. Rosalyn pushed the ignition button and listened to the BMW's engine rev before settling into a low idle. After adjusting her seatbelt she looked in the rearview mirror. Tyree waved. Rosalyn returned the wave before entering the stream of traffic that rushed past Ma-Musu's. She glanced back at Tyree. In the rearview mirror, he became a stranger again. She pressed on the gas without considering whether or not he was still behind her.

* * *

The Lakewood subdivision had become noticeably quiet with the shortened days of autumn. Canopied oaks lined the main thoroughfare. The trees' thinning leaves exposed a moonless sky accented with scattered clusters of stars. The cool night air had begun its calming effect when Rosalyn noticed Tyree's car slowing to a stop in the gravel driveway behind her. She glared into the rearview mirror and watched his headlights dim before he got out of the car.

"So, now you're a stalker, Tyree?"

"Hold up, Rosalyn. It's nothing like that. I was driving along and realized I hadn't really told you about this ring business. I..."

"Damn it, Tyree. I thought we said our goodbyes at the restaurant. Don't make me feel like it was a mistake to meet you there."

"Rosalyn...."

"No, Tyree. You need to get back in your car and go home to Charlottesville. Isn't your wife expecting you?"

"That's what I wanted to talk to you about. Jackie and I are separated. I haven't seen her in days, Rosalyn."

Rosalyn stared at him, feeling her lower lip tremble.

"Okay, Tyree, so you and your wife aren't together. I've had a nice evening up to now, but if you don't mind I'm really tired and would like to go inside."

A dog barked. Rosalyn turned in the direction of the sound. She could make out the shadowy figure of her next-door neighbor in the window.

"Rosalyn, if you'd give me a minute, I can make sense of this whole thing."

The neighbor's door opened and she called Winston in.

"Is that you, Rosalyn?" the voice asked. "Is everything okay?"

"Yes, Tina. Everything's fine. Sorry we got Winston excited."

The woman waved and slowly closed the door. Her silhouette remained in the window. Rosalyn stared in the direction of her neighbor's house a moment longer before turning back to Tyree.

"Okay, Tyree, we can go in for a moment but once you've said whatever you feel you need to say you've got to leave."

Inside the house, Rosalyn motioned Tyree toward the living room. She figured now would be as good a time to let Tyree know how she felt. They continued talking. Tyree revealed how things had changed after catching his wife cheating. He'd tried to make things right but his wife—and his heart—just wouldn't go along with it. That had been a year ago. Long work hours and ill feelings had moved them further apart and closer to divorce. Now it was only a matter of time.

When Tyree slid his hand onto hers Rosalyn felt no desire to move. A tear crawled down her cheek. Tyree gently wiped away the one that followed. Rosalyn did not know why she was crying— a feeling of weakness engulfed her. Tyree's lips gently caressed hers. She closed her eyes. When his lips traced a path down her neck, there was no energy left. She helped him remove her blouse, exposing her breasts. Her nipples hardened when the warmth of Tyree's mouth surrounded them. Rosalyn stood abruptly but felt herself falling before leading him to the bedroom.

* * *

At first, the dog's barking seemed like part of the weird dream she was having. It mixed easily with another sound that droned a steady rhythm. It was then that Rosalyn realized that Tyree was lying next to her. She turned her head slightly, watched the movement of his chest and listened to the sound of his light snore. She was careful not to awaken him as she slid from beneath the covers. Their clothing lay scattered around the room. Rosalyn used one foot and then the other to feel for her terry cloth slippers. A crumpled condom wrapper caught her attention. A brief wave of relief washed over her—at least she hadn't lost control completely. Yet, she knew she had.

She pulled the bedroom door closed quietly and decided to let Tyree sleep. Bright sunlight flooded the living room. Everything looked the same, yet somehow different. Last night had been easy, but this morning was not—especially with the sun shining so bright. Worst of all, Rosalyn felt herself falling for Tyree. She sat in her favorite wicker chair in front of the patio doors and hugged her knees tightly to her chest. Rosalyn closed her eyes, allowing the sun's warmth to bathe her as she waited for the familiar feeling of control.

This morning it did not come.

* * *

In the weeks that followed, Rosalyn found herself spending more time with Tyree. Several major customers made it convenient for him to spend more time in Richmond. Besides, Tyree could run his e-business anywhere there was an internet connection. After several overnight stays, he moved in with Rosalyn. Soon the clutter around her bathroom sink included razors, shaving cream and Tyree's cologne. Rosalyn had even started buying condoms again – at least until she could get back on the pill.

It wasn't much longer before she realized that the strange feeling she was experiencing was love. She was sure Tyree felt it too. He was just the type of man she'd dreamed about—a real soul mate. Rosalyn even told her momma about Tyree—at least the part her mother needed to know. She couldn't bear to hear her mother's sermon on fidelity. She reassured herself that, marital status aside, Tyree was just the kind of man her mother would like. One day, she'd introduce her mother to Tyree—one day after the divorce.

The uncertainty of Tyree's marital status created a ripple in Rosalyn's otherwise orderly routine. Tyree's wife wasn't trying to help things along either—especially now that she'd found out another woman was in the picture. It soon became safer to avoid the volatile subject of divorce. Each time she and Tyree made love, it felt like another piece of her had fallen away revealing someone she didn't want to be.

Work seemed to be the only place she retained some degree of control. The Colson Thomas contract would be the fifth major sale she'd completed this year. Even with the slight distraction, business was good. Rosalyn enjoyed the staccato clicking of her nails on the computer's plastic keys. As usual, the numbers added up. Anne buzzed her phone.

"Rosalyn, call on line two."

"Good morning, Rosalyn speaking."

"Is this Rosalyn Ross?"

"Yes, this is Rosalyn. May I help you?"

"Yeah, you can help me. In fact, I think we can help each other. I'm calling about Tyree Johnson."

"I'm sorry. I don't understand. What did you say your name was again?"

"I didn't. Besides, you don't have to worry about who this is. Call me an interested party if you like. Tyree is married and it would be wise for you to break off this little affair before it's too late."

"Too late? I think you're mistaken. We're just friend..."

"Friends! You're not a friend. You're a booty call—a ho, somebody to pass time with."

"Look, I don't know who you are but..."

"But nothing! You just need to leave my man alone. It's bitches like you..."

"I beg your pardon!"

"You beg my what? I don't believe this shit. Just stop fucking around with my husband, bitch."

"Look, I...," The phone clicked.

Rosalyn held the receiver for a moment before hanging up. She had never felt so humiliated in her life. She didn't know what to think. The office walls seemed to swell, then shrink, smothering her. She couldn't breathe. She looked out into the office at Anne. The young woman seemed oblivious to what had just occurred. The phone buzzed again, rudely penetrating Rosalyn's self-absorption. Anne's voice did not register the first time.

"Rosalyn. Do you want to take this call?" she asked in an almost exasperated tone.

Rosalyn paused; inhaled, then slowly placed the receiver to her ear.

"Roz, do you have the Thomas report?" a familiar voice asked.

"The Thomas report? Yes, it'll take just a moment for me to put my hands on it."

"Well, could you e-mail me a copy as soon as you can? Colson Thomas just dropped in and he wants to review his contract. I think you have the latest revision. You're welcome to join us if you like."

"No, no, Bob. If you don't mind, I'd like to sit this one out."

"Sure. You sound a little strange, Rosalyn. Is everything okay?"

"Okay? Yes, of course. I was in the middle of another call. I'll email you the file."

"Great. I'll let you know how the meeting turns out, okay. Thanks."

The phone was silent again. She placed the phone carefully on the cradle. Rosalyn looked up just in time to see Anne look away.

* * *

Rosalyn had not meant to argue with Tyree that night. She just needed to know where she stood. The phone call had been enough to convince her that he needed to be a little more aggressive about pursuing his divorce.

"Tyree, you here?"

"I'm on the computer, Babe."

"So, have you heard anything?"

"Heard anything? Heard anything—about what?"

"Tyree, how can you sit there and act like you don't know what I'm talking about?"

Tyree peeked over the computer and smiled. She knew that he thought he had some sort of control over her with that smile. She averted her eyes.

"Have you even talked to your lawyer?"

"Lawyer? Well, no. Not today. I mean these things take time."

"I'm not getting a good feeling about this whole thing Tyree. I mean, couldn't it jeopardize the divorce proceedings if somebody finds out that you're shacking up with another woman before things are final?"

"Shacking up? Look, Roz, it's going to work out. Just a little more time and—"

"That's what you've been saying for the past few weeks," she snapped. "You're not giving me much to go on."

"Rosalyn, this isn't one of your business deals. This is my life—our life. You know how I feel about this whole thing. You know how I feel about you. Look, if you don't mind I'd rather not talk about this tonight."

Rosalyn turned away. She took a few steps towards the bedroom and felt the weight of Tyree's hand on her shoulder. Tears blurred her vision.

"What's wrong?" he asked.

"I think you know what's wrong, Tyree. I'm tired of sneaking around."

"Who's sneaking around? I told you how things are. What do you expect me to do? Rosalyn, I love you. I wouldn't do anything to hurt you. Just work with me, Baby."

"Tyree, I want you to leave." Rosalyn's back stiffened. "Maybe once things are settled..."

"Leave? Rosalyn, what are you saying? You don't want me here? I thought you understood."

"Tyree, I thought you understood too."

* * *

The first of the flowers arrived a few days after he'd gone. They came every day. Although Rosalyn was certain she'd convinced Anne that they didn't matter, it was more difficult to convince herself. Nevertheless, she decided not to respond to Tyree's flowers or his equally incessant calls. The week had begun with Anne excitedly placing the flowers on Rosalyn's desk and ended with the exchange of tight uncomfortable smiles as the flowers were set beside the trash can.

When the flowers and calls stopped, Rosalyn began to feel the void left by Tyree's absence. She finally decided to call him at the only number she had—the number on the back of the business card from the first night. There was no answer. Now, she could no longer balance the burden of work with the troublesome weight on her heart. One vacation day from the office turned into a week. After the second week, she decided there was nothing left to do but go on with her life.

* * *

It was a Monday morning when Rosalyn returned to work. The office, bright and unfamiliar, was a welcome change from the consuming darkness waiting for her at home. She was relieved that there had been no need to provide the actual reason for her unusually long and unplanned vacation. Allen seemed to have determined his own reasons for the absence, and waved away her attempts to provide any explanation. He assured her that a few days away from work were a minor eccentricity compared with those of her peers. She left Allen in anxious anticipation of the safe refuge of her own office.

"Good morning," Rosalyn said when she reached Anne's desk.

"Good morning, Ms. Ross...I mean Rosalyn. How are you feeling?" The young woman's sincerity was obvious.

"I've felt better." Rosalyn was in no mood for conversation. "I'm anxious to get back to work. I know there's a ton of stuff I need to catch up on."

"Rosalyn, I just want to say that I'm sorry about what happened," Anne said abruptly and began fidgeting with the pen and pencil lying before her.

At first, Rosalyn assumed Anne was referring to her absence from work, but decided she must be talking about the absence of flowers and phone calls.

"Well, sometimes things just don't work out. Sometimes it's for the best," she said, partly to Anne, partly to herself.

"The best? I'm not sure I understand."

"Well, I'll miss the flowers, but sometimes you have to get on with your life."

"The flowers?" the young woman's face twisted in horror. "Then you don't know?"

"Know?"

"It was in Friday's paper." Anne reached into the left-hand drawer of her desk. "The funeral was yesterday. I saved the article."

J. Marcus Evins

Rosalyn snatched the folded newspaper from Anne. She did not feel the young woman's hand on her shoulder or hear the words of condolence. Rosalyn's eyes skipped over the page, but she could not—did not want to—understand the words. She blinked against the tears and read the article again:

> *The three-car collision claimed the life of Tyree Johnson. The thirty-five-year-old Charlottesville native is a recent recipient of the Virginia Small Business Award. He is survived by his mother and father. The accident that occurred on 64 East, between Charlottesville and Richmond, ended the life of one of Virginia's most promising entrepreneurs.*

Rosalyn continued reading until she felt her legs give way. She did not understand the loss of balance or the slow-rolling darkness into which she drifted. She did not see the newspaper float slowly to the floor or hear Anne's scream.

The End